ENCHANTED
AGAIN

*Erotic
Bedtime
Stories
for Women*

Nancy Madore

ENCHANTED
AGAIN

*Erotic
Bedtime
Stories
for Women*

MIRA

Spice

MIRA is a registered trademark of Harlequin Enterprises Limited, used under licence.

Published in Great Britain 2009
MIRA Books, Eton House, 18-24 Paradise Road,
Richmond, Surrey, TW9 1SR

© Nancy Madore 2008

ISBN 978 0 7783 0319 0

85-0309

Printed in Great Britain
by Clays Ltd, St Ives plc

BIRDS OF A FEATHER

Birds of a feather
flock together
and so do pigs and swine.
Rats and mice will have their choice,
and so will I have mine.

Pansy's spine arched reflexively where Jack's hand gently prodded her forward, and a shudder crept menacingly along the length of it. She stepped timidly into the room ahead of him, hardly mindful of her actions or the events that were unfolding around her. She seemed more in a dream than real life, as detached from the events as a figurine in a game of chess. For the moment at least, she felt more like a spectator than a participant.

The instant that Jack shut the door behind them, however, Pansy suddenly snapped out of her dream state and came fully alert, and even the air all around her seemed to crackle with life. Jack, too, abandoned his cool demeanor and was seized with a violent passion, grasping a fistful of Pansy's hair and jerking her head around so that her face was directly beneath his, with her lips parted for his approaching kiss. Pansy awoke to an explosion of sensation, and she clung to Jack frantically as he captured her lips in an all-consuming kiss that devoured the last of her reserve. She pressed her body against his with a sigh, causing him to kiss her even more passionately. His hands began moving deliberately over her clothing, finding buttons and zippers and clasps as he expertly removed every stitch without ever interrupting their kiss. Pansy was stripped to the skin before she even realized what Jack was doing, and though she normally had reservations about having her body so utterly exposed, Jack's unyielding, take-charge manner left her with no time for objections—neither uttered nor even imagined, for that matter—and no choice but simply to enjoy the wonderfully vulnerable sensation of simply submitting to another's pleasure. Pansy felt a slow, languid tightening in her womb that pulsated outward, causing the flesh between her legs to tingle and swell and moisten.

Once her clothes were removed, Jack took hold of Pansy's hair again and gently pushed her head down toward the floor. She twisted awkwardly at the waist at first, but then bent her legs and moved onto her knees, supposing that he wanted her to take him in her mouth, but he kept pushing her down even farther, until her elbows too rested on the floor. With a mixture of apprehension and delight she succumbed to the position and waited breathlessly for what he would do next. She was keenly aware of the dirty hotel-room floor where she waited on knees and elbows, but it only seemed to accentuate the moment, making it all the more thrilling. She had only the briefest of seconds to consider any of this before she heard a long swooshing sound from behind her where Jack stood. Even as her mind was registering the sound of his belt sliding out from his belt loops, Jack swung it around with vigor and landed it with a loud, resounding crack across the underside of her buttocks. The sound rattled her eardrums with a peculiar ring before the sting of the blow struck her consciousness. There was a subsequent volley of lashes that followed, some four or five at least, before she managed to cry out. She was stunned by how much the blows smarted, and all of her desire of just seconds before seemed to freeze in that instant. She made an effort to get up.

Jack held Pansy down with one hand on the small of her back, but he did not immediately resume the lashes. Instead, he positioned himself so that he was straddling her, with one leg on either side of her, and he grasped her hair again and gently pulled her head back so that he could look down into her face.

"You can't leave before you get everything you came here for, Pansy," he said in a surprisingly composed voice. He paused to scan the contents of the floor all around her and picked up something near her leg before continuing in the same matter-of-fact tone. "And whether you realize it or not," he said, "this is part of what you came here for." At this point he began, ever so gently, stuffing Pansy's panties into her mouth. Her eyes grew even wider at this, so he explained, as if as a side note, "This is just to cut down on the noise. Okay?"

There was nothing in Pansy's experience to come close to preparing her for the sharp thrill that shot through her when she heard these words from Jack, so, without even considering what they meant, she found herself vigorously nodding her head in agreement. Jack kept pressing her panties between her lips until her mouth was forced wide open. She continued to stare up at him in wide-eyed astonishment.

"Now, Pansy," he resumed calmly, "you have done nothing but put yourself down all the way over here, remember?" Pansy merely stared at him.

"*Remember?*" he repeated more forcefully. She nodded, but only because she realized he expected her to.

"Good," he said. "I'm glad you remember that. Because that is what you did. You said awful things about yourself. Think about it. You said all those things because deep down you want to be punished." He looked down into her face expectantly after saying this. With one hand Jack held Pansy's head back so that he could see her face. With his other hand he began to gently caress her cheek. Pansy's mind was starting to work again. She tried to recall what she had said. It was not unusual for her to put herself down; she did it continually. But her mind balked at the idea that she wanted to be punished. On the contrary, she had always believed her self-deprecating comments were designed to forestall others from drawing the same conclusions. When she was hard on herself it seemed others were prompted to contradict her.

Jack could see by her expression that she was considering what he had said, so he continued. His voice was soothing. "When you're punished for something you don't like about yourself, it makes it better." For some reason these words sent conflicting sensations simultaneously rippling through her; one of panic, the other of arousal. "You'll see," he concluded, keeping a tight hold of her hair to keep her from squirming as he picked up the belt and resumed the quick, steady lashes over her buttocks and thighs.

Stinging pain and mortification came in a brutal downpour that lasted for several moments; long minutes where Pansy forgot her arousal and her nudity and her guilt and every other thing that had been a part of her consciousness before. Initially she felt something akin to hysteria, and was even overcome with an urge to erupt into wild laughter. But quickly her laughter turned into sobs, and the hysteria faded away in the sharp reality of the all-consuming pain and heat spreading through her. At one point she became immersed in her efforts to escape the lashes, but upon the realization that she could not evade them she gradually accepted them, and in the end she was consumed with merely enduring the harsh onslaught with the anticipation that it would eventually come to an end. And although she had ceased her efforts to escape, her hips bobbed and jiggled rebelliously, seemingly in an effort to predict where the next lash would fall and futilely attempting to dodge her assailant's level eye. The skin of her backside burned hotter and hotter with every blow and Pansy could do little more than squirm and cry out in muffled sobs. The beating continued until Pansy was conscious of nothing but the searing pain that lit up her flesh like wildfire.

Then quite abruptly the blows stopped, and Jack dropped the

belt on the floor beside her. Pansy's eyes were still wide and frantic, and her hips continued to move in the rhythmic motion of her struggles. She was breathing heavily from her exertions and her gasps for air mingled with her muffled sobs. Jack pulled her head back again until her eyes met his, and she suddenly became still and ceased her crying. Even her tears seemed to halt on her cheeks. They stared at each other for a long moment. She felt as if he was observing her from within. He leaned closer and tenderly kissed her wet cheek.

"You took that well," he said gently. Something within Pansy jolted, but outwardly she merely continued to stare silently into his eyes. His other hand began moving lightly over her blazing haunches. She couldn't contain a slight moan when he touched the tender flesh. There was a strange combination of disbelief and acute attentiveness all around her and she struggled to ascertain what was real. Jack caressed her bottom thoughtfully, moving his fingers tentatively over the rising welts in her flesh. Very leisurely he let his fingers roam all around the area, and eventually he slipped a finger between the two round mounds of her buttocks, sliding it up and down along her crack. He slowly continued guiding his finger up and down; extending the span with every stroke until at last he reached her labia lips and pressed a few fingers into their silky folds. His fingers slipped in easily and Jack thrust them in and out brusquely, reveling in her soaking wetness, and accentuating the slopping sounds to add emphasize to his next remark. "You see," he said, "how much you wanted that?"

Pansy simply stared up at him. She felt as if she was drugged. Her flesh ached more acutely where he fingered her playfully than where the swollen welts still raged. She felt a slight tugging in the back of her head where he still held her by the hair. "Do you see that, Pansy?" he asked her again.

She could not speak through the panties in her mouth. The pain of the lashing was subsiding into an achingly hot tenderness that pulled at her womb and spread warmth throughout her lower body. Slowly she nodded. This simple admission caused her swollen sex glands to contract. Jack felt the contraction with his fingers.

"You're really a very good girl," he said huskily, causing more of the little contractions, and making her engorged sex sting. Jack's fingers moving in and out of her only managed to tantalize, not to satisfy. "We could take your punishment one step further, Pansy," he murmured. Her eyes were still fixed on his, and they widened slightly when she heard his words. "This time it's up to you," he assured her quickly. Her eyes bored into his. "I know your bottom hurts," he continued. "I can see that it hurts because it's so red and hot and swollen." Again he caressed her burning flesh. "But in order to get the full amount of pleasure— to get what you *need* from it, Pansy—you have to want it. You have to want it so much you'll beg for it." Pansy closed her eyes when she heard this. She dreaded what she was about to do even though she had no doubt that she would do it. How could she stop this now? Wasn't she already here, naked, on her hands and knees, getting carpet burn on a dirty hotel-room floor, with a virtual stranger, having already given him more of herself than she had ever shared with her husband? The most difficult part— the part where she'd agreed to come here with Jack in the first place—was over and done. To stop now would be to go home with all the guilt and none of the satisfaction. She could do no less than to see it through to the end.

Besides all of this, Pansy had never been so aroused in her life, and she knew that some small part of her really did want this. She opened her eyes. Jack was still watching her intently. She nodded her head in the affirmative. She saw him smile and felt a brand-new thrill of fear. He carefully removed the panties from her mouth. "Well?" he prompted.

"I...want it," she said, self-conscious. Her mouth was very dry.

"Ask for it."

"Will you punish me again?" she asked, feeling her face burn. But her eyes didn't look away from his.

"Beg for it, Pansy."

She paused only a moment before continuing awkwardly. "Please...Jack...please punish me again. Punish me harder this time!" And suddenly she meant it. Her hips were already swaying back and forth in anticipation of the blows to come.

"It will hurt more this time, Pansy," he said, looking to subjugate her a little more with every word. "Your flesh is raw from the punishment I already gave you. Are you sure you want more?"

Pansy faltered, recalling the pain. Jack smiled to see her hesitation. He wanted her broken. She began to tremble. He waited patiently for her answer.

"I'm sure, Jack," Pansy said after another moment. And all of a sudden, she *was* sure, even yearning for what was to come. "Please, Jack, please! I need you to punish me some more." She was overjoyed when she saw that he was pleased by her words.

"It will be good after, Pansy," he told her, stuffing the panties back into her mouth. He paused to touch her face affectionately. "I promise you that."

Her sex felt as if it was consuming her. She braced herself for the blows to come. He had not lied. The pain was twice as intense when it was inflicted on her raw flesh. Her hips bounced and jerked miserably as the blows fell over them and the flames of pain licked up along the length of her. She cried out and thrashed with all her might, knowing no one but Jack could hear or see her, and that it pleased him to see her so. In her wild abandon and absolute suffering she felt as if she was being released from something terrible, even though the incredible pain and heat was virtually consuming her.

Pansy was nearly beside herself by the time the second beating finally stopped and Jack threw down the belt for a second time. Without a word he immediately began removing his clothes. Her hips continued to rock back and forth and she moaned absently. She had rested her head on her arms, and gradually became quiet as it occurred to her that the worst was finally over. Her buttocks were rutted and inflamed and quivering. Her mouth was still held open wide with the panties. When Jack approached her she looked up at his hard, throbbing sex in wonder.

"Keep your head down," he said hoarsely, adding approvingly when she complied, "Good girl. Now bring your hips up nice and high for me…higher." He guided her hips up so high that she was obliged to unbend her knees and distribute her weight between her hands and feet. "That's it," she heard him murmur, and at long last she felt the hard length of him slide easily into her aching hole.

"Mmmhhh," she moaned, shuddering, and she heard his responding moan mingled with laughter.

"I've never seen anyone need a spanking that badly," he said, driving into her with hard and rapid thrusts. "You must have been really bad to need all that punishing."

"I…am," she tried to tell him though her words were garbled. She enjoyed these kinds of demeaning innuendos while in the throes of passion, and wanted to encourage him to continue in the same vein.

"Did you need to be punished because you're an adulterous whore?" he asked, pounding himself even more violently into her. He found this kind of talk exciting, as well.

"Yes!" she cried unintelligibly, slipping her fingers over her clitoris.

"That's it," he coaxed when he noticed her arm reaching between her legs to touch herself. "No need to be shy with old Jack. I know what cheating sluts like you like even better than you know yourself." He could see his words were exciting her even more. He wanted to hear more of her replies. "Have you ever been spanked like that before?" he asked her.

"No."

"Your husband doesn't spank you like you deserve?" he queried, thrusting harder and harder.

"No," she choked out again.

"But you deserved it, didn't you, Pansy?" he asked.

"Yes," she cried out. Her fingers were enthusiastically rubbing her clitoris.

He grasped her bright-red buttocks and began roughly kneading them with his hands as he continued to batter her with his thrusts. "You can still feel it, can't you, Pansy?" he asked her, knowing full well by her moans that she could. She responded in the affirmative. He squeezed her buttocks harder. He saw that she liked these painful reminders by the way her movements became more and more frantic with every squeeze from his prying fingers. Seeing that she enjoyed it, Jack became increasingly crude with her. "You'll remember it tonight, too, when you fuck your husband, won't you?" he asked her, and when she paused over the reminder of her husband, he repeated, "Won't you, Pansy?" It was at that moment that she climaxed, ironically, while she was crying out that she would indeed remember this later that evening when she was in bed with her husband.

Almost immediately after the last waves of pleasure passed, Pansy felt a peculiar detachment from Jack, even though he continued to drive himself into her, all the while telling her what a "cheating whore" she was. She kept her head down and pushed her hips toward him, hoping he would finish quickly. "Oh, yeah," he groaned. "Push that pussy out for me." And with that she at last felt him erupt inside her. Her arousal was fading fast now, with morose quickly following on its heels.

Jack remained joined with her for much longer than she would have liked him to, but finally he pulled himself out of her and went over to the bed and collapsed on top of it. She stood up, unsure of what to do next. Awkwardly, she pulled the panties out of her mouth. She realized that Jack was still watching her when she heard him laugh. This pleased and annoyed her at the same time.

She moved with controlled calm, aware that just beneath the surface there was——lying dormant until she was alone——a wealth of recriminations and anguish over what she had just done. For the moment, she walked around in a kind of daze, picking up her scattered items of clothing and clumsily putting them on. Jack merely watched her quietly from the bed.

When she was fully dressed she faced him self-consciously. In spite of her jumbled emotions she managed an awkward laugh. She waited for him to say something.

He surprised her with, "Are you okay?"

This seemed too personal somehow, so she brushed it aside with a small wave of her hand and in a shaky voice she replied, "Of course."

He saw her discomfort. "Look, Pansy," he told her. "I want to see you again. I like you. I know it got a little...well, let's just say I lost my head."

In spite of her regret Pansy felt a brand-new kindling of desire from his words. "I don't know, Jack," she said hesitantly. "I've never done anything like this before, and I feel…I feel——" She stopped, at a loss for words.

"You enjoyed it, Pansy. There's nothing wrong in that."

"I know," Pansy answered quickly. She did not want to think about the things they had done and she certainly didn't want to discuss them. "It's not that. I mean…it's…I don't know what it is. I need to think."

"I want to see you again, Pansy," he repeated. He suddenly seemed terribly vulnerable to her.

"I have to go," she said. She approached him on the bed where he sat watching her and lightly kissed his cheek. She wasn't sure what else she was supposed to say or do. "Bye for now, Jack," she said.

Once she reached the shelter of her car, Pansy slumped down and let out a long, shaky sob. She was all at once assailed with so many conflicting sensations that she couldn't even pinpoint what she actually felt. Overall there was a sensation of distress so potent it fell over her like a dark blanket of misery. She wept bitterly for several moments and then her tears stopped abruptly. As she forcibly resumed the familiar activities of her life, like turning the key in the ignition and shifting the car into Drive, she determinedly fought the revulsion that was steadily creeping over her.

"It's going to be okay," Pansy said out loud. "It was a onetime thing that I won't ever do again." She tried vigorously to pinpoint what it was that was bothering her so much. Certainly there was no love lost between her and her husband, and even more certainly there had been no real wrongdoing on her part, especially in light of her husband's many indiscretions. And yet, this was the first time she had ever been unfaithful to him. Even so, she could not believe that the simple act of adultery, committed within such a marriage as theirs, could bring about such anguish. She was actually feeling afraid; but of what? Images of her affair with Jack kept tumbling into her consciousness and, though she recoiled at the reminders, when she forced her mind to receive them she found that they still had the power to arouse her. Yet this realization only seemed to make her feel worse. How could she have allowed herself to be treated that way? How could she have begged for it like she did? She could still feel the wetness of her panties from having held them in her mouth for so long and her revulsion and fear returned. Was she depraved?

On a deeper level that she could not yet dwell upon, Pansy faintly acknowledged that she had never felt such pleasure as she had with Jack. She continued to scrutinize her feelings over the matter as she drove home, struggling to achieve some sense of calm before having to face her husband. This mere contemplation of her husband brought forth such a sense of panic that she nearly lost control of the car. Her mind had only to mingle the thought of her husband with the memories of that afternoon to put her in a state of absolute terror. She knew well how abominable the things she had done with Jack would be to her husband. Were he to find out, he would most certainly destroy her. This, then, was the primary source of her fear. Anger came at her from every direction at the realization. Yet she whispered frantically, over and over again, "He must never find out!"

When at last she arrived home, Pansy appeared calm, except for a slight trembling. She entered the house tentatively. Tom was there. She could hear his voice, loud and argumentative, as he shouted objections at someone, most likely over the telephone. She was still steeped in morbid fear and regret, and longed for a hot shower. She dreaded seeing Tom more than usual, but oddly enough, the sight of him as she paused in the doorway of his office, slumped in his chair, angry and arrogant and bitter, seemed to fully exonerate her of any culpability. She struggled to wipe the grimace from her features as she stared silently at him, recalling absently how her mother once warned her that frowning might make her face stay that way. She intended to move away from the doorway before capturing his attention but, like a bystander at a gruesome accident, she couldn't seem to pull herself away.

"Tapes malfunction every day," he was saying to the person on the other line.

Especially when you're around, Pansy thought.

She reflected that she felt different. Perhaps what she had done today had changed her somehow. But if she had changed, Tom had not. He was the same self-absorbed, miserable bastard. He looked up suddenly, barely registering her presence before proceeding to look through her as if she were no more than a picture on the wall.

"Yeah, yeah," he said into the phone. "You act like this bum deserves the royal treatment or something. He's the scum of the earth."

Innocent until proven guilty, Pansy thought.

Tom slammed down the receiver suddenly and immediately launched into a tirade, addressing her, seemingly, but nevertheless oblivious of her.

"Goddamn paperwork is going to keep me up all night," he said. "They need to decide if they want me to sit around dotting i's and crossing t's, or if they want me to get out there and serve and protect." This was a familiar theme for him, but by now it was glaringly plain to Pansy that by "dotting i's and crossing t's," Tom was not referring to some pointless red tape but, rather, he spoke of the actual tasks involved in investigating a crime—tasks which Tom felt he was above having to perform. He relied solely on his instincts when he decided whose rights to violate, and those instincts had been schooled over the years with the various prejudices he had acquired, all of which he considered "intelligence," and which rarely coincided with the evidence that kept cropping up to make him look bad. The appropriate processing of evidence was a thorn in his side, and those who pressed for details were, to him, troublemakers.

Pansy knew from experience that Tom particularly disliked being disagreed with.

She warred with the muscles in her face that were reflexively assuming an expression of acute contempt. "They don't appreciate you," she muttered perfunctorily, but her lips and tongue cringed over the words, and they came out sounding like an accusation.

"Damn right, they don't," he said, looking directly at her then, perhaps to see if there was any insincerity in her remark; for if he had any sense of reality he would never be able to trust such a comment. He got up and stretched. Pansy's eyes moved over him, noting with loathing the way his ill-fitting uniform emphasized the unsightly bulges that stretched out across his abdomen and hips, giving him an androgynous appearance from the waistline to his thighs. She wondered if he had ever actually physically pursued a suspect and then, quite unexpectedly, a small snort of laughter burst from between her lips. She immediately covered over it with a cough.

Feeling compelled to say something in the silence that followed, Pansy asked, "Is this the same case you've been working on all week?"

Tom let out a long sigh. "Yeah…the Foreman case. This new jackass at the D.A.'s office keeps sending it back to me…finding things to nitpick over." Pansy had no doubt that the "things to nitpick over" were really holes in the case—holes that the former district attorney would have ignored, pressing forward blindly only to push for a plea in the end. That way everyone came out a winner. Everyone except the accused, that is—if he or she was innocent. And what were the chances of that?

"What's the matter this time?" Pansy asked, stalling until she could find the right moment to escape. She wondered that he didn't notice how different she was. She was certain she must look different. But then, even she couldn't identify what it was exactly that had changed about her. All she knew for certain was that she had changed. She shuddered. Tom went on, oblivious of any change. He was oblivious of *her,* she realized suddenly.

"This D.A. actually accused me of harassment!" he said, thrilled for an audience to talk to, even if it was only Pansy. "He just won't accept the fact that the guy is guilty."

"What did he do?"

"He killed his wife!" Tom said, looking at her as if to say, *How do you like that?* "He killed his goddamn wife!"

She wondered. It was one thing to accuse someone of murder; it was another entirely to prove it. Coming from Tom she found it hard to believe. She felt an instinctive aversion to the positions he took on nearly everything now. She wondered about this new district attorney. She secretly admired him. So, he refused to play ball? Well, that was refreshing. Although, she knew from experience that the D.A. would eventually come around. They always did.

She watched Tom, mesmerized, as he poured out his troubles with the case to her. She struggled to find any redeemable qualities in him but failed. She wondered why she married him. Poor, impotent, misunderstood Tom! She pitied the people he came up against, and another wave of fear and dread came over her. Thank heavens he hardly ever noticed her. He had no inkling whatsoever that less than an hour earlier she had been in a hotel room, groveling on her hands and knees, begging to be beaten with a belt.

Finally Tom wound down enough for her to make a graceful escape, which she did with a sigh of relief. A sense of guilt lingered over her, gaining strength with each little pang of discomfort that reminded her of her time with Jack. She pondered over the guilt for a moment; she thought she had gotten over that in the car. It occurred to her that the guilt was for herself, not Tom. The love between her and Tom had been gone for many years now, but she had stayed, and this suddenly bothered her. Yet how could she leave? As inept as he was at everything else, Tom did manage to somehow keep a roof over her head. She was certain she could not manage as well on her own. Things were difficult enough as they were. It seemed to her that this was an impossible world to survive in all alone, and it seemed more difficult every day. In the event of a divorce, Tom, with his connections, would see to it that she got nothing. She would have to start over from scratch. Who would take care of her? She thought about Jack and shuddered. There was nowhere for her to go.

But the thought of Jack lingered and grew stronger. Little flash-backs of what he had done to her kept playing themselves out in her mind, giving her almost as much pleasure as the actual events had. The memories sent simultaneous surges of shock and excitement through her. But what shocked her the most was Jack's interest in her to begin with. Why had he chosen her? She knew there was nothing remotely outstanding about her. Most men didn't even notice her. She had never possessed any one particular characteristic that drew them to her, but then again, she didn't feel she was especially unattractive either. There were things that she saw in herself that she felt were overlooked...perhaps Jack saw these things, too. She recalled how persistent he had been with her when they met. He had approached her quite unexpectedly in the coffee shop just around the corner from where she lived. She had gone there every morning for years, and then one day he was there. She noticed him immediately because he was the first patron of the bustling little shop ever to notice *her*. His eyes were always on her when she happened to glance at him, and he smiled unabashedly when she caught him staring. It was Pansy who would, at these moments, look quickly and guiltily away.

It took only a few mornings of this before Pansy and Jack began exchanging small greetings of acquaintance, such as a smile and nod of the head, or a quick "good morning." Pansy was curious about him but had no thoughts of satisfying her curiosity. Soon Jack began talking to her while they waited together in line, which he would unapologetically saunter into at whatever place Pansy held in it. He did this so casually that no one thought to question him, least of all Pansy. He would lean in and say confidential things in a low voice meant for her ears only. Sometimes he made comments about the other customers in the shop and other times he would tell her little things about himself. These comments, made in hushed tones, seemed inordinately intimate to her and she became more and more certain as the days went by that he was propositioning her. Yet she couldn't quite believe this could be true, and later, reflecting upon it, she would actually laugh at herself. But the next morning there Jack would be, standing so close that she could feel the heat of him as he commented on something innocent enough in and of itself, but in a tone and manner that once again had her pondering over his meaning.

One morning Pansy impulsively voiced her conclusions about his behavior.

"Why are you flirting with me?" she asked him.

"I don't know," he admitted with a laugh. "All I know is that I want to do things to you." Those words, spoken in his low, determined tone while his eyes were boring into hers, had been her undoing. Although she managed somehow to resist a few more of his advances, she knew the moment he had uttered those words that she would not be able to rest until he had done whatever "things" it was that he wanted to do with her. And aside from her bursting curiosity over what those things might be, the fact that he wanted to do things at all, and that his mind had even conjured up the things to begin with, had been a copious feast for her undernourished sense of self.

Pansy stood under the hot water in her shower as her thoughts volleyed back and forth between Jack and Tom, exhausting her with the conflicting feelings both men aroused. She felt a kind of ecstatic horror when her fingers first identified the welts Jack left on her buttocks and thighs, which brought with it a wave of exhilaration so unsettling that she had to brace herself against the wall of the shower to keep from falling down. God forbid that Tom should come rushing to her aid if she did fall, only to discover those welts. This brought her thoughts back to Tom with annoyance. And all of these sentiments only left her feeling more confused when she reluctantly turned off the quickly cooling water and stepped out of the shower. She dried off and shrouded herself in her most matronly nightgown.

For a reprieve, Pansy's thoughts wandered to the case Tom was working on. She wondered about the man he accused of murder and she found herself once again ticking through Tom's many faults. It annoyed her that he could sit there and complain about having to produce more evidence when he was so likely in the wrong. Once she might have debated the matter with him; but now she knew only too well what it would cost to disagree with anything he said. Tom did not like to be crossed. He could never bear to have any negative suggestion made against him. Strange then, how casually he was able to point his finger at others, especially when he had the power to actually destroy their lives when he did so. She thought about the man who Tom was so rigidly pursuing. Tom had ranted and raved about the difficulties he was having with the case, but he had never mentioned a single fact that proved the man had committed murder. Did the man he accused really kill his wife? Was Tom actually right for once? After all these years with Tom, Pansy had difficulty imagining Tom being right about anything. How could he be? He had absolutely no relationship with the truth. He despised all forms of it, and even lied to himself, regularly and perpetually. He rarely looked at any single thing objectively. But thinking of Tom for too long acted on Pansy's mind like a depressant. She forced him from her consciousness as she nestled down in their bed, where she let Jack once again creep into her thoughts.

Pansy asked herself what it was about Jack that caused her to think of him so often in the short time that she had known him. He was the opposite of Tom in every way. Lean and strong, with raven hair and coloring to match, he was all at once to Pansy beauty and danger and excitement. Dark and baleful, it was difficult to know what he was thinking. He did not whine and complain, as Tom often did. He was mysterious and perhaps a little treacherous. But to Pansy's mind he could not be cruel or evil. He was not empty; he was closed, and there was a difference. Tom, for all his ranting and raving, hid a hard, malicious soul. Pansy laughed at herself suddenly. Here she was, defending Jack, as if it mattered. She would likely never hear from him again. Or worse, she would see him at the coffee shop and he would completely ignore her. And yet, she wondered. How could their experience together have changed her so much without having any effect on him?

Pansy was still awake hours later when she heard Tom approach their bedroom, but she quickly rolled onto her side, facing away from his side of the bed, and feigned sleep. Tom shuffled around in the dark room, clumsily undressing. The bed groaned under his heavy weight. Pansy sighed.

Suddenly and unexpectedly Tom's hands were all over her, tugging at her nightgown awkwardly. Surprised, Pansy sprung around and rolled onto her back before his hands could reach her swollen buttocks. She wondered over his untimely advances. He had not touched her in months. Perhaps he had sensed a change in her after all...

Tom was still struggling ineffectually with her nightgown, so Pansy raised her hips to make it easier for his bungling hands. When she was bared from the waist down, she mechanically raised and opened her legs for him as he approached. He began thrusting himself at her, doubly annoying her because, as usual, he had made no preparations or allowances for her to accept him and, even worse, he wasn't even anywhere near the point of entry where he was blindly and stubbornly jabbing forward. Was he ever able to get any single thing right? she wondered with exasperation.

Pansy reached down and grasped hold of Tom's penis with exasperation, maneuvering it so that at the very least it would have a place to go when he thrust forward again. The lack of foreplay did not overly disturb her because thoughts of Jack had kept her in a continuous state of arousal and wetness since she left him. Tom groaned in surprise when he felt how wet she was. He automatically assumed that he was the cause of her excitement; just as he automatically assumed it was her own failure when it was otherwise. But he was genuinely pleased by her wetness, whatever the cause, and it increased his excitement as he began pounding himself into her. This conclusion to the events of her day had a strange effect on Pansy. Thoughts of her affair mingled with her absolute hatred for Tom to create an effect that suddenly seemed terribly exciting. She moved her hips rhythmically beneath him so that her clitoris rubbed against his body, further surprising and delighting him. "Pansy," he moaned, slowing his thrusts and switching gears suddenly from merely using her body to making love to her. She preferred the feeling of being used by him, however, and his sudden gentle lovemaking quieted her passion considerably and, even worse, brought out more feelings of guilt. It occurred to her that her feelings were always subject to the actions of the people around her. She tried desperately to simply enjoy the rare moment of mutual goodwill between her and her husband, but it was no good. She was too aware of the man that Tom was, panting and sweating copiously from the simple exertions of ordinary lovemaking while his flab battered her from above. She bit her lip and wished for it to be over.

At the coffee shop the following morning Jack strolled confidently into line next to her, standing so close that his hand could lightly brush the small of her back without anyone around them noticing. She was shamefully relieved and delighted to see him.

"I can't stop thinking about you," he murmured, leaning in so his warm breath touched her ear as he spoke. As improbable as his words seemed to her mind, her heart clung to them fiercely.

"Me, too," she whispered breathlessly. Her heart pounded. *Why me?* she kept wondering.

"This afternoon," he said.

"Oh…I don't know…" She paused. So soon? The welts still

hurt. And while the memories kept her in a constant state of arousal, the thought of actually doing those things again frightened her.

"This afternoon, Pansy," he repeated more firmly. A thrill shot through the center of her.

"Okay," she agreed with equal parts exhilaration and apprehension.

She walked around the next few hours in a fog. She could think of nothing but seeing Jack again. She whiled away the hours in a fever, trying to occupy the time in between. One of the things she found to do was to bring her husband and his cronies lunch at the police station.

Pansy's excitement was palpable when she stepped into the precinct where Tom worked. He had been pleased by her generous offer to bring him lunch, but did not wonder too much over it, taking it in stride as his due. It didn't even occur to him to wonder if her exuberant smile and starry expression was for anyone other than himself.

Pansy tried to appear unperturbed, but her mind had difficulty staying on what she was doing. Tom and his friends noticed this only so far as the inconvenience they felt that their sandwiches were all mixed up. Pansy merely laughed when they pointed out her mistakes. But in a sudden instant her laughter died and her face went slack. The men around her did not even notice the alteration in her, preoccupied as they were with getting their lunches in order.

Pansy's gaze landed on a photo lying on Tom's desk. Jack's face stared up at her. A strange sense of unreality came over her. Random thoughts flitted through her mind as she struggled to achieve a blank expression. After several moments she attempted to speak.

"Who's that?" she asked no one in particular, pointing at the picture of Jack.

"That's him," Tom replied with his mouth full of food. A clump of something greenish in color flew from his mouth and landed on Jack's face. "That's John Foreman, the wife killer."

"Oh," Pansy said. *Of course it is,* she thought. She had a strange urge to throw her head back and laugh hysterically.

"Tried to make it look like an accident, but I have no doubt he killed her," her husband continued. As she looked at her husband she distracted herself by wondering why he always began a new sentence after taking a huge bite of food. She looked again at the picture of Jack. The green glob on his cheek made him seem rather pitiable. Thoughts raced through her mind. One carried the realization that it was not coincidence that brought her and Jack together. And yet, her heart rejected this.

Still, the more serious issue was that Jack was accused of murder. She wondered why this wasn't her primary concern. If it were anyone else but Tom accusing Jack perhaps it would bother her more, but knowing Tom as she did, it was hard to give the accusation credence.

She was less than an hour away from her meeting with Jack. What if Tom was actually right for once? What if Jack really was a killer? Was it even safe for her to meet him alone in a hotel room? No one else in the world would know where she was. Thoughts kept pouring through her mind in frantic disarray. Always upper-most among them was the question of why Jack had pursued her to begin with. Had he approached her because she was the wife of his accuser? What did he ultimately want from her? This, more than anything else—even the potential danger she was in—filled her with an overwhelming sense of despair. She sat down in a nearby chair, suddenly weary. All of the energy and happiness of only moments before had vanished.

Tom and his companions had continued talking, oblivious of any change whatsoever in Pansy.

"He's a clever one," Tom was saying. "I'll give him that. Always covers his tracks."

"You'll get the bastard," one of the others chirped in.

Pansy only half listened, concentrating all her efforts on breath-ing evenly. It was a struggle to remain composed. She tried to soothe herself out of the overwhelming confusion. Why should she care what Jack's motives were in seeing her anyway? What was he to her? But an all-consuming sense of hopelessness enveloped her. Nothing good ever came to her. Everything was suspect. She looked at Tom with perverse loathing. Everything associated with him brought her anguish, she thought unreasonably. She wished fervently that he was dead. As was her habit during these crucially unhappy moments of her life, she distracted herself by pondering her husband's exis-tence, finding comfort in conjuring up reasons why Tom might in all likelihood die an early death. It seemed not only probable, but inevitable. There were so many factors in favor of it, and it gave her hope to go over them, methodically and analytically. Why, his very position as a police officer was purported to put his life at risk, although Pansy could not imagine him ever being heroic or anything like that. More likely his arrogant disregard for the rights of others would eventually anger someone enough to provoke violence. But there were many other risks to Tom's life that she had found to deliberate over. On this occasion, as she watched him practically inhale his sandwich, she found herself wondering how it was possible that Tom's arteries, which by now had to be lined with numerous residual coagulations from years of habitual ingestion of every sort of saturated fat, never managed to halt the flow of blood and end his miserable life. How much longer could they hold out? Even as she thought these thoughts, she noticed all around his desk evidence of his slovenly eating habits, including several stale donuts and wrappers from fast-food restaurants. And yet, there he stood, ranting and raving like a healthy young toddler; pudgy and dimply and ruddy. His continued good health seemed a personal affront to her.

Pansy glanced at the clock and wondered what she should do. It seemed obvious now that Jack was only using her, but she still wanted to see him. Once again she blamed Tom, who had created in her such a desperate hunger for affection that she would crave the touch of any man who would have her. She couldn't bring herself to listen to Tom and the other overstuffed peacocks of his precinct for another instant so she abruptly stood up and left the police station.

Although Pansy counted numerous reasons not to, she found herself hastening to get to the hotel room Jack had reserved for them, and when she arrived she was breathless and trembling with desire. In her present state of mind she wondered if she should even mention what she had discovered. She was terrified of losing whatever it was that brought Jack into her life, and suddenly it didn't matter what it was. She was deeply troubled as she tapped lightly on the hotel-room door, and in the next moment, when she looked into Jack's dark, troubled eyes she started to cry.

"I was at the police station before I came here," she blurted out. "My husband is a cop. But you already knew that." She sobbed miserably as the words spilled impulsively from her lips.

Jack didn't move or speak. He only smiled. Pansy was taken aback by this at first, but then she felt relieved. She couldn't have borne it if he had made up an obvious lie. She stopped crying and looked at him. Ruefully she succumbed to the slight pulling sensation at the corners of her mouth and dumbly returned his smile, but she said, "You have nothing to say?"

"What would you like me to say, Pansy?"

She would have liked him to say that he actually liked her in spite of everything else. She would have liked to hear that he had enjoyed being with her the day before and especially that he wanted to be with her again in the future. "Why?" she asked him. She was terribly afraid he would say the wrong thing.

Jack laughed at her. "Would you believe me if I told you that my dealings with your husband are purely coincidental and have nothing to do with us meeting each other?"

"No," but she was pleased by the manner in which he asked her this.

He moved closer to her, approaching cautiously. "Would you believe that I saw you with him once and couldn't get you out of my head?"

"Definitely not," she replied with outright laughter this time.

He became serious all of a sudden, standing very close to her and looking down into her face. He reached out a hand and lifted a lock of her hair. He held it a moment, seemingly studying it. Pansy was absurdly flattered by the gesture. She waited breathlessly for what he would do or say next.

"Would you believe…" he continued contemplatively as he played with her hair, "that I thought you deserved a little happiness being married to a prick like him?"

"Well, maybe you thought that…but I find it hard to believe that was your reason for…being with me."

"Does the reason matter so much?"

She paused, afraid to fully expose herself to him. "No," she sighed. "The reason doesn't matter. Only that you actually want to be with me, and not just for revenge."

He dropped her hair suddenly and grasped her hand, placing it firmly over his groin. She quivered when she felt his hardness. "Does that feel like revenge?"

"Because my husband can never find out about us," she continued.

A small, almost imperceptible change came over Jack's face when she said this. All the humor left his expression and he looked at Pansy with a mixture of irritation and indifference. The irritation did not bother her half as much as the indifference. She wished they could put this behind them and begin on a different note.

"Look, Jack," she began.

"What if I told you that your husband *is* going to find out about us?" he said spitefully. "I mean, what am I supposed to do with the video of us if I can't show it to your husband?"

Cold steel seemed to close over Pansy's heart when she heard his words. It was suddenly difficult for her to breathe.

"You're lying," she choked out.

"Am I?"

She looked around the room. There was no evidence of a camera anywhere, but she realized it would most likely be hidden. It occurred to her that both hotel rooms had been secured by Jack before she had arrived.

"I'm leaving." But she couldn't bring herself to move. Her eyes were wide with fear.

"Pansy, Pansy, Pansy," Jack said then, all of a sudden smiling again. His anger had abated as quickly as it had appeared and he was once again good-humored and charming. "You're so much fun to tease," he said smoothly. "There's no video of us. I wouldn't want to be caught in a video like that any more than you would." He began to laugh wholeheartedly, as if at the absurdity of her believing such a thing. But Pansy was deeply shaken.

"I don't like that kind of teasing," she said, upset. Her excitement had been squelched as thoroughly as embers doused with ice water.

"Then you shouldn't be so naive and trusting," he said with cheerful finality. The subject was abruptly closed and Jack was determined to move past it. He approached Pansy again and this time he put his hands on either side of her face, holding her just below the jawline in a firm but gentle caress. Her breathing stopped at the intense longing that came over her from this simple contact. She gazed up at him in abject adoration mingled with anguish. He appeared to her as a sumptuous feast, perhaps a poisonous feast; but like an animal, wild and starving, she would devour every last morsel to her gluttonous death. Jack saw the blatant hunger in her eyes and it caused the blood to rush to his groin in a violent surge. He continued to stroke the sides of her face with his thumbs. "Should you?" he whispered huskily.

Pansy was beside herself with a wish to appease him. "No, I guess I shouldn't," she whispered back, although she had forgotten the question. She felt weak and somewhat foolish, too. She vaguely wondered if Jack found her lack of self-control contemptible. But at that moment, there was such a look of tender passion in his eyes that it startled her. She looked away from him, saying, "I feel like a fool."

"You're no fool," Jack told her adamantly. He held her face in both his hands and forced her to look at him again. His expression was grave. "No woman has ever revealed her feelings so openly, right there on her face, with me before, Pansy," he told her. "It's truly humbling, and I'm the one who acted like a fool." Pansy was stunned by Jack's admission and silently waited for his next move, floating helplessly in a deep sea of arousal, and knowing no relief without him.

Jack continued to lightly caress Pansy's face as he went on talking to her, moving leisurely over his words, meandering in and around the pleasure to come. His voice was low and gentle, like his caresses. "But you shouldn't look at me like that," he repeated huskily. "Someone should have taught you never to let a man catch you looking at him like that." Pansy just kept staring into his eyes and listening to him, hypnotized by his voice and the gentle, steady strokes of his fingers on her face. She watched him with an almost ludicrous devotion. But Jack appeared to find nothing ludicrous in her expression, and he continued speaking to her in the same vein, tantalizing her with his words. His voice was so heavy and laden it seemed to be moving over her, even fondling her. "Perhaps I should teach you why you shouldn't look at a man the way you're looking at me now." He noticed that her eyes widened with anticipation when he said this, and he couldn't suppress a laugh. "You would like that, wouldn't you," he said, amused. "You would enjoy a lesson from Taskmaster Jack?"

Pansy began to shake. His unhurried attentions produced a bounty in her desolate existence that she could not resist. She nodded her head shamelessly to his rhetorical question, as if to assure him that yes, she would indeed welcome any lesson he would care to give. Jack laughed once again, and his desire seemed to increase suddenly in reaction to hers. "Let me see the marks I put on you yesterday," he said. "No, just turn around and take down your pants. Yes, like that." He stared at the red and purple welts on her bared buttocks and thighs. Pansy stood quietly trembling with her pants halfway down her legs. The cool air made her more aware of the wetness between them. Jack, as if reading her thoughts, reached down to touch her and with a moan he let his fingers wallow in the silky fluid.

"Christ, Pansy," he murmured. He moved onto his knees behind her and grasped her hips violently, causing her to cry out. "Bend," he said simply before pressing his face between her legs and burrowing his tongue into her wetness. Pansy was bent awkwardly at the waist, light-headed from the dizzying pleasure he was giving her. His tongue wriggled and writhed its way into her, first into her front passage and then into the back, repeatedly switching back and forth between the two as he ravished her thoroughly. Pansy struggled to maintain her footing as she basked in the heady sensations that were rushing over her. She positively loved the way he opened her up and exposed her to his every wish as he took and gave pleasure in equal parts. She knew she would let him lead her anywhere, no matter if it brought her pain, shock, embarrassment or anything else. But even before she could fully consider the possibilities of where Jack might lead her, he was already taking her there.

Jack grudgingly pulled himself away from her, pausing to kiss her buttocks on and around the welts. "I won't spank you again until you heal," he told her. Pansy captured from this remark the promise that they would be seeing each other more in the future. "I have something else in mind anyway," he added offhandedly.

Pansy thrilled to his words. She noticed that his eyes were fixed on something across the room as he spoke, and she followed his gaze to an odd little statue that she hadn't noticed before. It sat upon an elaborate footstool next to the bed. The statue was of a vicious-looking gargoyle with a sadistic grin on his hideous face. She wondered suddenly that she hadn't noticed it. The gargoyle held a sword in its hand, the tip aiming downward and the handle turned outward and up, so that it was pointing toward Pansy and Jack. Pansy did not fail to notice that the handle of the sword was of a similar shape and size of a man's penis, perhaps a bit larger. She felt a mixture of dread and longing curling up within her. Jack's eyes remained fixed on the statue.

"Pansy," he began slowly and thoughtfully, "take off your clothes." As she removed her clothing he walked over to where the statue stood. He seemed to be studying it. "Come here," he said after a minute or two. She shook off the last of her clothing and went to him. He looked her over. There was a lazy smile playing at his lips. "I want to see you ride the gargoyle's sword handle." Pansy closed her eyes. It had been exactly what she was thinking, and yet…

"Now," he demanded, sitting down on the bed. Pansy was uncertain of how to proceed. That she would do it was evident; yet it was extremely awkward. She didn't know if she should face the gargoyle or put her back to it. There was also the difficulty of getting onto the sword handle in such a way that she would be able to move up and down on it. And all the while she was painfully aware that Jack was watching her. She moved closer to the statue and saw that the object she was about to mount nearly reached her waist in height.

It would have been easier had it been slightly lower, for now she would have to accomplish her task on tiptoe. She decided to face the statue so that she could rest her hands on it for leverage. She positioned her feet on either side of the gargoyle and placed her hands tentatively on its repulsive head. Its hideous face seemed to be looking directly at her from this vantage point, and its lips twisted into a lecherous smirk. Very carefully she maneuvered herself over the tip of the handle, easing her body down on it ever so slowly. It was larger than it first appeared and much stiffer than most man-made objects for that purpose. It was as hard and cold as marble, and terribly irregular. She gasped as she struggled to push herself down farther on it. Its solid length was foreign and extremely menacing, although startlingly arousing, too. She was never so well lubricated to take on such an object and she slowly and cautiously inched herself down farther and farther, literally forcing herself lower and lower with each downward thrust. Even with her extreme wetness she could feel the solid edges pulling at her insides. It affected her in the same way that the previous day's beating had; leaving her weak and confused and craving, and fully unable to reason again until she found a release.

"That's it," Jack encouraged. "Just a little farther and you'll reach the end."

"I can't," she cried, even as she struggled to take more of it inside her. If only it were the tiniest bit flexible, she thought. But it was her body that was obliged to flex and yield to the hard edges of the gargoyle's sword handle. She gasped loudly as she wiggled and squirmed her way down the length of it. She clutched the gargoyle's head in her hands as she fought to get her body farther down on the rigid handle. "Ooooh!" she cried.

"Just a little more, Pansy...for me." The sound of Jack's gentle coaxing gave her strength. She grunted loudly as she finally succeeded in taking the last bit of the sword's handle inside her.

"That's a good girl," he praised her enthusiastically. "Now ride up and down on it." Pansy gripped the gargoyle's head firmly as she began to painstakingly move up and down over his handle. Her moans were mingled with little gasps and shrieks. Her pleasure was as intense as her suffering. She was no longer aware of how she performed for Jack as he watched her with eager surprise, and she was only vaguely aware that she had lost control and entered some forbidden place that she had never been to before.

"I'm afraid," she burst out in between gasps.

"Don't be afraid, Pansy," Jack chided her. "I'm here with you." And he came up behind her and kissed her shoulders and neck and pinched her nipples firmly between his fingertips. He moved one hand lower and began massaging her clitoris carefully, so as not to inhibit her movements over the statue. "That's it," he encouraged. "Go all the way down. I don't want to catch you going only halfway."

Pansy obediently drew her body up as far as she could on tiptoe and then descended all the way back down, over and over again, wailing and moaning like a woman possessed while Jack continued to cajole and caress her toward her climax. Her cries came louder and deeper the longer she rode the stiff and jagged shaft. She was in a state of arousal that surpassed all boundaries, but even if it had occurred to her to stop she would not have dared displease Jack by doing so. With dogged determination she pressed on tirelessly. Her tender insides clung to the statue as she pulled herself up, catching on the various ridges in its form, only to resist those same ridges when she pushed herself back down over it, so that every single movement had to be coerced, in spite of the moisture that poured from her body. The guttural sounds escaping her lips as she pumped her body up and down over the gargoyle seemed more suited to the gargoyle himself. Pansy absently wondered if perhaps it was the gargoyle, and not her, who uttered the sounds; for in spite of his hard, cold exterior, she was suddenly convinced that the gargoyle had become a living thing. She stared down into his grinning face as her legs continued to propel her up and down, up and down, along his rigid sword handle. And she knew suddenly that others had ridden the gargoyle's sword before her. His eyes seemed to mock her, taking in all of her appearance; from the tears on her cheeks to her parted lips, to her bouncing breasts. And with that notion it suddenly seemed that she actually was making love to the gargoyle. It felt as if he was ripping her apart, but it was her own legs that continued to drive her up and down over him. She knew that Jack was watching her as closely as the gargoyle watched her. He was looking over her shoulder, staring down at her with one hand crudely pinching her nipples while the other expertly stroked her swollen clitoris. If she stopped short of going all the way down on the sword handle he gently scolded her. When her cries became too loud he tenderly shushed her. She fervently wished that she could stay there, in the room with Jack and the gargoyle forever, as her release washed over her, and she screamed from the force of it.

But in spite of her earlier wish and the powerful passion she had felt, Pansy was profoundly relieved when it was over, and in the very next instant she was filled with so much remorse that she burst into tears. She struggled to remove herself from the sword handle, which had suddenly become excruciatingly painful. Jack helped her off the statue and pulled her close to him.

"Hey!" he said, genuinely concerned over her distress, which was nearing hysteria. "Pansy, its okay," he kept trying to soothe her, but he was at a loss for words. He wrapped her up in his arms and pulled her down onto the bed. He held her pressed so close to him that she had to struggle to breathe. His body remained aroused and hard, but he simply held her. "I'm sorry, Pansy."

She looked up at him, momentarily shocked out of her grief by his apology. Her surprised expression amused him. He kissed her tenderly, but then more passionately as her arms slipped up around his neck. And then she was lost all over again in her desire for this man she hardly knew, except that he wanted her for whatever reason.

Later, Pansy put her clothes on in silence. She perceived Jack's annoyance over her obvious regret.

"When can I see you again?" he asked impatiently. It suddenly occurred to Pansy that he was perhaps as unnerved by his desire to see her again as she was by her own.

"I don't know," she replied evasively.

"I see," Jack replied, failing to keep the irritation out of his voice. He was silent for a moment, and then, "I guess if I get bored I'll always have the videos."

Pansy stopped dressing and looked at him. "Don't worry…" He smiled at her. "They're for my eyes only."

Pansy stared at him. She felt a wave of nausea so powerful that she could taste the bile in her mouth. When he first mentioned a video, it seemed easy to believe it could have been a joke. Or perhaps it was easy for her to believe that with her desire for him looming over her like a shroud. But now, in the aftermath of that desire, with him bringing it up a second time, it seemed certain.

When the nausea passed, Pansy turned away from him and picked up the last of her clothing, dressing as quickly as she could. Then without a word she walked to the door and turned the knob.

"Pansy, I was kidding," she heard Jack say. She opened the door and walked out into the hallway. "Pansy!"

She continued walking down the hall and out of the building.

The instant she reached her car, Pansy dissolved into tears. *Why did I do it?* she kept asking herself. She wondered why every decision she ever made in her life had to carry with it such a high price. She continued in this vein of self-recrimination and self-pity until the tears were depleted. Then, once the despair receded she turned to anger.

What right, she raged inwardly, did people have to always take advantage of her? Jack, like Tom, had immediately assumed that because she was amenable she was weak. Why did everyone always have to try to get one over on her? She was filled to overflowing with impotent rage and suddenly Jack's taunt about the video recalled itself to her mind. In the next instant something peculiar happened. It seemed to Pansy that everything suddenly stopped. It lasted only a second or two, but it definitely stopped, leaving the hairs on the back of her neck tingling with life. The silence of it startled her. Afterward she might have thought she had imagined it, except that Pansy was certain that something had shifted in the interim. She struggled to pinpoint what happened.

Driving home, Pansy slowly realized that she was now looking *in* at herself from the outside, as well as *out* of herself from the inside, both at the same time. It was as if she was seeing her life from two different perspectives. She was suddenly filled with a strange calm as her thoughts began to collect themselves, seemingly of their own accord. All at once she perceived that she had other choices, choices that were already formulating into plans inside her mind. By the time she arrived home she was at ease with her thoughts.

Tom had once again arrived home before her. As on the previous night, he was talking to someone on the telephone in his study. She felt an odd sense of déjà vu that clashed momentarily with the parallel minds that were at war within her consciousness. The sound of Tom's voice, which usually caused her skin to prickle and twinge was tonight not nearly so bothersome, perhaps due to her preoccupation. She stepped into the doorway of his office and looked inside. A little rush of adrenaline trickled through her when she saw him, and she realized this was a result of the plans that were formulating in her mind.

"How's the case coming?" she asked him, smiling in secret and snuggling more cozily within her blanket of loathing. Her voice sounded a tad shrill in her state of overexcitedness. She felt strangely disconnected to everything around her as she tentatively sampled the role her parallel mind was creating.

"I'm getting nowhere," Tom complained with a sigh, scarcely noticing her. "If there isn't a break in the case soon, that son of a bitch is going to walk."

"Hmm," she said, trying to keep the joy out of her voice. "That's too bad." She was aware of a sense of being slightly off-kilter, but she was too excited about the drama that was—or was not— unfolding—she was becoming more and more unclear about which of these it was—and the things she would—or would not—do. Even so, to simply play along, for the time being, with these contemplations as they evolved within her consciousness and its parallel minds filled her with giddy excitement. She fairly skipped up the stairs and into their bedroom, where she went directly to her husband's secret hiding place and reverently pulled out his handgun. The icy steel of the gun, rather than bringing her abruptly to her senses, actually intensified the sense of unreality that was all around her. An alarm did sound in the farther-back reaches of her consciousness, but the madness that had consumed her was stronger, and it seemed to gain strength from the certainty of cold, heavy metal in her hands. A hysterical laugh welled up in her throat as she felt another surge of adrenaline run through her. *This isn't really happening,* she thought.

Even so, Pansy flipped the cylinder and checked to see if there were bullets inside. There were. Next she noticed the silencer in the gun case and was surprised by how easy it was to attach it to the gun. She pulled out an overnight bag that she kept under the bed, and placed the gun inside it, along with a pair of Tom's shoes and various articles of his clothing. When the overnight bag was stocked with these things she slid it back under the bed and waited.

"I think I'm going to go downstairs and read for a while," she told Tom several hours later. They were lying side by side in their bed. Tom was nearly asleep but Pansy was wide awake.

"Sure," he mumbled from beneath the covers. Pansy quietly slid the overnight bag out from under the bed and took it downstairs with her.

Less than thirty minutes later, she found herself staring thoughtfully at Jack's house from the inside of Tom's idling four-wheel drive. She knew for certain now that Jack had made those morning visits to her coffee shop solely for the purpose of seeking her out, for in examining his file on Tom's desk she discovered that he lived and worked all the way across town, with too many coffee shops in between them to count.

An excess of adrenaline was soaring through Pansy's bloodstream, giving her an almost supernatural sense of self. She barely noticed any discomfort or awkwardness as she went through the motions like a person in a dream, although everything all around her seemed foreign and unnatural. She had put Tom's shirt and pants on right over her clothing, and stuffed her feet into his shoes with her own shoes still on. She drove Tom's car without altering a single thing, not even adjusting the seat, making it so she had to sit on the very edge of it in order to reach the pedals. She performed all of these activities at the direction of her parallel mind, like an actor playing out a role in which the director has every last detail planned out, and she did all this without being fully cognizant of where it all was leading and without knowing if she would actually carry it through to the end.

Pansy pulled Tom's cap down low on her forehead as she quietly stepped out of his car. In spite of the layers of ill-fitting clothing, she moved as stealthily as a spider across the street and toward Jack's house. It was dark inside except for a dim light coming from one of the windows. Pansy walked instinctively toward the darkest side of the house, approaching it as if she had been there before. She strode cautiously along that side of it and then around the corner, careful to make her steps consistent and natural. She peered into the windows as she went. When she came upon the back door she reached out a gloved hand, prepared to attempt the lock with a master key she took from Tom's police key chain, but when she grasped the doorknob and turned, it was already unlocked. She smiled, realizing suddenly that Jack would not bother locking his doors, his reasoning likely being that if someone was determined to get in, they would do so. And, of course, he was perfectly right.

Pansy closed the door soundlessly behind her. She could hear television voices in the near distance. She pulled Tom's gun out from the waistband of her pants and flipped off the safety switch as she tiptoed through Jack's house, keeping the gun semi hidden at her side. The adrenaline flooding her system left no room for other emotions, except a lingering sense of unreality for everything around her. She looked around the dark rooms with mild interest as she moved onward, wondering absently what would happen next. She moved in the direction of the sounds coming from the television.

He was asleep. Pansy could see that immediately from the way he was slumped in his chair, even though he was facing away from her. She approached him slowly, expecting him to jump out at her in the next instant. But Jack didn't move, not even when she stood directly in front of him, staring at him. From deep within her she could feel stirrings of desire, but that was in her other mind. She waited for him to sense her presence and wake up, but he did not.

"Jack," she whispered at last. When this failed to rouse him she repeated it louder. "Jack!" There was a ringing in her ears. She kept the gun hidden at her side, although she now wished she did not have it. It seemed terribly heavy and burdensome all of a sudden.

Jack jerked awake at the sound of her voice. "Wha...Pansy?" He looked surprised, but not annoyed to see her. He stared at her in wonder. "What are you doing here, Pansy?" His voice was husky from sleep, and Pansy felt another wave of desire. His waking eyes were now taking in the strange clothes and oversize shoes. His expression went from wonder to uncertainty and he started to get up, but Pansy brought the gun from her side and pointed it at him.

Jack actually laughed; a spontaneous burst that lasted only a split second. "Pansy?" His voice was high with disbelief, but the smile was slowly fading from his face. "Is this a joke?"

"You mean, am I *teasing* you?" she asked with meaning. He didn't have to pretend not to know what she was referring to. Dawning came slowly, but she waited patiently without elaborating.

"Pansy, I swear to you," he said, completely serious now, "I would never, ever do that. There's no video."

"Did you kill your wife?" she asked him abruptly. It was the first time she really thought about it and she was curious. In the bizarre frame of mind she was in, it seemed more relevant than it had been when she was her other self.

"No, Pansy, I did not kill my wife," he said wearily.

She was becoming painfully aware of her finger on the trigger of the gun, and revulsion was quickly replacing her earlier rush of adrenaline. She realized suddenly that she could not kill Jack after all. In fact, her parallel mind had unexpectedly disappeared and now she was all alone with the horror of her situation. Jack seemed to comprehend some of this from her expression and he sagged back down in his chair in relief, although the gun was still pointed at him.

"Christ, Pansy," he said weakly. "I would never have said those things if I'd known they'd hurt you so much." She was staggered by the genuine compassion in his tone. She would have fully expected him to be angry, or perhaps even try to hurt her. Her earlier anger had by now dissolved into nothingness, as did all her previous angers. And yet they still lingered dormant inside her, unrecognized and unavenged. Pansy was immobilized with despair and uncertainty. She looked into Jack's troubled eyes and she felt a jolt from deep within her that caused her entire body to stiffen, including her finger that had remained on the trigger. The gun suddenly went off with a resounding *thunk*. Without even aiming, Pansy had shot Jack directly in the chest.

For the third time in two days, Pansy cried bitter tears of anguish and remorse, lamenting what she had done and issuing promises into the stifling air around her. One moment she was bemoaning her misfortunes and the next raging against the forces that seemed forever to be working against her. Eventually, as always, her thoughts came back around to Tom; fat, loathsome, useless Tom. Always her grief led her back to him.

But even as she stirred up her ongoing resentment of Tom, it suddenly occurred to her that something was different this time. She came alert with a newborn hope. Was it possible that she had fixed Tom once and for all? Her mind put all the events of the night together neatly and concisely as she quietly drove his car into their garage. It was Tom's car that had driven to—and quite possibly had been seen at or in the vicinity of—Jack's house. It was Tom's shoes that made footprints all around Jack's house, Tom's gun that fired the shot into Jack's heart, and bullets marked from Tom's gun that ultimately killed Jack. It wouldn't even be a lie when she told the police that she didn't know for certain whether or not Tom had remained home that night, having spent the night in the den where she had supposedly gone to read. Even if Jack had taped videos of their affair, which she doubted now, they would only add to Tom's motive and further explain his hatred for John Foreman. He had been obsessed with the man, and it would not be hard to prove that he had killed him.

Pansy was all at once exultant again. How perfectly just that Tom should feel the burn of being accused for something he didn't do. How many people had felt that same burn because of him, including possibly even Jack?

Pansy deliberately fell into a routine of inertness in the weeks that followed. She spoke almost never, steering clear of everyone and everything. The uncertainty of what might happen kept her in a constant state of acute watchfulness, and her worst fear was that Tom would not be linked to the murder after all. She knew firsthand how bungling and corrupt the men of her husband's precinct were, and it seemed more and more probable that the many subtle hints she had dropped would all be for nothing. Often she remonstrated with herself for not leaving some small possession of Tom's near Jack's body, but she had not wanted to make it too obvious, bringing suspicion in from the other end.

Just when Pansy had all but given up hope, John Foreman's murder investigation at last took a turn in Tom's direction. She could hardly believe her good fortune when at last they took him away. She remained quiet and thoughtful throughout the investigation and ensuing trial, appearing to all who observed her as the grief-stricken wife. She testified reluctantly of her inability to fully verify Tom's whereabouts on the night of the murder, and her reluctance was at least partially genuine, for she was absolutely terrified that she might slip and say too much. The prosecutor had to drag every last word from her quivering lips, and this too made it all the worse for Tom.

As for Jack's threat about a video, Pansy need never have

worried about that. There were no videotapes, and no one ever came forward to link Pansy with Jack on the two occasions when they had met in hotel rooms. She had even worried that a stray hair of hers may have appeared on Jack's body or clothing, but if such a thing had existed, the police never bothered with it. The police, who were Tom's peers and cut from the same cloth as him, had set their minds at the first hint of culpability upon his guilt, and once their minds were set they, like Tom, were loath to change course. It was, for them, a staggering tragedy, and they were equal parts sad and superior, shaking their heads at the difficulty of being a police officer and the statistical likelihood of it driving a person over the edge.

Tom was ultimately obliged to spend the rest of his life in solitary confinement, evading aggrieved convicts as he pondered what had happened.

"I would visit, Tom," Pansy told him one day over the phone. "But let's face it. There hasn't been anything between us for a long time now. To visit you would be to prolong the inevitable. You should just get on with your new life there."

But Jack was not so easy for Pansy to forget. She thought of him often, especially the last few moments they had shared together, when his thoughts had been for her. She came to think of their short-lived relationship as a great love affair, all the more poignant for having ended so tragically at the pinnacle of their affection.

Eventually Pansy was moved to go out and date, out of sheer dread of living alone more than anything else. One of Tom's associates at the precinct had expressed an interest, catching her off guard. She was charmed by his bemused demeanor and awkward advances. She sympathized with the challenges he faced, working so many unrewarding hours at the precinct and having no one to properly care for him. Surely with her help, he would have more success with his cases and perhaps even lose some of the excess weight he had put on from constantly eating in fast-food restaurants. Here, at last, was her second chance in life, and Pansy decided to seize it.

Perhaps things would be different this time.

* * * * *

CURLY LOCKS

Curly Locks, Curly Locks,
will you be mine?
You shall not wash dishes,
nor feed the swine.
But sit on a cushion
and sew a fine seam,
and sup upon strawberries,
sugar, and cream.

Carol sauntered into the café and flipped her curls confidently as she looked around the room. She quickly caught sight of Mary and Jane, sitting at opposite ends of a small round table. She was, as usual, the last to arrive.

"Ladies," she murmured without apology as she approached the women.

"Well! Here she is at last," said Jane. She eyed Carol with mild reproach, adding dryly, "And looking like a million dollars, too, as usual." Coming from anyone else, Carol might have interpreted such a remark as jealousy. But Jane, she knew, was neither impressed nor envious of her appearance. On the contrary, such comments were of a condescending nature, carrying within them an intonation of reproach for time wasted on frivolous and pointless endeavors. Carol had tried time and again to explain to Jane the importance of maintaining an image of beauty and femininity, but she soon realized that those were the efforts that were wasted. She once spent a full hour, for instance, outlining the merits of having acrylic nails applied and maintained on the tips of her fingers, but in the end it was a futile conversation that left Jane—who simply cut her fingernails with a nail clipper—more frustrated than ever with Carol, and vice versa.

In truth, Jane was as different from Carol as a person could be. Each was an utter enigma to the other; Jane being a staunch feminist who exhausted most of her energies fighting—or more specifically, complaining about—the battle of the sexes, and Carol refusing to believe any such battle existed. Men were, to Carol's mind, easily won over without a battle, and if there were any inequities between her and the men in her life, she was satisfied that she had somehow managed to tip the scales in her own favor after all. Women who felt differently were, in her opinion, simply not making the most of their opportunities. Carol felt that Jane, for instance, would get a lot further with the opposite sex if she expended some of her energy on her appearance, and less on fighting for equality.

Excluding these differences in opinion, Jane's feminist viewpoint had benefits. She made the perfect friend, having ready at all times an endless supply of rationale for just about every feminine behavior, while at the same time possessing a wealth of incriminations and suspect motivations for those behaviors that were male. This aptitude for adapting all her conclusions to her feminist viewpoint was wondrously supportive, especially in matters relating to her friends' relationships with men. No matter what scenarios Carol or Mary presented for discussion, it was already preordained that they—the women—would be the innocent victims, while the men would be cast as insufferable villains. She had come to rely on Jane for these little affirmations about her correctness in all that she did. And aside from these very supportive endorsements from Jane, there was the added benefit of appearing so much more attractive by comparison whenever Jane was around.

"When you have a million dollars to spend…" teased Mary, who openly envied Carol's many good fortunes, but in such an innocuous manner that it was flattering instead of threatening.

The waitress came over when she noticed the last of their party had arrived. "Drinks before you order?" she asked.

"Oh my, yes," cooed Carol happily. "I definitely think a drinkie is in order. I'll have a Sex on the Beach, and oh…if you could *supersize* it I would be ever so grateful." The women giggled at the suggestively made remark. Carol brought a genuine merriment to her jokes that infused even the most repetitive ones with new life.

"I'll have an iced tea," said Mary, and to Carol's disapproving look she added, "Some of us have to go back to work, you know."

"Nooo!" whined Carol, childishly clinking her bracelets on the table. "Come on! How often do we get together like this?" Although it was actually every week, Mary conceded.

"Okay," she said to the waitress, rolling her eyes with feigned reluctance. "*One* drink then."

The waitress didn't appear to care whether she had one or fifty. Trying to keep the annoyance out of her voice——clearly implying that she was not a mind reader——she asked, "*What* will you have?"

"I'll have the same as her," Mary said, blushing slightly. "A Sex on the Beach."

"Make it three," Jane told the waitress, and the woman left them.

"Whoa!" Carol laughed. "What an attitude on that one."

"So much for her tip," Mary added, slightly miffed.

"Is that very nice, Mary?" scolded Jane with a laugh. "Think how you would feel in her place."

"I think I would make a little more effort if I expected a tip," mused Mary.

"You know," Carol interjected thoughtfully, "I bet I would make a damn good waitress." At this, all three burst into loud laughter, but a moment later Carol was mildly offended. "Seriously," she said.

"What do you care?" asked Mary, who candidly and regularly expressed her belief that Carol had no cares or worries worth considering because she had a husband who was rich.

Jane, on the other hand, was of the opinion that Carol was wasting her life by living vicariously through her husband. As always, she took up the opposite viewpoint from Mary's, and said, "I think Carol would make an excellent waitress." But then she added as an afterthought, "God knows she's accustomed to serving her *master*."

"Oh, for God's sake, Jane," said Mary. "She doesn't work half as hard for her money as we both have to."

"Um, excuse me, ladies," interrupted Carol. "I'm sitting right here." The waitress arrived with their drinks. Carol thanked the woman profusely. "You *are* an angel," she gushed happily. Then straightaway she swallowed several mouthfuls of the tangerine-colored liquid and instantly felt better. Their conversation would be easier to take after a few of these. "Actually," she continued once the waitress was out of earshot, "if I *were* a waitress I would at least make an effort to bring some fun to my customers, along with the food and drinks, of course."

"And think of all the experience you have," said Jane, bringing the topic back around to her original point, "from waiting on Harvey hand and foot."

This kind of remark, which usually rolled right off of Carol, corresponded a little too closely with her own thoughts of late. She had been feeling that perhaps her life was going nowhere, and it seemed appropriate that her husband was the reason. After all, hadn't he been the main preoccupation in her life all these years? What might she have done with her time if not for having to always be thinking about him?

"Hand and foot?" echoed Mary. "What a crock!"

As usual, Carol's two best friends were at odds. They both were peculiarly interested in her life. Jane seemed to feel that every woman should be burning her bra while climbing mountains—both of these things made Carol shudder—while Mary was in the unpleasant position of already having to climb mountains in order to survive—and she wasn't feeling very liberated by it.

"Come on," replied Jane. "She sets her clock by the man. 'Oh dear, is it four o'clock already!'" she mimicked. "'I had better get home to Harvey!'"

"Well, what of it?" interjected Mary. "Don't the rest of us punch a time clock, too? I recall mentioning that I have to get back to the office."

This dispute might have gone back and forth in this way throughout their lunch if Carol had not abruptly interrupted them.

"Do you girls think I'm wasting my life with Harvey?" she asked.

They were both so unused to Carol sounding uncertain about anything, that they at first only stared at her, stunned. Then both of them answered at once.

"Yes," said Jane.

"No," said Mary.

"Do *you* think you're wasting your life?" asked Jane, excited by the prospect of Carol reaching the epiphany Jane felt she should reach.

"Well…I have wondered lately," Carol admitted.

"What could you have done without Harvey that you haven't done with him?" Mary asked her sensibly. "Or, even more importantly, what would you *do* without Harvey?"

"I don't know," replied Carol. "Maybe I would become a waitress."

"In that case, I think I would blow Harvey tonight," Mary told her.

"Oh, that's nice, Mary," Jane said. "Encourage her to further subjugate herself to him."

"Do you have any idea how much ass Carol would have to kiss to get the same kind of cash from waiting on tables that she gets from Harvey?" Mary asked her.

"Money isn't everything," said Jane piously.

"It isn't?" Both Mary and Carol asked this at once.

"No!" said Jane haughtily. "It's about self-respect."

"How much self-respect do you suppose that waitress has while putting up with our shit?" Mary asked her, forgetting for the moment her own earlier resentment for the waitress. "Or, for that matter, how much self-respect does a working mother have, when she is guilted into showing up for work instead of staying home with her sick child? Or a secretary who is browbeaten into picking up her boss's laundry?"

"Self-respect comes from within a person," said Jane in a sanctimonious tone. She had that untouchable sense of correctness that was as formidable as any religious faith. "You just *know* you are doing the right thing because you are doing it yourself. Self-respect comes out of that."

"Mmm," thought Mary. "You mean like when you borrowed money from Daddy to start up your business?"

"That is entirely different!" stormed Jane, becoming overly defensive all of a sudden. The vehemence of her tone caused Carol and Mary to exchange glances. Getting help from her father for the business had always been a sore spot for Jane, but lately any mention of her business at all seemed to have the power to upset her. They watched as Jane gulped down half her drink in an effort to compose herself. When she put down her glass she frowned at Mary. "I did not have to subjugate myself to my father for that."

"Perhaps not, but you can hardly sit there bragging that you did it entirely on your own, either," replied Mary in a gentler tone. "And besides, when did sex with the hubby become subjugation? Some of us would be pretty happy for a husband to screw right about now." Mary had a very simple and explicit viewpoint on things, and the reasoning of a woman who spent years being single and struggling on her own. Though she tried forming relationships with men again and again, she had never been able to capture the attention of one long enough to retrieve any sense of security or strength from him, let alone to form the kind of commitment required for marriage. Most people who knew her agreed that it was not any deficiency in Mary that caused her relationships to fail but, rather, it was simply that she longed for a relationship so wholeheartedly that it terrified the men who came in contact with her.

"Will you just be quiet for a minute and let Carol put in a word?" remarked Jane. Turning to Carol, she continued, remarking condescendingly, "I'm sure there are many dreams Carol had for her life that Harvey has squelched." She stared at Carol expectantly.

Carol paused, sipping the last of her drink noisily as she thought about it. The conversation was becoming a little more intense than usual, but Carol thrived on the attention. It was, perhaps, the glue that held the three together, that Mary and Jane were content to discuss Carol's life. Mary's issues were, although more real and pressing than Carol's, rather tedious and impenetrable, and Jane, on the other hand, never wished to discuss her problems. "I'm not really sure," Carol admitted at last. No squelched dreams appeared to come to mind.

"You see that," said Jane. "Harvey has her so engrossed in his life that she doesn't even know what she wants anymore."

"Jesus Christ, Jane!" Mary exclaimed. "Is that what you call women's liberation? To simply blame everyone else for everything?"

And in the next instant their friendly luncheon had become a heated debate between Mary and Jane about what feminism was and was not, and when the meal was over Carol left the café more than a little tipsy and considerably less than content. Usually these little gatherings cheered her, but this time she came away feeling depressed. Suddenly the emptiness of her life seemed to spread out before her in a wide expanse of nothingness that left her feeling desolate. What was there to look forward to?

She got into her car and drove, but she didn't want to go home. She set out on the highway heading south, her destination for the moment undecided. She felt an overwhelming sense of dissatisfaction with everything. Was it possible that Harvey had squelched all her dreams? Why couldn't she remember any dreams? All her thoughts and wishes had, for as long as she could recall, been connected to shopping, or getting her next corrective surgery, or attending her next party. But what did it all mean? Wasn't she supposed to have a purpose that extended beyond making herself happy in the moment?

Her melancholy was abruptly interrupted by an unfamiliar and eerie awareness creeping over her, even as her car simultaneously began veering inexplicably off to one side of the road and out of her control. Little by little her consciousness registered the sounds of crashing metals and breaking glass, and she could feel the sharp and shocking—yet peculiarly unreal—punctures to her flesh. Even as she comprehended these things, which appeared to be happening in slow motion, there was a violent rush of chemicals flooding through her bloodstream, giving the situation a supernatural effect that removed, for the moment, all terror, and put in its place an almost detached curiosity in the events as they occurred. At length, other cars rushed in all around her, and Carol felt her vehicle being slammed and twisted in all directions.

Once the initial uproar of the crash was over there was mostly silence, except for vague whimpers and occasional shouts, none of which Carol could make any sense of. She perceived only that the initial rush of comforting chemicals to her bloodstream was quickly wearing off and that they were being replaced with a very intense fear. She felt wetness all around her, and concentrated on not thinking about what it was. She focused all her energies on listening attentively; painstakingly assessing the noises around her, not in an effort to make out what they were, but searching for one distinct sound in particular. She waited single-mindedly for what seemed like hours, listening keenly and anxiously for the longed-for sound, and wishing earnestly for the moment when it would come. When at last it did come, she had to strain to be sure she heard it, barely audible at first, but quickly growing louder as the sirens of the ambulance approached, closer and closer. Only when she was certain the sound she awaited was the sound she heard did she finally stop listening and begin to cry.

In what seemed to be only an instant later, Carol's body jerked convulsively and her eyes opened to shockingly bright light. Abruptly she closed her eyes again. She knew instinctively not to move. There was pain everywhere—pain in places she couldn't even identify. She felt so incredibly weak that she wondered if she was fully alive. She longed to hear a voice. She tried to alert someone nearby that she was conscious, but it took three strenuous efforts to finally produce a slight moan.

"She's awake!" Was that Mary's voice? Carol tried to open her eyes again, but they kept snapping shut several more times before she was ultimately able to keep them open for any length of time.

"Lights," she croaked inaudibly, squinting and blinking uncontrollably.

"It's the lights!" Mary said to someone else in the room. "Turn them down!" She spoke in a harsh whisper, overemphasizing every word.

"Is that better?" Carol heard Jane ask.

"Jane?" She didn't dare move her head. Her eyes were finally able to focus without the harsh glare of fluorescent lights, and Mary's concerned face came into her view.

"My God, Carol," Mary whispered more calmly. "Take it easy now."

Someone took her icy hand into their warmer one and Jane's face came into view. "It's okay," Jane assured her in an authoritative tone. "You are going to be okay." Carol closed her eyes in relieved gratitude. Good, sensible Jane always knew what to say to make her feel better.

"Harvey's here, too," Mary added. "He has been right by your side the whole time. He only just left to get us more coffee."

They were covering all the foremost questions on her mind.

"What happened?" she managed to say.

"You were in a car accident," Mary told her, omitting all details of the accident itself, including that the police had been questioning Carol's alcohol levels or that it had been determined that the crash was her fault. "Everything is going to be fine," she assured her.

"My face?" Carol hardly dared to ask the question that was most prevalent in her mind. It had not even occurred to her to wonder if anyone else had been hurt or if she had been responsible. She held her breath as she waited for Mary to answer.

"Not a scratch," Mary told her. "Your injuries were all mainly in your—" She stopped there because Jane poked her. Carol caught a glimpse of Jane shaking her head at Mary from the corner of her eye.

"What injuries?" cried Carol frantically. "Tell me!"

"There might be some minor injuries to your back," Jane told Carol after a moment's hesitation. "The *doctor* will explain." Jane gave Mary a warning look.

"I want to know now," Carol insisted.

"There is really nothing to tell," Jane told her. "We are all still waiting to hear what the doctor has to say."

"Here's Harvey!" Mary blurted with an audible sigh of relief.

Mary and Jane left the room so that Harvey could discuss Carol's condition with her privately. In truth, Carol was remarkably fortunate to have suffered so few injuries. But those injuries were in her back and lower body, and there was the distinct possibility that she would never walk again. Neither of her friends wanted to be in the room when Carol learned this.

"I'm exhausted," Mary told Jane in the hospital waiting room. "I think I'll go home and get some sleep."

"I'm going to stay until the results of Carol's tests come back," Jane said determinedly.

Mary looked at Jane in surprise, but then a grateful smile came over her tired features.

"You've been a rock through all of this," she observed. Impulsively she kissed Jane's cheek before she left.

It wasn't until the following day that the tests came back conclusively that Carol had not suffered permanent damage to her spine and that, with hard work in rehabilitation, she could indeed expect a full recovery.

The news affected everyone differently. Jane was overjoyed.

Mary, once the worst was over, reverted to her old attitude of open envy, marveling cynically over the unbelievable good luck that Carol possessed. Harvey was optimistic and encouraging, fully focused on Carol and her healing.

Carol, who had been anxious but full of hope while waiting for the test results, suddenly became dejected upon hearing this news. She could not understand how people could call her fortunate or how the news of her condition could be interpreted as good. An extended period of laborious effort stretched out before her, impossibly dull and difficult, all for the purpose of getting her life back to where it was before the accident. She fell into a deep depression and seemed to grow more lethargic every day. She refused to begin her treatment, insisting that all she needed was a different doctor. The hospital staff became patiently disapproving, while Harvey and Mary were becoming openly frustrated. Only Jane remained unwaveringly sympathetic, spending hours upon hours by Carol's side, providing a never-ending supply of consolation and reassurance. Even Carol's inane and shallow chatter, which she would normally have found grating, Jane endured good-naturedly, even seeming to enjoy it and responding in kind. Meanwhile, Carol's condition continued to deteriorate, and no one seemed certain about exactly what to do.

One night, long after visiting hours were over at the hospital, a shadow fell over the sleeping body of Carol. It hovered motionless over her for perhaps half an hour.

In the dark room the woman stood staring at Carol thoughtfully. After a long while she removed a necklace from around her own neck and carefully placed it around Carol's. Then she leaned over Carol's body, very close—so close that her lips hovered just above Carol's, and she could feel her faint, regular breaths brush against her face. Very gradually, and with exceedingly subtle, almost imperceptible little gasps the woman began to inhale Carol's breath, pulling it in between her lips more and more vigorously as she went, until she was actually extracting the air from the deepest part of Carol's lungs. While she did this, the woman willed Carol to let go, concentrating all her energies on pulling Carol herself out with the oxygen she was taking from her body. The woman continued in this way for a very long time, pulling Carol's breath in purposefully and straining single-mindedly to subdue and capture Carol's very soul.

Carol came suddenly awake, but she did not struggle. She stared up in stunned surprise into the face of the woman bending over her. The woman stared back into Carol's eyes without faltering. In fact, it seemed her resolve was strengthened by Carol's sudden waking. She drew the breath from Carol's lungs even more violently, pulling with all her might while her eyes burned into Carol's, effectively forcing her will into Carol's consciousness. The woman labored tirelessly and resolutely without giving even the slightest consideration to failure. Carol's body shuddered with small, involuntary jerks as she gasped for the air that was being drawn out of her. At length the woman could feel Carol beginning to yield and once again she sucked in her breath with renewed force, doubling her efforts. Carol simply stared up at her, motionless and dazed.

There was a slight but definite release all of a sudden, and the woman felt an overwhelming thickness in her throat and lungs as she drew in one last long breath and everything that came with it. A wave of dizziness swept over her and she fought the nausea that followed it. She struggled to compose herself, realizing that there was little time to waste now that the first part of her objective had been so well accomplished. She pressed the offending entity down into the deepest part of her, where it seemed to settle without any kind of resistance. Carol's body slumped lifeless on the bed.

The woman leaned over Carol once again, this time focusing all the energy and the strength she had remaining into breathing life—her life—into Carol's body. Giving herself over completely to the years of restrained privation and longing, she forced all her innermost desires to the fore and concentrated and held them at her center, lying just below her heart in the space it held between her lungs. The intense and deep-rooted emotions were easily captured and contained, for they had been a part of her existence for as long as she could remember, beleaguering her always. Her constant cravings for the things Carol possessed were far more powerful than any lingering attachment she felt for the things in her own life. Uppermost in her thoughts was Harvey—kind, sweet, wonderful Harvey! Her yearning for him over the years had become painful. She concentrated on Harvey now, along with all the other things of Carol's that she coveted: the beauty, the money, the freedom. The only thing that separated her from these things that she yearned so earnestly for was the body she inhabited—a mere shell that should not have the power to keep her from them. She visualized Harvey's eyes, seeing her as Carol, and the intensity of her efforts doubled. She must succeed or it would not be worth going on. She could not survive another day of her own existence.

The woman's determination became a kind of frenzy that seemed to give her superhuman strength. She pushed the air out of her lungs and into Carol's body with remarkable force and in painfully long breaths destined to take the very life from her. Each failed attempt left her gasping for air and reason, but only for mere seconds before she tried yet again. With each of these extended exhalations she poured out all of her keenest desires, kept secret for so long. The irregular breaths, stretched out to such a degree, had the effect of making her giddy and light-headed. She began to believe that she was Carol, and that those things she had spent her life pining after were finally hers. Her conviction seemed to ease the burden of her task, and she could feel a distance forming between what was her life and what would be. She mentally threw the past behind her and grasped frantically at the future in front of her. It happened in a mere fraction of a second, in an easy, sliding shift that was almost imperceptible. Seemingly out of the blue she was lying on her back with a heavy weight upon her. Looking up, she saw that the weight was actually her own body; for she had collapsed over the body of Carol—her body now! She felt weak and terribly disoriented, but overwhelmingly content. It had happened. She had really done it! She relaxed then, losing consciousness.

Carol struggled to finish her physical-therapy exercises for that day. Her muscles shook violently from her efforts, which were impressive for anyone, but astounding for Carol. No one could believe her remarkable transformation over the last few weeks. It was supposed that the near-death experience she suffered that night in the hospital had caused the dramatic change in her; for she had been sluggish and depressed up until that point. Even the hospital staff had come to doubt that she would achieve any kind of recovery at all. But the inexplicable relapse, or perhaps the long period of unconsciousness that followed it, seemed to infuse Carol with a new lease on life.

Harvey was the one who was most amazed by the change in Carol. He had never before, in any circumstance, seen such determination in her. She was progressing so well that her body was not only healing but appeared to be in the best shape of her life. Harvey was filled with admiration for her, and he did everything in his power to help and encourage her.

During this time of convalescence, another change had taken place between Carol and Harvey. It seemed they were growing closer than either had ever dreamed possible. It appeared that Carol had suffered some memory loss through her ordeal, and in the process of Harvey reacquainting her with their past, the two had begun replanning their future. Instead of feigning interest in the things Harvey told her about himself, as Carol had always seemed inclined to do before the accident, she now asked him questions that demonstrated a genuine interest. Harvey found himself wanting to open up to her more. He rushed to the hospital to see her at the end of each day. And he responded in more ways than one to the new interest she was showing in him; something in the way she looked at him now caused a stirring deep within him. He had never before desired her so much, but now when he made advances she hesitated still; only this time it was not in the mocking way she had done before the accident, but with a shyness that was unusual for her. She was not teasing him, but seemed genuinely timid.

Given these developments, both Carol and Harvey were as nervous as newlyweds when at last the day came for him to take her home from the hospital. Carol wandered around their house, looking at everything as if she were seeing it for the first time. She literally scrutinized the items in every room. Harvey brought her suitcases to her bedroom. "I'll leave you alone to rest," he told her considerately.

"No!" she protested, surprising him with her vehemence. "I want you to stay with me."

"Sure," he told her. "I'll stay with you as long as you like."

Carol raised her eyes to meet his. "I want you to stay here with me all night," she told him quietly, but her voice held a calm determination.

"Won't my snoring disturb your sleep?" Harvey asked.

"I don't think that's going to bother me anymore," she said without elaborating.

Harvey sat on the bed while Carol examined the items in her various closets and fished through her dresser drawers. At last she discovered a gorgeous nightgown of pale silk that sent shivers of delight over her fingers where they brushed against it. She leisurely lifted the lacy garment from the drawer, deciding at once that she would wear it for Harvey on this very special night. It was a sheer, peach-colored slip of a thing that would do little more than cast a shadow over her lovely body. She turned to Harvey, holding it up. "Do you like this?" she asked him.

"What do you think?" he replied with a laugh.

Carol handed him the feathery garment. She stood before him, capturing his gaze as she began slowly unbuttoning her blouse. How many times she had dreamed of this moment!

It was peculiar—Carol's body was not perfect, but for her it had always represented perfection. She realized now that perhaps it was the way Carol had accentuated all the finer attributes she possessed that made her seem so. Or maybe it was merely the way Carol carried herself, making even her imperfections seem beautiful and sensual. She had never liked or accepted her body before, so she had never been able to find comfort or sensuality within her own skin. Always her movements had felt awkward and stilted, making it impossible for her to enjoy that body, especially in the presence of a man. With each intimacy she hid herself away to change, creeping about in the dark and feeling her way into bed.

She had never brazenly flaunted her body before a lover, but having admired Carol's body for so long, she was now, for the first time in her life, not only able to do it, she was longing to. She could easily have been an exhibitionist for the pride she felt in displaying herself for Harvey's pleasure. Her pulse quickened as she drew her blouse back off her shoulders and let it fall to the floor. The bra she wore underneath was lovely; a work of intricately woven lace that cupped and enhanced the look of the luscious breasts that were finally hers. No one had ever remarked on her former breasts—but then, she had never troubled herself to package them up in anything as lovely as the brassieres Carol owned. Perhaps they would not have seemed so commonplace if she had; but that didn't matter now. She had lovely breasts and the beautiful lingerie to wrap them in. She watched Harvey's face carefully as she reached around behind her to unsnap the bra and let it, too, fall to the floor. His eyes glowed as he stared, rapt, at the vision of her as she presented herself to him. She savored the expression on his face, and the little shivers of arousal it caused to course through her body. She could not resist running her hands over the soft, well-cared-for breasts, cupping them and even playfully pinching the nipples. Harvey's eyes widened as he watched her. She wondered if Carol had ever touched herself this way while Harvey looked on. From what she had gathered from her many discussions with Carol about her life with Harvey, sex was a tool she used to get what she wanted. She would be the one to reap the benefits of that now. All the years of teasing and tormenting

Harvey had cemented him to her forever. Carol had acted out of indifference and self-centeredness, but for Harvey it had created the illusion of value that was beyond anything he had thus far been able to achieve. Now, she would step in and love Harvey as she had always longed to do, openly and without a single worry of ever losing him.

She shimmied off her skirt and panties with amazing sensuality, exposing the rest of her perfectly groomed body to her long-awaited husband. She felt so extraordinarily sexy standing before him in the dimmed light. All was perfection and she was free to feel desire without the slightest sense of embarrassment or shame. She felt like posing and romping for Harvey in fact, uninhibited by any misgivings over her appearance, either real or imagined. She had admired and envied this body for far too long to see anything amiss in it now.

She moved closer to Harvey, offering herself to him with pride. But when he reached for her she turned her body around and raised her arms. "Would you help with my gown?" she asked demurely. He slipped the sheer nightgown over her shoulders. It fell over her curves perfectly, reaching midway over her hips. She turned back toward Harvey.

Now it was Carol's turn to watch in admiration as Harvey undressed for her. She stared at his strong, muscular body, enthralled, but was suddenly frightened when he came to remove his boxer shorts. She stopped him before he could do so, gently guiding him to sit on the bed. Then she sat on his lap, bare bottomed, taking his hand and pressing it between her legs, eager to have him touch her there and admire how pretty it was, and how ready she was for him. She couldn't wait to experience firsthand how it felt to be cherished and loved—truly loved—by the man of her dreams. But also she felt strangely timid; trembling and terribly vulnerable. She allowed herself to feel all these emotions, confident that she, as Carol, would be able to get what she wanted from her own dear, sweet Harvey. She knew he would never hurt her. She was amazed that any woman would take such a man for granted.

Harvey seemed to be dealing with his own set of emotions. He was surprised and delighted by this new behavior in his wife, though he had already begun to realize that things were improved between them since the accident. Still, it was as if all the years of trying to get close to Carol had finally led to this long-awaited moment. He could clearly see her need and vulnerability as she came to him now, completely unguarded and without the haughtily teasing manner she used to approach him with, and he suddenly realized how much he needed to have her come to him like this and how much it strengthened the bond that had been building through the long years of yearning and waiting and hoping. He had loved her through it all; now his heart seemed to be filling for her all over again. He took her in his arms, being especially gentle with her at first, but through her eager encouragement becoming more urgent also.

The first thing Carol was conscious of as she curled up next to Harvey was his incredible warmth. It drew her toward him instinctually, and she settled contentedly within the protective curve of his body. The heady pleasure of it stunned her momentarily. She had imagined his embrace hundreds of times, and yet, she had never been able to come close to bringing together all of the incredible aspects of its reality. The heat radiating from his body acted like a magnet to her cool skin. Reflexively her hands moved over him in an effort to capture some of it through her fingertips. For her, his warmth underscored his gentle strength and innate kindness. The former Carol had often mistaken Harvey's kindness for weakness. Not so with her. She found it almost unbearably attractive, especially when combined with his gentleness, which was made all the more exquisite by his hard, sinewy body. She fought the overwhelming emotions that assailed her and tried to concentrate only on the feel of his warm skin beneath her fingertips. Her cravings of a lifetime had not even begun to be fulfilled and yet, it was already almost too much for her to take. She felt like a starving person who suddenly eats too much too quickly. The sudden overabundance caused her to feel slightly sick. She tried to quiet herself by slowing all of her movements. Harvey, seemingly aware of her anxiety, simply held her tenderly, allowing her to set the pace.

When she had gained control of her emotions, Carol turned her face up toward Harvey's and his lips immediately came down over hers in an all-encompassing kiss. She had known it would be like that, so all at once gentle and passionate. She whimpered faintly as his tongue, soft and wet and warm, took possession of her mouth.

His breath was sweet; his lips tender and demanding. Her arms went around his neck and she pressed her body closer to his. Once again she was staggered by the heat penetrating off of him. She reveled in the way it felt to move her body alongside his. She pressed her breasts hard against his chest, holding him tighter in her arms, and moving her hips forward to rub against the hard length of him. There was a fullness bearing down deep within her womb that diverted her attention from everything but Harvey. Her desire was almost too strong for her to bear, and she repeatedly reminded herself that she was here to stay, forever. Harvey continued to kiss her leisurely and passionately while she moved her body sensually against him. His hands caressed her face, moving along her jawline and lightly rubbing her neck in a possessive embrace that left her feeling giddy and weak. She felt so desirable— and so much desire! Her breasts felt full and weighty as she moved them against his muscular chest. Harvey kissed her tirelessly, perhaps realizing that she would not be able to bear it if he stopped. When at last he did pull his lips away from hers, he looked hard and deep into her eyes, as if searching for something he'd missed before. She stared back at him helplessly, wondering if he saw the intense passion she felt there. She noticed the clear surprise in his expression, and she suddenly knew for certain that Carol had never really loved him.

"It's been so long," he whispered. She closed her eyes, fully enthralled by the sound of his voice. How lovely it was, more pleasing than any other she had heard before. Once again she felt surprised delight that she was really here with him, and that his soft, husky voice was addressing her. How utterly exquisite it was to have entitlement to him as his wife. Had she been born in this body she doubted she would have known how to bring this about; but she was here now and it had all been brought about for her. Each and every night, from this day forward, Harvey would walk through the front door of their house and come home to *her*. She could make whatever she wished of it. She could grow bored and lazy, as so many women did, or she could make an effort to nourish the rich bounty of feelings that existed between her and Harvey, keeping them alive and healthy. It was so remarkably easy. Strange that so many women should work so hard to escape this. Her decision had been made in an instant, although the desire and longing had been with her for as long as she could remember. The opportunity, when presented, made everything strikingly clear. All the anger and struggling and hopelessness; it all amounted to no more than simple frustration over her inability to have what she wanted. To complain was infinitely easier than to work for the things one wanted and needed, but it offered none of the satisfaction. If she and Harvey grew indifferent this time around, it would not be her actions that brought it about.

But she knew somehow that it would never be that way between them again. Harvey had remained loyal to Carol for this long in spite of everything, and there was no reason to fear that that would ever change.

Carol was now ready to embrace all the things that had overwhelmed or frightened her before, but she still forced herself to take it slow. Her fingers inched their way beneath the waistband of Harvey's boxer shorts. She was anxious all at once to get her hands around him, curious to know fully the most intimate details of the bargain she had made. Her fingers felt around greedily for him, quickly locating and then wrapping themselves about his solid thickness. She was pleased and delighted by what she found. Best of all was his irrefutable hardness; proof of his desire for her and promise of the pleasure he would give her. She ran her fingers all along the length of him, discovering him through her sense of touch, and then slowly and affectionately began to stroke him. She could hardly wait to feel him inside her, and she shivered suddenly as a sharp thrill ripped through her at the thought.

Harvey moaned over the pleasure Carol was giving him with her hand. He kissed her again and this time his hands simultaneously began to roam over the luscious curves of her body. She trembled with anticipation as his fingers traveled ever so gently and unhurriedly along the flesh of her inner thigh. She wanted to take in and set to memory every interchange and sensation, but there were suddenly too many to note. Harvey's tongue was mingling with hers in a deep kiss as his fingers at last reached the top of her thigh and lightly brushed across the lips of her labia. Up and down, and back and forth, his fingers struck gently and persistently over her distended flesh, teasing her, until the little lips parted for him and he was at last inside, sinking into her wetness. They both moaned over the feel of his touch to her silky desire, each breathing in the other's breath.

Harvey became impassioned all of a sudden, and it seemed that his hands were everywhere at once. Where Harvey's seductive tenderness had warmed Carol before, his aggressiveness now lit her on fire. She wrapped her arms around his neck and opened her legs wide to him, signaling her surrender and readiness for him. She wanted him inside her.

But Harvey surprised her by holding back still, no doubt with the desire to prolong their time of pleasure. He lingered untiringly over her body, not only using his hands to explore every part of her but also now employing his lips and tongue, pausing with dramatic effect to kiss or lick some part of her perfumed body. He kissed the tip of one breast and leisurely curled his tongue around the nipple before slipping lower and pressing his tongue into the cleft of her navel. Continuing down at a painfully slow pace, he leaned in between her legs, kissing her inner thighs lovingly and murmuring huskily, "I want to taste you first."

His words sent little ripples of pleasure pulsing through her. Her legs trembled uncontrollably as he moved between them, and her whole body jolted when his lips touched down. He only kissed her tenderly first, intimately, and then when she was certain she could bear it no longer he began licking up and down the length of her, running his tongue along her slit until her lips parted and opened to him. Carol clenched her hands, grasping the sheets on either side of her, and shut her eyes tight. Harvey's tongue seemed at first abrasive to the delicate skin of her inner flesh. As he delved deeper into her she could feel the stiff coarseness of his facial hair on her sensitive inner thighs. Oblivious to the mild abrasiveness of his advances or how they were further inflaming her, Harvey continued to devour Carol with enthusiasm. She clung to the bedsheets perilously, admonishing herself all the while that she must not think of anything but what he was doing to her; she must let herself *feel* it. In her mind's eye she visualized Harvey's beautiful face settled determinedly between her legs, and imagined seeing each individual action as he performed it. She pictured his mouth, so full and sensual, often with a hint of humor playing at the corners, but serious now as it kissed and licked and nipped at her, bringing her pleasure even while it subdued her. She wished it would go on forever, or at least until she could become accustomed to the sheer wondrousness of having Harvey loving her this way. Perhaps in time she would be able to have him thus without the excruciating exhilaration that distracted and ruffled her so much that it inhibited her ability to find satisfaction. Harvey seemed to sense her quandary, and so he took his time, sucking and pulling at her labia insistently while massaging her clitoris with his tongue, gently coaxing and coercing her arousal to the fore. Her sex quivered and contracted for him, and before long her hips were rocking back and forth wildly against his face, until Harvey decided he could wait no longer.

Harvey rose up over Carol, pulling her legs up and apart as he positioned himself in between. She looked up into his face with wonder, still not quite able to believe that she was with him and that in the next moment he would be inside her. The seconds seemed interminable as she waited breathlessly. Harvey tormented her further by holding back the moment of entry to slide the tip of his hardness up and down along the length of her opening. As he did this he closed his eyes, seeming to revel in the exquisite feeling of her warm and silky-smooth wetness on his sensitive skin, and building up both of their passions to overflowing. The throbbing arousal within them had progressed to the point that it had become achingly acute, causing sharp little stings of desire to pierce their swollen tissue. Carol's hips moved up and down as she waited for the moment when Harvey would come into her. And when the moment finally came, Harvey thrust himself into her with gusto, causing both of them to cry out. Carol could feel her engorged flesh clinging and grasping at Harvey's shaft as he pushed himself in and out of her. His delay in penetrating her had enhanced their pleasure to such a degree that, instead of merely feeling Harvey's thrusts, Carol could actually feel the friction all along her inflamed insides. She began to drown in the incredible sensations that rushed over her. Harvey leaned down to gently kiss her, barely grazing his lips over hers. The soft brush of his lips and breath against her face was so tenderly poignant that, for one instant, she was immobilized and unaware of anything but Harvey. There was an intimacy to the moment that she had never dared dream of experiencing. To her, Harvey's unconscious acts of tenderness were far more intimate than anything he could do to her body.

Carol moved her hips against Harvey's aggressively. She was torn between the desire to seek out her release and delay it. As powerful as the building tide of pleasure within her was, she longed to linger in the moment and savor every minute detail. She wished she could preserve the memories of each and every movement and gesture for eternity, to treasure like little keepsakes that she could call upon in times of need. She had learned through painful experience that genuine pleasure was hard won and often didn't last. She would not allow herself to take Harvey for granted, even though he had already proved he would endure much. She did not trust that part of her former self that was still within her. Her insecurities caused her mind to keep leaping greedily at the future, wondering over things that she could not at the moment foresee or control. She hungered for Harvey with an intensity that teetered on possessiveness. She wanted to capture and keep every aspect of him within her. She wished she could crawl inside him and stay there. But these thoughts spoiled the mood and inhibited satisfaction, so she struggled to enjoy the here and now, and leave thoughts and plans for the future for another time. Harvey—wonderful, warm, loving Harvey—was here, inside her, and his every thought was of her in this moment. This moment, at least, she could take him to her as fiercely as she pleased.

Carol clasped her arms and legs more tightly around Harvey and pulled his face toward hers, slipping her tongue into his warm, inviting mouth. It thrilled her to note his immediate response to her every single action. He felt her urgency and immediately responded in kind, picking up the pace and increasing the intensity of his thrusts. She gyrated her hips frantically against him, bringing about a delightful friction for her sensitive clitoris each time it came in contact with Harvey's body. Harvey realized why she was moving in this way and kept his own movements light and steady so as not to distract her. Carol was again delighted by his lovemaking, recalling how less knowledgeable lovers from her past had mistaken her movements for something else, interrupting and thwarting her satisfaction in their impatience to reach their own. Unlike them, Harvey—wise, considerate Harvey—allowed her to set the pace, patiently waiting for her to be satisfied. In fact, he set out to help her along by moving his hands over her body, turning even the most nonsensual parts of her into erogenous zones. With this encouragement from Harvey, Carol was able to go deeper and deeper into herself as she continued her rigorous movements single-mindedly. She rocked her hips up and down in just the way that felt best, faster and faster and with more and more force until at last the delectable little waves rolled over her, again and again, making her entire body quake and jerk. It was the first time she had ever achieved this satisfaction with a man inside her.

Harvey, who had up until now been satisfied to take only as much pleasure as it would assist Carol's pleasure to take, was suddenly overcome with a violent lust. Carol's body had become even more softened and enticing from her climax, and her inner walls clung to him persuasively as he moved in and out of her. Even so, he held back and slowed his movements for as long as he could, luxuriating in the soft, clingy feel of her, and then gradually quickened his pace, giving himself over completely to his passion.

Now it was Carol who ran her hands over Harvey's body while opening herself even more fully to his vigorous thrusts. She lovingly coaxed and cajoled him as he got his satisfaction from her. When he released himself into her she felt her heart soar with delight from the thrill of it. She could have wept, but instead pulled him close to her and held him almost violently. He did not pull away, staying willingly in her embrace.

After a moment, Harvey leaned up on one elbow to examine Carol's face. His expression was pleased, but slightly puzzled, and she smiled at him, genuinely happy for the first time in her life. His look told her clearly that it had never been this good between them before. She told herself that it was better now because he was with *her,* the new and improved Carol. The Carol she always should have been. She could not resist reaching her hand out and tenderly touching his face. He kissed her then and she could feel his happiness, too. How easy it was to please a man who loved you. How impossible to please one who didn't. But she reminded herself that she would never have to think about those men again.

Harvey rolled off Carol's body eventually, and she was aware of the cold air all around her. But he did not go far, and when she moved toward him he took her to him, curling his body around hers and embracing her with his arms held tightly around her, holding her close.

"Are you sure you want me to stay with you all night?" he asked her. The question shocked her. How could Carol have ever allowed him to leave her bed?

"Quite sure," she told him adamantly. She did not explain that she could not bear it if he left her after what they had just shared. She tried not to think about the many men who had roused themselves from her bed after intimacies in the past. She snuggled up against Harvey, knowing that she would never wish to sleep alone without him again.

Carol was too excited to sleep, but she lay contentedly in Harvey's embrace, thinking about all that had happened and trying to accept her incredible new life. In a little while Harvey began snoring. It made her smile. The sounds of his breathing were loud but repetitive and steady, and for some reason they brought tears to her eyes.

Always a bridesmaid, never a bride, the old saying came to her mind. She had thought of it countless times but this was the first time it made her laugh; for this night was, for her, the true equivalent of a wedding night. Surely no bride had ever begun her life so optimistically, or so blissfully. She longed for morning to come so that she could get on with her life with Harvey. Enough of sleeping and waiting; she wanted to *live* her life! She fell asleep with the tears still on her cheeks, lulled by Harvey's hearty snores into a deep and peaceful slumber.

Before dawn Carol came sleepily awake. It was still pitch-dark as she once again came to terms with her new surroundings. Harvey was already gone from their bed. She sat up, looking all around her as her eyes became adjusted to the dark. Memories of their lovemaking the night before rushed back to her and she smiled. She heard the toilet flush and realized she must have been roused when Harvey got up to use the bathroom. She lay back down on her pillow, happy and at peace.

She waited contentedly for Harvey to quietly make his way back to the bed. She was filled with desire for him all over again. He settled himself under the covers beside her, careful not to wake her. Carol snuggled up closer to him, delighting once again in the wonderful heat of him. Immediately his arms came around her, strong and gentle, and she felt her body yearning for him. She marveled over how wonderful it all was; that she could reach for him and he would actually pull her to him, or that she could want him and he would respond. She turned her face into his chest and kissed the warm, muscular flesh again and again, all the while feeling his heart drumming steadily beneath the surface with her fingers. His arms tightened around her. She tipped her head up toward his face and he, in perfect accord with her yet again, bent his head down toward her and touched her lips with his. To Carol, Harvey's response was so incredible and exquisite and esteemed that it was almost painful to endure. She prayed the novelty and thrill of it would wear off just a little, before she lost her mind. Their kiss was lazy and affectionate but quickly becoming more passionate. Pressed up so close against Harvey, she could feel him growing hard against her. She slipped her hand down inside the band in his boxer shorts and grasped his growing hardness. Stroking him all the while, she brazenly turned her body on its side, facing away from him, and pulled up her nightdress while simultaneously pressing her bare bottom into the curve of his groin, wiggling around his hardness so that it settled in between her cheeks. Needing no further encouragement Harvey pressed himself into her soft wetness from behind, holding her firmly in his arms while he found his pace with her in this position. She lay on her side with her legs bent toward her body to accommodate him better. They had not exchanged a single word. Harvey took her swiftly and urgently this time, holding back only until she was satisfied and then releasing himself inside her with a groan.

Neither moved away afterward; they merely drifted back to sleep while still joined in the embrace of their lovemaking. Carol lay silently in Harvey's arms, feeling truly safe and protected for the first time in her life. His warmth was almost overwhelming with the blankets over their bodies, holding the heat in, but she could not bring herself to move away from him. She would rather suffocate than move away. Yes, at long last this was where she belonged.

Several weeks later no one would have guessed that she had been through any kind of trauma at all when Carol stepped into the little café with a confident air, swishing her lovely curls this way and that as she looked around the room.

"Surely this can't be the Carol I've come to know and love," someone asked her from behind. She turned to see Mary laughing at her. "I don't think in all the time I have known you, you've ever been on time!"

Carol laughed. "A near-death experience will do that to a girl."

"You look amazing."

"I feel amazing," Carol responded happily. "Let's get a table."

Mary stared openly at Carol with an almost incredulous expression on her face. She seemed to sense something different about her.

"A Shirley Temple for me," Carol told the waitress when they were seated. When Mary heard this her expression became one of genuine shock. Carol laughed. "I'm driving."

"Of course," said Mary. "You're perfectly right." Things seemed to be changing too quickly for Mary to comfortably absorb.

There was silence for several moments. Neither appeared to know exactly how to broach the subject that was uppermost on their minds. A palpable sadness hung in the air around them.

"I went to see Jane," Mary said at last.

"Oh?" queried Carol, keeping her expression fixed. "How was she?"

"The same."

"What's going to happen to her?" Carol wondered halfheartedly.

Mary sighed. "I don't know. I guess for the time being they'll keep her in that place."

There was another pregnant silence. Mary seemed to be struggling for the right words. "What on earth happened that night?" she asked at last.

"I have no idea," Carol said, also carefully choosing her words. "I was so drugged up during that time it's all kind of fuzzy," she lied. "All I really remember is Jane freaking out." She shuddered all of a sudden and that was genuine. She looked at Mary, repeating the account that she knew Mary had already heard from Harvey and the nursing staff. "She kept screaming that she was *me,* over and over again."

"Did she say anything else?" Mary wanted to know.

"Not that I can recall," Carol said, pretending to consider the question at length. She paused a moment and then asked in a casual tone, "Did Jane say anything to you?"

Mary shook her head. She had noticeably paled. "I do remember thinking she seemed a little overly interested in your recovery, but I had no idea she was so affected by what happened. I thought she was just being a good friend."

"I feel responsible somehow."

"How could you be?" Mary asked her soothingly. Then she added, "But I have to admit, if any of us was going to lose it, I never would have thought it would be Jane. I really thought she had it together."

"I don't think Jane ever confided in us about everything that was really going on in her life. I think she had more problems than she let on," Carol said.

"Did you know she was on the verge of losing her business?"

"I had heard that afterward, yes," Carol replied.

"It seems so strange without her here."

"I know."

Their drinks came then. Carol raised her glass. "To Jane," she said. There were tears in her eyes, but they were tears of joy.

Mary touched her glass to Carol's. "To Jane."

* * * * *

DESPERATE DAN

Desperate Dan, the dirty old man
washed his face in a frying pan.

Claire walked into the shoddy little restaurant and tried to ignore that all eyes were on her. It was nerve-racking being the object of so much attention. She had never received so much as a second glance when entering a room back in Chicago, but here in this small town she was practically a celebrity. She was actually the first person to move to Anamoose, North Dakota, in over twelve years. None of the locals could believe she had done it. It was always the first question she was asked by the people she met: What on earth made you come here? Which meant she was asked it a lot, because even though it was a town of just over three hundred people, it was inevitable that she would meet every last one of them. She always answered the question with the same unwavering reply: that she preferred peace and quiet for her work, and furthermore—she would always add—she absolutely adored living in the country. This seemed to satisfy the askers, even though any one of them might have reasoned that there were plenty of quiet little country towns that were not quite so…bygone as theirs. Anamoose looked like a town that had been passed over and left behind, giving it a sense of eeriness that was just as tangible as the old, decrepit buildings that lined the streets. But if her questioners were at all skeptical of her explanation they never mentioned it to Claire. And she could hardly have told the plain-faced, straightforward inhabitants of Anamoose that her real connection with their town originated more than thirty years ago, when she was just a small girl learning to read and happened to come across the name Anamoose on a label on a jar of her favorite rhubarb jelly. It would have seemed strange indeed to have attempted to explain that she remembered the name all these years because, to the ears of the whimsical child she was back then, there was a pleasing ring to it that made it seem a kinder, friendlier place than the one she presently found herself in. She used to repeat the name out loud, again and again. She tried to imagine what a place called Anamoose would be like. Sometimes, when she was angry, she was apt to think, I shall go to Anamoose someday, and live happily ever after there. It was a childish fancy that carried over into a troubled adolescence and then stubbornly remained through adulthood, becoming by then almost a mantra to get her through difficult times. Like religious people look forward to ascending upward toward the heavens someday, so Claire always imagined going to Anamoose.

Even so, Claire never really believed she would ever go. As long as there was even the tiniest thread of hope that she might someday assimilate herself to the city where she was born and raised, she continued the struggle to exist there. But each time she came close to building any real ties, it seemed the fast-paced city of Chicago would metamorphose into something new altogether, leaving Claire behind to start all over again. Yet always there remained some small bond that was too hard won to simply walk away from. The deciding factor came at last when her fiancé, David, broke off their engagement. Theirs had been a convenient but shallow connection that impressed her more than anything else by its very existence, and it fizzled into nothingness with almost as little fanfare as the original proposal. But with that final blow Claire at last admitted to herself that there was nothing real to keep her there. And once the decision was made it was remarkably easy. There were no close friends to bemoan her leaving, and no other male admirers to pine over her. Even her mother had moved on and left Claire behind, sitting tranquilly by herself, day after day, in a tiny room at the full-care facility that housed her, having settled herself into a pleasant and mysterious place of her own making. There was hardly anyone for Claire to notify that she was leaving; not even so much as an employer to which she must tender her resignation. She worked from a small office in her apartment, for a company far away, who mailed her checks in exchange for completed manuscripts of newly updated textbooks. It was all very technical and Claire was proficient at it, so there was little communiqué necessary between the parties at all. Her landlord was the only person with whom she was obliged to discuss her move away from the city, aside from the post office. Her landlord seemed genuinely disappointed to lose her, complaining that she was the only tenant in the building who paid the rent on time every single month; whereas the postal employee she spoke to was much less affected, abruptly sending her to the self-serve desk where she could fill out a form and mail it back to them.

But to the residents of Anamoose, North Dakota, her life was a different matter entirely. Claire was received with a remarkable amount of interest by everyone she encountered, from the clerk at the market to even the men she passed working outdoors. And as for the employees of the Anamoose Post Office, they took down her information as if it was of the highest importance, and the post-master himself filled out the little change-of-address card for her, going to great lengths to assure her that every piece of mail that was addressed to her would be delivered correctly and on time.

All this was frightening to Claire at first. Her distrustful mind could not help wondering what all the attention she was getting was going to cost, and she doubted that she would be able to foot the bill. She knew there was little that was particularly notewor-thy about her and that in any other town she was more apt to dis-appear altogether into the woodwork. She realized that it wasn't something extraordinary about her as a person that was causing the interest, but simply that she was a new face in the stale little town. And furthermore, her coming to Anamoose from the city suggested she must be chic and sophisticated, if not beautiful or charming. In time, she knew the novelty would wear off and she would become just like everyone else in the town, and this thought appealed to her. To finally belong somewhere and be known by the people around her was all she had ever hoped for. All of her previous relationships had been shallow and fleeting, leaving her to wonder if she even possessed the skills required to develop lifelong connections. But now, she believed and even knew that she would find those kinds of connections in Anamoose, just as she always dreamed she would from as far back as when she was a child.

During her weeks of notoriety, Claire's presence never failed to trigger a response from the men she happened to encounter. Although she applied the same common-sense reasoning to this phenomenon, there was nevertheless something awakened in her from this new kind of attention that caused her no little distress and anxiety. She found herself longing for things she had spent years forcing out of her consciousness.

There was one man in particular who stirred more than the usual amount of discomfort with his curiosity over her. Claire guessed him to be in his early fifties, and felt he might have been attractive if not for the deep scars that covered his face and neck. The unsightly marks gave him a menacing appearance that bordered on frightening. Glassy blue eyes stared out intently from this homely visage with an expression that contained a combination of interest and humility. Claire was alarmed by the realization that she was never in the strange man's presence when his blue eyes were not fixed on her. His interest seemed to extend much further than anyone else's in the town, male or female. She wondered resentfully if he felt she was, in her own unspectacular way, a suitable match for him. She found herself painstakingly avoiding him.

It took only a few weeks for Claire to develop deeper ties within the sociable community of Anamoose than she had formed with the inhabitants of Chicago over a lifetime. One of these was with Maggie, who owned the Widow, the only restaurant in town. Claire was quickly becoming its most regular customer, being a terrible cook and discovering that she enjoyed the company of people when they actually took an interest in her. The atmosphere at the Widow was exactly what Claire might have imagined it to be, had she thought to create a friendly little restaurant in the town of her dreams. It was warm, lighthearted and loud. The first time she stepped into the place had proved to be a bit harrowing, as conversation had immediately stopped and all eyes had turned to look at her. But now when she came through the doors of the quaint little restaurant she was acknowledged with some hearty hellos and friendly nods of the head.

Maggie smiled warmly as Claire slipped onto a stool at the bar. The two had taken an immediate liking to each other. One reason for this was that Maggie was closer to Claire's age than the majority of the women of Anamoose, who were either terribly old or extremely young. Maggie was just in her forties, and full of bright energy.

"How's it going over there today?" Maggie asked cheerfully.

Claire sighed. "I'm having a few problems," she said. This was the way most of their conversations began. Maggie was, for Claire, the Anamoose Information Center. She discussed the problems and difficulties she encountered with Maggie and trusted all of her advice. "The most pressing thing is that I have to get the water heater fixed. I turned up the temperature, like you suggested, but it's only getting worse. The water's barely even getting warm now."

"Oh dear," said Maggie. "I was afraid of that." She gave Claire a small smile. "Looks like you're going to need Dan."

"Dan?" Claire tried to remember if she had met anyone called Dan.

"Yeah." Maggie sighed. "He's our Mr. Fix-it around here."

"Where can I find him?" Claire asked.

"Look no further," Maggie chirped. "Dan!" she called loudly over Claire's shoulder, looking out across the room behind her.

Claire turned, following Maggie's gaze to a back corner of the restaurant, and discovered glassy blue eyes staring intently at her. She was certain he hadn't been there when she first came in. She turned back to Maggie, but couldn't catch her eye.

"We need your services over here," Maggie was saying to Dan.

"I don't think..." Claire started to object in a low voice, but then closed her mouth when she realized that she didn't know how to put into words her innate objection to the man.

Dan approached them slowly, coming to stand behind Claire, slightly to the right of where she sat and close enough that she could feel his nearness. She turned awkwardly to meet his eyes and said with a stiff smile, "Hello."

He nodded. Maggie introduced them, quickly going on to explain Claire's dilemma with the water heater. She ended with, "When do you think you could get to it, Dan?"

Dan was silently thoughtful for a moment. Although Claire had turned away from him immediately after he had acknowledged her, she knew—she could feel—that his glassy blue stare had remained on her profile throughout Maggie's explanation. She felt his eyes on her still. Her face burned as she waited for his reply. When he didn't answer she turned to meet his blue gaze.

"I might be able to get over there tomorrow morning," he said finally. His voice was quiet and low.

"Great!" Maggie raised her eyebrows at Claire. "That's one down," she said with satisfaction. "What's next?"

In spite of the tension she felt, Claire laughed nervously. She wished fervently for Dan to go away. She could still feel his eyes upon her. She tried to pretend he wasn't there, uncomfortably continuing her conversation with Maggie. "You wouldn't know anyone who can type, would you?"

"Mmm…" Maggie tapped her chin with her finger. "I think Brenda does some typing…" Her voice trailed off as she thought about it.

Claire, meanwhile, concentrated on ignoring Dan and his intimidating stare. She felt him beside her and wondered why he didn't go away. Her face continued to burn under the heat of his gaze. She tried unsuccessfully to concentrate on what Maggie was saying. She felt as if there was a constriction in her chest and struggled for breath. Suddenly unable to endure it a moment longer she turned toward him, not even certain of what she would do or say, but in the next instant she gasped in shock to see that he was no longer there. She looked anxiously all around her, but Dan was nowhere to be seen. She turned back toward Maggie on her stool. The heat in her cheeks was quickly cooling as the blood drained from her face. When had he left? How could she have felt him there so distinctly if he wasn't there? She looked at Maggie. "Where did he go?"

"Who?" Maggie asked.

"Dan!"

"He went out the front door."

"Oh."

"Anyway…" Maggie was still discussing typists and resumed the conversation where she left off before Claire interrupted her.

"What's his story?" Claire asked suddenly, interrupting her again.

"Who…Dan?"

"Yes."

Maggie looked at her curiously and then released a small shrug. "I'm not sure Dan has a story," she said.

"I wouldn't be too sure about that," interjected a voice from a few seats down along the bar. Claire turned and saw that it came from a young, grinning man, heartily wolfing down the luncheon special.

"What do you mean?" she asked him.

"Be quiet, Bruce," Maggie said. "Don't pay any attention to him," she told Claire.

"I want to know," Claire insisted.

"She's going to hear it sometime, Maggie," said Bruce. He smiled at Claire, clearly delighted to have a new audience for what was obviously an old story. Other people in the café were now listening in and some of the other men were chuckling quietly. "Around here he's known as Desperate Dan, the dirty old man."

"Why do they call him that?" asked Claire.

"Because they're a bunch of mean-spirited, immature—" Maggie began, suddenly becoming outraged.

"Because he's a perv," Bruce interrupted her, shrugging his shoulders. In the silence that followed, it occurred to Claire that this was all Bruce was going to say on the matter, and now he was simply finishing his lunch while waiting for Claire's reaction.

Maggie picked up the subject from there. "Some of the guys around here like to tease Dan because no one has ever seen him with a woman," she explained. "He's always been a little strange, so someone started repeating that rhyme and it just kind of stuck." She gave Bruce a reproachful look. "They have absolutely no basis for calling him a pervert."

"I wouldn't be too sure about that," said Bruce knowingly, as if his uncertainty, in and of itself, were a statement of fact. Another trickle of snickers could be heard along the bar.

"Oh, just shut up, you fools!" said Maggie suddenly. She

tossed the towel down and made to turn away, but Claire stopped her.

"Maggie, should I be letting him in my house to fix my water heater?" she asked. "I didn't want to say anything before, but he does kind of give me the creeps."

Maggie looked at her squarely. "I have known Dan all my life," she said solemnly. "Believe me when I tell you, he is truly harmless."

"Are you sure?" Claire asked.

"I would trust him a lot further than I would trust Bruce here," Maggie said with a deliberate glare at Bruce, who accepted this as good-naturedly as if Maggie had handed him a compliment.

Claire was mildly comforted by this, but nevertheless found herself thinking about "Desperate Dan" all that afternoon and later that night. Was it true that he had never been with a woman? Is that why he stared at her with that strange, concentrated gaze? Did he look at all women like that, or was there something about her in particular that aroused his interest? She shuddered when she recalled what Bruce had said. *Desperate Dan, the dirty old man!* That keen stare he fixed on her really did project a sort of desperation from behind the eyes. But did desperation automatically signify perversion? She slept poorly, tossing and turning until early morning, when at last she fell into a deep slumber.

She was startled out of her sleep by a sharp knocking.

Confused, she reluctantly pulled herself up and peered out the window. Desperate Dan stood on her stoop, waiting. She came suddenly awake, stumbling around her bedroom in search of a robe. The knocking came again, louder and more urgently this time. In her dazed state Claire found it alarming. Finding a bulky robe at last, she rushed toward the front door while putting it on and pulling the ties tightly about her waist. She threw open the door just as Dan was about to knock a third time.

His eyes took in her appearance from head to toe while she struggled for the appropriate words. "I'm sorry. I guess I over-slept." She wondered what time it was. He simply stared at her in silence.

"Um, okay, well…I guess I should show you where the water heater is," she said, feeling annoyed with him already. She turned and gestured suddenly for him to go ahead of her. She felt almost frantic to get his eyes off of her. Dan moved ahead of her grace-fully, carrying a large tin box full of tools in one hand as he went. "The stairs to the basement are just down the hall to the right," she informed him.

"I know," he said simply.

"Oh," she said. "Yes, you probably worked here before…with the previous tenants." She felt stupid saying this. He didn't reply.

"I can't seem to get the water hot enough, and the small amount of heating it provides doesn't last very long at all," she continued nervously as she followed him down the stairs.

"I know," he said again. He turned and fixed his disturbing gaze on her face. "I can take it from here," he told her. He continued to stare at her as he waited for her to leave.

"Okay," she said. She noticed her voice had a shrill edge to it. "Okay then," she said again, a little more smoothly. "I'll just go back upstairs then." Still he just looked at her. "Okay," she said yet again and turned to leave. To her embarrassment he did not move a muscle until she was all the way up the stairs and through the doorway. He just watched her as she went, and it took all her effort not to break into a run to get up the stairs and away from his gaze. When at last she had escaped his penetrating eyes she shut the door behind her and collapsed against it. No wonder they called him names, she thought. He deserved it.

She dressed quickly, aware that Dan could be coming up the stairs any moment. No doubt he would stare just as openly and calmly if he found her half-naked as he did when she was clothed. The thought of this caused a strange thrill to shoot through her and she shuddered in horror. But she dressed even faster.

In the end, she had time to make coffee and breakfast and still had fifteen minutes more to wait for Dan to finish with the water heater. During this time she was peculiarly aware of him in her basement. It was disturbing to know that he was likely more familiar with her new home than she was. She waited anxiously for him to finish. She felt unable to begin her day while he was there. At last she heard him trudging up the stairs. She paused nervously, uncertain as to whether she should meet him at the top of the stairs or wait for him to find her in the kitchen. She picked up her checkbook and then set it back down on the counter. Then she picked up a cup of coffee and tried to take a sip but it felt too awkward so she simply held the cup and waited. He was taking his own sweet time about it and she sighed with exasperation as she waited for him.

He did not call out to her but came directly into the kitchen. He stood in the doorway and looked at her. Without even realizing she was doing it, Claire began grinding her teeth.

"Finished?" she asked, tipping the cup over her bottom lip casually, but somehow missing her mark and spilling coffee down the front of her shirt. She laughed nervously. "Oops." He merely stared at her and waited.

"How much do I owe you?" she asked, wiping the coffee away with a towel. She felt strangely mutinous against his unrelenting gaze all of a sudden and fought off the urge to stick her tongue out and cross her eyes.

"I had the part, so just the labor…say, seventy dollars," he said blandly.

"Well, uh, I think I should pay for the part, too. I mean, even though you had it already doesn't mean it didn't cost you something when you bought it." He didn't reply to this, but just kept looking at her thoughtfully, so she continued, "What if you need that same part for someone else's water heater?"

"All right," he said agreeably. "Another eighteen dollars or so for the part makes it eighty-eight." His eyes never glanced away from her face, not even when he spoke.

"Okay then." She tried to sound as unperturbed as he was, but her hand was trembling as she began writing out a check. Every movement felt awkward. She could feel her face turning red in response to his unwavering gaze. She wanted to tell him how rude it was to stare. She scribbled her name on the check and with an exaggerated flourish ripped it away from the pad. But in the next instant she saw that she had performed this last gesture a little too aggressively, tearing the top edge off the check and leaving it without a number or a date. She held it up with a little laugh of disbelief. "Oops," she said again. Dan shifted his weight from one foot to the next and continued to watch her with interest.

She filled out another check, removing it from the pad with much more care this time, all the while filled with annoyance and thinking, "Desperate Dan, the dirty old man." She recited the little rhyme over and over in her mind as she wrote, achieving from this some small measure of revenge against him for the discomfort he was causing her. She could not wait for him to be away from her, but felt strangely morose when he was finally gone.

With Dan and his unsettling stare still affecting her, Claire drove out to meet the typist Maggie had recommended. Brenda was a wholesomely feminine woman whose primary function was taking care of her husband and their two children, but who was excited by the prospect of making some money while she did it. She explained to Claire that she had learned to type in high school and had honed her skill over the years by communicating online through instant messages. She bragged that everyone she chatted with online, whether professionally or personally, always remarked on how quickly she was able to send a reply. Claire tried to appear properly impressed by this, even though it didn't matter to her how long Brenda took to type the documents since she was being paid by the page. She informed Brenda that the most important thing was that the typing be accurate.

"That's the other thing," Brenda continued enthusiastically. "No matter how casual the chat, I never leave out punctuation or caps like other people do. I always write everything out exactly the way it is supposed to be." Claire smiled. This would not have held much water with an interviewer in Chicago but here in Anamoose it was pretty impressive indeed. And Claire was impressed. She marveled that this ordinary housewife, whiling away the more tedious hours in an online chat room, had the conscientiousness to care whether she capitalized and punctuated.

Brenda was putting together refreshments for her guest in between disruptions from her children or the necessity to scold them from time to time, so Claire settled in for a lengthy chat. Dan was still on her mind and she wondered how she could maneuver the conversation in his direction. She wanted to know what Brenda thought of him. It was a given that Brenda knew him; everyone knew everyone in Anamoose.

"How do you like Anamoose so far?" Brenda asked her.

"Oh, I love it!" Claire responded, surprising herself a little with the realization that she was not just being polite. It was true. She had never been happier; except for the unrelenting attentiveness she continued to get from Desperate Dan. "I'm nearly settled into the house and have already been working on repairs." She paused a moment, hoping Brenda would ask about the repairs so she could bring up Dan.

"Oh?" replied Brenda. "Nothing serious, I hope."

"Only the water heater," Claire said, discarding the matter with a little wave of her hand. She moved guardedly toward the topic she really wanted to discuss. "*Dan* fixed it for me."

Brenda stopped what she was doing and looked at Claire a moment. Claire felt that Brenda knew what she was getting at, but Brenda seemed suddenly cautious.

"Yes, it would be Dan to fix it," she said simply.

"Is Dan your fix-it guy, too?" Claire asked.

"We've hired him for things Ben can't do," Brenda said. Did Claire imagine it, or was there a defensive tone—almost as in an admission of some kind—in this statement from Brenda?

Claire bit her lip. "He's a strange man, that Dan," she ventured.

"How so?" Brenda asked, looking at her again.

"I don't know…kind of creepy, you know, the way he stares." She said this with a nervous little laugh.

"Dan is really a very kind and sweet man," Brenda said rather abruptly. "He wouldn't hurt a fly."

"Well, I find it unnerving," Claire insisted, disappointed that Brenda, like Maggie, didn't seem to want to say anything disapproving about Dan. She decided she would have to discuss Dan with the men of Anamoose to get to the truth about him. Perhaps the women felt sorry for him.

"Do you really?" Brenda asked with a little smile.

Claire decided it was best to change the subject. She brought out the project she wanted Brenda to type and their discussion remained on the documents until Claire left.

After one last stop at Maggie's diner Claire promised herself she would spend the rest of the day working at home. Stepping into the Widow, she was once again surprised and delighted when she received the nods and words of welcome from the inhabitants therein.

"How's the water heater?" Maggie asked her.

"I haven't tried it out yet," Claire said, thinking of Dan instead of the water heater. "We'll see."

Maggie leaned in conspiratorially. "And no trouble from Dan?" she teased.

"No," Claire said, adding before she could stop herself, "Just that creepy stare."

Maggie's eyes suddenly took on a dreamy expression. "Those blue eyes are intense, aren't they?" she said.

"Yes," agreed Claire. "Does he…look at everyone like that?"

"The people he looks at, yes," Maggie said. She leaned in closer. "Harmless!" she said with emphasis and then walked off to pick up a plate of food for a customer.

Claire swiveled her bar stool so that she could glance around the room. No sign of the young man, Bruce, who had claimed to know something about Dan. Then all of a sudden she spotted Dan himself, sitting alone at a table in a far corner of the room. His gaze was on her and their eyes met. She waved without smiling.

He gave her a slight nod and continued to stare. She turned her stool back around so she was facing front again. She tried to remember how long she had been talking to Maggie before and exactly what she had said. She realized with relief that Maggie had known Dan was there and that was why she had discreetly lowered her voice during most of their conversation, causing Claire to inadvertently do the same. She felt an overpowering urge to turn and look at Dan again but resisted it. She no longer felt like eating, so she thanked Maggie for her help and left the restaurant.

When she arrived home, Claire found inside her mailbox a package wrapped neatly in brown paper and tied with brown twine. There was no postage or even an addressee. Someone had placed the package in her mailbox by hand. She carried it into the house and pulled off the brown packaging paper hastily. As she opened it she thought of Dan. She sensed the package came from him.

Beneath the brown wrapper was a plain white cardboard box, just under a foot long and about four inches wide and deep. Claire opened the box with interest. She gasped when she looked inside.

It was immediately obvious that the gift had been made by hand. But that was far from the most startling thing about it. Inside the box was a sculptured replica of the male genitalia, somewhat enlarged, and expertly carved from a cream-colored substance that was solid but clearly pliable. The workmanship and detail was impressive. At the very base of the sculpture there was a large metal nut and bolt fixed securely, suggesting that the sculpture was perhaps detached from something else, and not merely an object unto itself.

Claire stared at the contents of the box in disbelief. She was aghast. Utterances of outrage lodged in her throat, nearly strangling her. She knew for a certainty that Dan had done this. *Desperate Dan, the dirty old man.* This was going too far, she thought angrily. This was not acceptable. She picked up the telephone, prepared to call the police. The phone shook excessively with the trembling of her hand and she hesitated as she stared at it. A long moment passed. Very slowly she put the phone back on its receiver. She began pacing up and down alongside the table upon which the white box sat, its contents within untouched. She was completely unnerved and hadn't the slightest idea what to do.

The worst part of the conflicting emotions warring within her was the embarrassment she felt. She tried to pull herself together and reason it away. She had done nothing to encourage such behavior. She had tried to act naturally around him in fact—or as natural as was possible with him staring at her. But this rationalization did nothing to ease her mind.

At length she stopped in front of the white box and once again looked at the object inside. It suddenly occurred to her that it wasn't guilt over encouraging this overture that caused her embarrassment, but rather her wish to actually touch it. It was horrible and debased, and she knew she should throw the unwanted gift into the trash or turn it in to the police, but she couldn't bring herself to do either of these things. And what was even worse—

much worse, in fact—was that she was alarmingly aroused. She could not remember ever being this aroused before. Even during all those years while she so fiercely loved and adored David and positively craved his attentions, she could not recall feeling such an all-consuming and nearly painful arousal. It seemed to transform sense, reason and principle into nothingness. It made the unthinkable inevitable.

Claire wrapped her fingers around the sculpture and lifted it out of the box. It was incredibly lifelike, and deceivingly rigid for its designed malleability. All around it there were bumps and ridges that emulated the real-life form it was modeled after, right down to the thick, engorged veins that trailed along the length of it. It was impossible to hold it without envisioning it inside her. She held it against her cheek for a moment, fighting the urge to slip it in her mouth. It was beyond unthinkable, and yet she found herself sliding it across her lips. Closing her eyes, she could visualize precisely Dan's intense gaze watching her as she touched it with her tongue.

Suddenly she became aware of her surroundings and looked around self-consciously. The windows were curtained but she did not want to take any chances. She took the package into the bathroom and quickly removed her pants and underwear. She slipped her fingers between her legs and slid them across her slick opening, making herself even more aroused. She moaned with compunction over what she was about to do. Although she hardly needed the additional lubrication, she opened her mouth wide to receive and wet the phallic sculpture. She longed perversely for Dan's eyes to be upon her now. She wondered if her behavior would provoke a change in the stoic expression of his glassy stare.

His craftiness could not be faulted. The sculpture was precisely the size and shape she would have wished for.

Claire worked the supple sculpture in and out of her mouth, savoring the excruciating arousal it brought her to do so. But all too soon this activity was far from enough to satiate her, and she slid it out of her mouth with sharp anticipation to feel it between her legs. She moved down onto the cold bathroom floor and raised her legs up high over her head—so high that she was able to rest her feet on the wall behind her. All of her movements and actions were contrived for the benefit of her fantasy that Dan's watchful eyes were there in the bathroom with her. She maneuvered herself in ways she had never done before, caught up entirely in the dream that Dan was there with her as she took pleasure from his creation, and that his intense gaze was upon her.

Opening her labia with the fingers of one hand, she gently worked the sculpture into her wet hole, moving it up and down when her body resisted, until she reached a point where she could take no more of it. She grasped the nut and bolt at the very base of the sculpture for leverage. She suddenly realized the purpose for the nut and bolt, and felt an intense craving such as she had never felt before in her life. She knew they were put there intentionally to remind her that there existed more than just the phallus-like sculpture. She was keenly aware that somewhere out there was an attachment that would connect the sculpture to something even more depraved and unnatural. In the height of her passion she could only feel a craving for whatever that attachment was.

She began to work the sculpture in and out of her body with one hand while rubbing her clitoris with the other. She closed her eyes tight as she struggled to envision Dan's eyes watching her use the object he created for her. She longed to cause a reaction in him, but wondered what the reaction would be. Would his expression become leering and derisive if he were to see her right now?

Claire gave herself over absolutely to the lust that had been taking control of her since she first laid eyes on the anonymous gift. She stroked herself furiously, thrusting the sculpture violently in and out of her body as she did so. When at last her release came, it brought a flood of pleasurable sensations so strong her entire body jerked and shuddered. The pleasure still lingered a few moments longer, but was followed by a rush of disgust that was almost as powerful as the arousal had been. She got up abruptly and dropped the sculpture into the sink. She dressed in a hurry, mopping up the telltale wetness furiously. Then she washed the sculpture with soap and water and dried it. She felt awkward now to even hold it in her hand.

She wanted suddenly to rid herself of the sculpture but could not bring herself to throw it away. At last she resolved to return it to the white box and bury it under a pile of clothing in her closet.

Distressed and fatigued, Claire went to the kitchen to make

herself a cup of tea. There was a deadline looming on one of her projects but she dreaded remaining in the house alone for the remainder of the afternoon. She preferred to go to Maggie's diner and sit amid the warmth and noise. Self-discipline overruled this idea though, and Claire set to work by sheer force of will. Once she began, she found she was surprisingly productive, and it was dark before she stopped to break—and then only for a quick bite from the kitchen before she returned to work again. Her wish to escape, along with her embarrassment over her earlier behavior, were practically forgotten.

But later, as Claire was clearing away her work from the day, she was once again overcome with a desire to see a friendly face. She looked at the clock and tried to remember how late the diner stayed open. She was generally not one to go out at night, but after such a long day she felt she could do with a drink and some companionship.

The diner was abandoned and dark, but as Claire was turning her car around in the parking lot, preparing to leave, she spotted the back of Dan's truck sticking out from behind one corner of the restaurant. Slowly inching her car to that side of the building, she caught sight of Dan himself, walking noiselessly away from the house that stood behind the diner—the house where Maggie lived. He was carrying his toolbox. Claire paused only a moment before driving out of the parking lot and into the street to go home. Dan had seen her of course, and he stood there thoughtfully, watching her drive away.

"Damn!" Claire said out loud, once she was out of his view. Why was he always everywhere she went? What was he doing at Maggie's house? She thought of the toolbox but recalled suddenly that Maggie's house had been fully dark. Her mind began to wander and she found herself conjuring up strange scenarios. She laughed at herself, but the thoughts repeatedly returned and she found it hard to sleep that night.

The next morning Claire was up early and rushed out to have breakfast at Maggie's diner. Maggie behaved the same as she always did, expressing jovial interest in her customers, particularly Claire.

"So, how's it going today?" she asked Claire when she got a minute free from the morning rush.

"Great," replied Claire. "I couldn't remember how late you stayed open, so I missed you last night for dinner." She watched Maggie's face carefully as she said this, but she could detect no apprehension over Claire's having been there after closing.

"I'm sorry I missed you," Maggie told her sincerely. "I normally stay open later if I know someone is coming by, but generally, if it's slow, I'll close around ten."

"I could have sworn I saw Dan drive away as I was pulling into the parking lot," Claire continued. "You weren't having any problems with your water heater, I hope." She couldn't tell for sure, but it seemed that Maggie might have tensed just a little. But Maggie's expression remained unperturbed.

"No," she replied thoughtfully, "no problems there." She paused a moment before adding, "Dan didn't even stop by the restaurant for dinner last night. As a matter of fact, I didn't see him at all."

"Oh," said Claire. "Perhaps he wasn't leaving here then, but just driving down the street."

"Yes, I bet that was it," said Maggie.

Claire was incredulous. There was no doubt she had seen Dan, with his toolbox in hand, walking from Maggie's dark house toward his truck the previous night. Was it possible that Maggie didn't realize that Dan was there? Claire doubted this and yet, what other explanation could there be? If Dan had been there, fixing something, it certainly would not be something Maggie would feel the need to lie about. Unless...but Claire stopped her thoughts abruptly in their tracks. She watched as Maggie efficiently managed her restaurant, telling herself that it was impossible that this straightforward, practical, sweet woman was so debauched as to participate in the sordid events that were currently popping up in her mind. But then, she reminded herself with morbid incongruity, who would expect—or even believe, for that matter—that Claire would have behaved as she had done the previous afternoon?

Claire left Maggie's restaurant and drove to Brenda's to see how the typing was progressing. She secretly hoped Brenda would be more talkative this time than she had been before.

"How long has Maggie been widowed?" she asked Brenda casually.

"Oh, heavens, it's been seven or eight years now since Scott died," Brenda told her.

"Strange, that such a vibrant woman hasn't remarried," remarked Claire.

"Maggie has never so much as gone out on a date since her husband's death," said Brenda. "She really loved him."

"Well," observed Claire, "she's still young."

"It's not that easy, even if she were inclined to date," said Brenda. "In case you haven't noticed, there's a shortage of men around here. Especially men our age. Those of us who married young got the pick of the litter."

Claire laughed. "Well, we're not living out on an island here in Anamoose. There are adjoining towns that have men living in them."

"That's true," admitted Brenda. "Still, I don't see Maggie dating anyone."

Claire paused nervously, trying to find the right words. "That handyman guy...Dan, is it? He seems to spend a lot of time over there," she began, trying hard to make it sound like a casual observation, but managing instead to sound very schoolgirlish about the whole thing.

Brenda looked at her a moment. "Dan and Maggie are just friends," she said.

"Is Dan seeing anyone?"

"No. Why?" Suddenly Brenda's eyes opened wide. "Are *you* interested?"

"No!" Claire said this a bit too adamantly, so she tried to rectify this by adding, "I don't even know him."

Brenda looked at her sideways. "The truth is, I don't know if Dan has ever dated anyone."

"Why is that?" Claire asked. "I mean, he's not the most attractive man...his face is...I mean, well, but I have seen less attractive people get married."

"With Dan it is not his appearance that keeps him from dating," Brenda said. "There is actually something attractive about him. Something that kind of grows on a person. I think it's Dan's choice not to have a girlfriend."

"Is he gay?"

"No," laughed Brenda. "He is most certainly not gay." But suddenly her expression changed, and she abruptly switched subjects. "I have to pick up little Bobby from his play group," she said.

Claire was disappointed. She was certain there was some mystery pertaining to Dan, but the women of Anamoose were not forthcoming.

At home, Claire was acutely aware of the gift she had hidden away in her closet. Since succumbing to its startling persuasion she had refrained from going near it or its hiding place. As she labored to concentrate on her work that afternoon her thoughts persistently meandered in the direction of the closet and the extraordinary sculpture that was hidden there. These thoughts she persistently and resolutely squelched, dragging her mind laboriously back to the task at hand; but the repeated efforts exhausted her and left her fully discouraged. She stared out the window at the pale sky that was as blue, it seemed to her, as the glassy stare of Desperate Dan.

Finally accepting that she would get nothing accomplished by staying home that day, Claire stuffed the unfinished manuscript into a leather bag and took it with her to Maggie's diner. She spotted Dan immediately—having lunch alone in his usual booth in the far corner of the restaurant. Claire could see that he was watching her. She smiled inwardly. She positioned herself strategically, several booths away from him and sitting sideways, so that her face was partially visible from his vantage point. Then she pulled out the manuscript and began to work, without difficulty at all this time, pacified at last by the steady, inexhaustible gaze radiating over her from across the room. Maggie brought coffee and Claire continued to work, fully engrossed. She worked until late in the day, when suddenly she looked up and became aware that Dan was no longer in the restaurant. But she was satisfied that she had never been more productive.

Returning home, Claire was both alarmed and excited to see a much larger package waiting for her on her stoop. It was wrapped in the same brown paper as the other package had been, and tied with the brown twine. She looked all around her for a sign of someone watching her, but there was no evidence of another soul about the place. As before, there were no marks to identify who had sent the package or who it was addressed to. Nevertheless, Claire new.

Once inside, Claire tore wildly at the knots in the twine and ripped away the brown paper used for wrapping. Opening the box at last, she stared at its contents uncomprehendingly. It appeared to be some kind of mechanical apparatus with folding tubes and connections and wires that frustrated her expectations. Tentatively she reached inside and clumsily removed the bulky contraption.

It quickly became apparent that whatever the instrument was, it was meant to stand upon three metal legs, like a tripod. At the center of the tripod there was secured a heavy circular revolving mechanism of some kind. Claire did her best to snap the gizmo into place, examining the parts as she set it upon its legs. She knew instinctively that somewhere this contraption held the mates to the nut and bolt at the base of the lifelike phallus that was hidden in her closet. Her heart raced as she tried to disentangle the jumble of metal into something she could understand.

Four hours later Claire gave up. She concluded that there must be parts missing still. She shook with a mixture of indignation, mortification and frustration. Her body ached from the hours of neglected arousal. She trudged off to bed miserably, her anger making it possible for her to avoid her closet and what she kept hidden within.

What was she to do? Her consciousness struggled to conquer the feelings of unrest and longing that besieged her. The whole situation was insupportable. There was nothing even remotely acceptable in her connection to the benefactor of these highly inappropriate gifts. But her awareness of how wrong it all was did very little to dampen her desire. She could not sleep. She stared wide-eyed at the ceiling in a sort of ecstatic stupor. She should be contacting the police and here she was, barely able to contain her emotions while she waited breathlessly for his next deplorable action.

The next morning Claire was surprisingly alert and optimistic. She had accomplished much in the week so far, and decided to continue on the path of productivity by riding out to Brenda's to drop off more typing. As she drove she tried to keep her thoughts on the manuscript and her new typist, wondering vaguely if being a wife and mother would inhibit Brenda's ability to manage all the work.

Brenda lived in a more rural part of Anamoose, where the houses were rarely in sight of their neighbors. Just beyond the long driveway that led to her house Claire spotted a truck pulled off to the side of the road and parked in a small, dirt clearing that was mostly hidden by trees. She passed Brenda's driveway and drove up beside the truck to verify that it was, in fact, Dan's. Stopping right in the middle of the street, she stared at the truck, and then looked all around her. Brenda's was the only other driveway by quite a distance. Dan could be visiting Brenda; he may well be her friend. No doubt they had known each other all their lives. Or perhaps Dan was hunting in the vast woods behind and in between the sparse houses. There were many explanations, none of which were any business of Claire's, but even so, Claire parked her car beside Dan's truck and walked surreptitiously through the woods toward Brenda's house. She noticed that one side of the house had only a single window, set up high. It was unthinkable, and yet, she found herself taking long, determined strides toward that side of the house so that she might poke around until she found a suitable window from which to spy through. The word *Peeping Tom* came to her mind but she brushed it away. She felt that she must see what was happening. She was certain things were being kept from her. She believed that in one of those windows she would find Dan, and that whatever else she saw there would shock her. Even so, she had to see it. She reached the house at last and then moved purposefully along the side of it, taking one window at a time, to carefully peer inside.

There was a small basement window at ground level that Claire almost passed by, but getting down on one knee and supporting herself with the side of the building she bent down carelessly to have a quick glance. Her head immediately shot back up. They were in the basement. Claire got down on her hands and knees and, very cautiously this time, peeked in the basement window.

Brenda's basement was considerably darker than the outdoors, so it took a moment for Claire's eyes to adjust. Even so, she instantly perceived the enormity of what she was witnessing. Her mind reeled as she took in the astonishing scene before her. Brenda was not fully visible from her vantage point, but Claire could see enough of her to know that it was indeed Brenda who was fully nude and splayed out on all fours on a low, sturdy table. Perhaps three or four feet behind the table upon which Brenda knelt, there stood a contraption much like the one Claire had received the night before, with the same type of tripod base firmly holding in place a revolving mechanism of some kind that was being controlled by Dan. At the moment it was circling at a sluggish pace, similar to that of a train engine that was just starting to warm up. Claire noticed that Dan had his hand on a large lever which increased the speed of the machine as he slowly moved it toward him. The circular motion of the apparatus appeared to power a long, metal arm that connected the machine to a phallic-like sculpture that was very similar to the one Claire had been given. With each rotation of the machine, the long, metal arm was thrust forward and back. With the increase of speed to the machine's revolving engine came an increase in speed to the thrusts of the long, metal arm.

Claire's eyes traveled the length of the cylinder as it firmly and steadily drove the phallic sculpture—which was fastened to the arm with a nut and bolt similar to the one at the base of her own sculpture—in between Brenda's labia and far into the softness beyond. Claire moaned involuntarily at the sight of it. She felt all at once incredibly drained by the powerful surge of emotions that flooded her consciousness during the seconds that passed while she comprehended the incredible scene before her. The initial, debilitating surge was past, but she was still affected by the conflicting sensations that lingered. Foremost was a sort of unspecified infuriation so palpable that it brought physical discomfort. This, she knew, was what caused her to shake so violently. The source of her fury was unclear to her. She told herself that what she was watching had nothing to do with her, and yet, she felt that she was at the core of it. She felt as affected as if she were somehow being physically attacked.

Joined with the unsettling frustration was a disturbing mixture of pungent revulsion and painful desire. The two emotions battled for control within her, finally leaving her with such a feeling of jealous longing that in that moment she actually abhorred Brenda. She bitterly wished it were she who knelt on that table, and she resented the forces that caused it not to be so. Her desire was so acute and palpable that she could almost imagine she felt the cold, hard table beneath Brenda's hands and knees. She watched impotently as the sculpture was powerfully and unrelentingly thrust in and out of Brenda's exposed body. Without a whisper of hesitation it mercilessly propelled the sculpture back and forth, with its whirring engine turning round and round all the while. Dan remained back near the controls of the mechanism, with his hand clasped firmly over the lever, moving it steadily but ever so slowly, so that the continuous thrusts of the arm gradually increased in speed. Throughout Brenda remained motionless, apparently helpless to move against its power. She seemed helpless to move away from or stop the unrelenting thrusts of the machine.

Claire could not drag her eyes from the sight of the sculpture being propelled in and out of Brenda's pinioned body. She watched Brenda tremble and shudder as she was obliged to accept the machine-driven phallus into her body again and again, and at an alarming force that no ordinary human could achieve. She wondered that Brenda could endure it, even as she yearned for it herself. She was aroused to the point that she couldn't even move. She could only continue to stare through the basement window, amazed and aroused and wickedly envious. Every new nuance of the event that she was able to capture caused her more discomfort. She could perceive Brenda's euphoric response even without being able to hear her cries of ecstasy. Brenda's demeanor as she quivered vulnerably at the receiving end of Dan's powerful machine was more telling than words. Claire could also observe that the thrusts from the machine were indeed powerful, for the flesh all around Brenda's opening pulsated violently from the force of each and every thrust, and the lips of her labia clung fervently to the irregularly carved material of the phallic sculpture. Claire noticed all of these things, and each new little observation increased her own arousal.

At one point Claire did finally manage to pull her gaze from the tantalizing image of Brenda's body accepting the thrusts of the sculpture to look once again at the amazing mechanism at work. Her eyes traced slowly along the length of it, wonderingly, longingly, and eventually they fell upon the man operating it. And she saw that Dan was watching *her!*

Jarred from her stupor, Claire jerked her head back and away from the window. Panic flooded her insides and made her suddenly hot. She sprung up from where she had been kneeling in the grass and ran at full speed across the yard and through the woods to her car. Dan had caught her watching. She wondered what her expression had been while she watched.

Claire got in her car and began driving but she did not want to go home. Nor could she bear to visit the diner. It suddenly occurred to her what Dan was most probably doing at Maggie's house that night. She wondered how many other women benefited from Dan's services. What a bizarre situation it was! These were Claire's thoughts on the surface of her mind, but beneath them there still stirred the conflicting emotions that had assailed her since that first package was left in her mailbox. Dominating every other emotion was a yearning that was driving her to distraction. She rode out of Anamoose and headed south; traveling through one town and then another while attempting to find some measure of calm.

Eventually the road had its effect and Claire felt sufficiently soothed to return to Anamoose. The long drive back further depleted her so that when she arrived home at last, she was too exhausted to feel much of anything. It was pitch-dark when she turned into her driveway, but she could clearly see Dan's truck parked there. Her entire body came alive at the thought of speaking to him.

Dan was sitting in his truck, with the driver's-side window down. The manner in which he parked made it necessary for her to walk by his open window in order to get to her house. She stopped when she reached him. She didn't speak, only looked at him.

"How's it working?" she heard him ask. It was so dark that she could not fully make out the details of his face. Only his glassy blue stare stood out clearly, which almost had a luminous quality at night.

"How dare you," she choked out in a low voice. She could not begin to give words to the feelings of outrage she felt over his audacity, nor could she come close to telling him how much she needed him to be even more audacious in order to stop the painful aching between her legs. And aside from all of this, she knew that he knew that the long metal arm that connected the sculpture to the mechanical base was missing from the parts he had sent her.

"I was just following up on the job I did to your water heater," he said with a small smile. It was the first time she had observed even the slightest amusement in his expression.

"No, you were not," she said.

At this he laughed out loud. "You don't have to use it, you know. Throw it out if you want to."

She didn't know what to say, so she remained silent.

"Or," he continued slowly, "you could let me help you enjoy it to its fullest potential."

"You are a pervert," she told him forcefully, but her voice was clearly full of anguish and she blushed.

"You seemed to like what you saw today."

"Why do you do it?" she asked, suddenly allowing her curiosity to come to the fore. "What do you get out of it?"

"Pleasing women is my fantasy and my pleasure. They don't have to do anything but allow me to watch while they get pleasure. Best of all, they don't have to feel embarrassed or guilty. Who cares what 'Desperate Dan, the dirty old man' thinks?" Claire blushed when he recited the rhyme. Dan didn't seem fazed by it in the least.

"Is Maggie one of your...recipients?" she asked.

"You were the one spying on Brenda," he reminded her. "No one will ever learn anything about you, or any woman, from me."

There followed an uncomfortable pause. He seemed to be waiting for her to reply. But Claire remained silent. It was all too new, and her sense of values was still so genuinely offended that any overture would have left her feeling debased. She fervently wished that it did not have to be her who made a step forward; if not for that she might gladly acquiesce to what he was suggesting.

"Suit yourself," he said at last, but he said the words gently and without anger. Claire watched him drive away, feeling suddenly inconsolable.

She avoided leaving her house for nearly a week. During this time she worked practically nonstop, infused with a strange energy that never seemed to burn out. The sculpture had somehow made its way from her closet to a new hiding place deep within the folds of her bedsheets, where it remained buried until those times when she reached for it and then the soft, malleable material suddenly came to life. It thrilled her to know that it was created for her by Dan.

But at long last, when she could evade the world no longer, Claire left the house in order to attend to some of the things she had been neglecting. One of these was the typing she had left with Brenda. She completed all of her other errands first before making her way down the quiet country road where Brenda lived.

"I've been worried about you," Brenda said, seeming genuinely pleased to see Claire. "I was going to call, but I've been so busy." Claire was taken back by the naturalness Brenda demonstrated with her. Clearly Dan had not informed her of Claire's violation of her privacy. She had never really worried that he would, but was nevertheless apprehensive about the prospect of seeing Brenda again. Under Brenda's guileless demeanor it was easy to slide into the old friendship that was developing and, if not forget then at least set aside, her surreptitious knowledge of how the woman spent her days when her children were away at school and her husband was far off in another state driving his truck.

Having so painlessly achieved all of her objectives thus far, Claire felt strong enough to venture once more into Maggie's diner. She was strangely excited, in fact, when she drove into the parking lot and noticed Dan's truck parked outside.

Once again, upon her entering the restaurant, there came a volley of greetings, inquiring where she had been all these days and how she was feeling. She realized with a start that it was the first time in her life that she had been missed. Her cheeks grew pink with pleasure. She stood at the bar to speak with Maggie.

Dan rose up from his booth in the corner and stood close behind Claire as he handed his bill and some money to Maggie. Claire could feel the warmth of his body where he stood so near her. She knew his blue gaze was fixed on her. Her heart pounded ludicrously inside her chest. She felt as if her tongue was choking her. She remained silently immobile while Dan concluded his business with Maggie and turned to leave. Something inside her cried out. Her pride fought it down, but only for a few seconds before it returned with double strength.

"Dan!" she heard herself call. She turned and he did, too. Her heart was pounding and she knew this was a life-changing moment for her.

"That other…thing…for the water heater…" She looked into his blue eyes urgently.

His tone was casual. "Yes, I remember," he prompted.

Her heart hammered painfully. She tried to match his casual tone but failed. "I would like to have that fixed as soon as you can manage it." Her voice sounded much too eager, she noticed, but the discomfort this caused her was nothing compared to what she would feel if she did not settle this with him right now.

"I can be over there this afternoon."

She could have wept. Working hard to check her emotions, she turned back to where Maggie stood watching her. She sat back down on the bar stool and met Maggie's eyes. There was no suspicion or censure of any kind in Maggie's expression. The ladies exchanged smiles.

This was, at last, the place where she belonged. Claire was finally home.

* * * * *

GEORGIE PORGIE

Georgie Porgie, puddin' and pie,
kissed the girls and made them cry.
When the boys came out to play,
Georgie Porgie ran away.

Daphne reluctantly placed the phone on its receiver. She could not leave Georgie another message, and yet, why didn't he call her back? She picked up another cigarette and lit it, inhaling deeply. She realized she had just put one out and reminded herself for the millionth time that she needed to quit smoking. Perhaps her appointment with the hypnotist Thursday would help. She didn't hold out much hope, but the friend who recommended the woman insisted she could work miracles. At this point, Daphne would try anything.

Her mind flashed back to Georgie. She was genuinely confused. He had seemed so sincerely interested in her, pursuing her so relentlessly that, when she finally gave herself to him, she thought for once she had gotten it right. And that night with him had been magical. But here she was three days later, and still no word from Georgie. Her mind could not accept that she had been so thoroughly duped.

Against her better judgment, Daphne ultimately found herself driving by Georgie's favorite bar. She had to go out anyway, she reasoned, for more cigarettes. She pulled into the parking lot and drove up and down in between the rows, looking for Georgie's car. But it wasn't there, and she began to wonder if something might have happened to him. This thought seemed infinitely more preferable to his dumping her after getting her into bed. She began to reason that it was far more likely that he had been incapacitated in some way than that he had gone through all the trouble of seducing her for a single night of sex.

With this same utilitarian logic, it did not seem entirely out of line for her to go to Georgie's house. In fact, it seemed rather uncharitable not to. The least she could do was to check on him and make sure that he was okay. He may be sick, or in dire need of help, and here she was offended that he didn't call. As she drove in the direction of where Georgie lived, she persuaded herself that she was doing the broad-minded and practical thing.

Even so, Daphne hesitated once she reached the parking lot of Georgie's apartment building. What if he really didn't want to see her? But her apprehension was squelched by a surge of excitement when she spotted his car. He was home! Her adrenaline ran high in anticipation of seeing him. She felt incapable of controlling her own actions. Yet she lingered in her car, lighting up another cigarette. She stared thoughtfully up at his building as she blew smoke rings out the window. She felt she ought to have an excuse of some kind for coming, but could think of nothing plausible. Everything that came to her mind seemed ridiculously transparent. Had she by chance left her missing earring there? That sounded pathetic, even to her ears.

I will simply tell him the truth, she told herself, purposefully opening the car door and making her way to his apartment. Her heart thudded vigorously at the thought of seeing him again, and whatever she ended up saying to him seemed trivial by comparison. Surely he would be as delighted to see her as she was to see him, and words would not be necessary. Without pausing for further deliberation, especially any that might lead to a change of heart, she hastily knocked—perhaps a bit too loudly—on Georgie's door.

Daphne heard movements from within the apartment and suddenly had second thoughts. But it was too late to escape, for she was standing in the middle of a long hallway and she could see that someone was already turning the doorknob. She actually jumped when the door flew open and Georgie appeared. He was undressed except for a pair of gray shorts, and his black wavy hair was tousled all around his head. His dark eyes registered surprise at first to see her, but then she thought she detected annoyance creeping into his expression. From behind him, she could easily make out the form of a woman, also scantily dressed in ruffled underclothes.

"Daphne," he said after a minute, as if he was just recalling her name. But she was already seething with indignant anger.

"Well, I guess this answers my question," she said in a shaky voice. But the implied clarification did not prompt her to leave. She looked at Georgie tragically. "Why?"

Georgie sighed, as if bored. "Why what?"

"Why all the pursuing? Why all the games? You can't have done all that just to get me into bed that one time?" She was incredulous.

Georgie cast a quick glance at the woman standing quietly behind him. "Please don't turn this into an ugly scene," he murmured.

"How *dare* you!" Daphne screamed. There were sounds coming from surrounding apartments, and she was aware that she was losing control, but she no longer cared. "You are a sleazy, no-good, manipulative—" The door slammed shut in her face before she could finish.

Daphne stared at the closed door in shock. She was trembling with rage and disbelief. She had an urge to kick the door but she resisted it. She stood there for a long minute before turning to leave. A woman was peering at her from a crack in a door that was slightly ajar. She walked dejectedly down the long hall and left Georgie's apartment building.

Back in her car, Daphne lit up a cigarette. She was more than anything else confused. Had she deluded herself into thinking that Georgie really liked her? No, she knew that she had not. She had not been the pursuer between them. It was quite the opposite. She had, in fact, been wary of going out with him from the get-go, sensing that he was much too smooth and good looking to be reliable. She had been shy and uncertain the first time he approached her, while he had been amused and intrigued by her reticence. He had been relentless, calling her many times. He even sent her flowers. When she finally agreed to go out with him, he had gallantly picked her up at her door. Aside from his devastatingly good looks, how could she possibly have known?

It was not until their third date that she finally yielded to Georgie's charm and good looks, melting into his arms and his bed. She was normally not at her peak performance when it was the first time with a new partner, but with Georgie everything came off seamlessly. Their bodies melded together in perfect harmony. She had even managed to reach an orgasm, which usually took her months into a relationship to achieve. She left Georgie that following morning believing they had begun something truly magical. But Georgie never called her again.

Daphne reflected that she probably should not have waited so long to sleep with him after all. With men like Georgie, it was the women who got more attached with each encounter. If she had gone home with him that first night, it would have ended the same, it's true, but at least she wouldn't have felt so much hurt over it.

She reached for another cigarette, but the pack was empty. She stared at it in surprise. Surely she had not smoked the entire pack already? She circled the street in search of a convenience store. She would never make it through the night without cigarettes.

By the time Thursday rolled around, Daphne was up to three packs a day. She puffed furiously on a cigarette as she squinted to read the road signs up ahead. She looked around nervously. Her quest had brought her to a seedier part of town, but what was more disturbing was the eerie silence all around. One would have expected to find some hoodlums loitering noisily about or perhaps to hear a few police sirens. The area appeared to be deserted. Up ahead she spotted the building she was looking for. It was run-down and decrepit like the rest of the neighborhood. She saw lights shining from within, and this reassured her. In truth, the creepy surroundings cheered her somewhat. They matched her idea of where a hypnotist might conduct business. Best of all, her depression had been replaced with curiosity. The session would be a diversion that might at least prove entertaining.

A bell rang when Daphne stepped inside the large open room that was a bookstore, antique shop and apparently a used-clothing outlet as well. The room smelled of strong incense, pleasant but a bit overpowering. She surveyed the odd collection of mismatched items that were scattered about the room without rhyme or reason.

A woman appeared from a room in the back. Daphne had envisioned someone with long, wavy hair overrun with streaks of gray and tie-dyed clothing that fell in loose layers all around her. But this hypnotist was actually quite chic in a snug-fitting skirt and blouse that might have been better suited for Wall Street, with neatly cropped hair that looked professionally colored and in all other respects well kept. The hypnotist approached Daphne with a clear, steady gaze and a friendly smile. She grasped Daphne's hands in hers and held them firmly for a moment, closing her eyes as if in deep concentration. When she opened her eyes to look at Daphne she appeared surprised.

"I, ah…have an appointment," Daphne began uncertainly.

"I know why you're here and I can help you," the hypnotist assured her with a knowing smile. "But first we're going to have to get you to relax just a bit. I'm Julia, by the way." As she spoke, Julia led Daphne to a long, deep-cushioned couch near the back of the room. "We'll have enough privacy here," she explained. "And I can still keep an eye on the store if a customer comes in."

It all seemed quite unorthodox to Daphne, but she was fully enthralled by it nevertheless.

"So," Julia began languorously, easing herself closer to Daphne on the overstuffed couch as she spoke. "Why don't you begin by telling me more about this little problem of yours."

"Oh, okay…um…" Daphne struggled to collect her thoughts. She was thoroughly distracted by her surroundings and Julia's nearness. Julia stared at her with wide-eyed expectation. "I started smoking when I was about…I think—" She stopped then because Julia had begun softly chuckling. She looked at Julia questioningly.

"That's not why you're here," Julia told her matter-of-factly. Daphne stared at her in silence. "Is it?" Julia prompted.

Two hours later Daphne left the hypnotist feeling like a different person. When she got into her car she immediately lit up a cigarette, puffing on it happily. She was filled with hope. She marveled at what a wonderful thing hope was. Hope created expectation, which, in turn, provided energy to make things happen. She giggled, excited, as she placed the key in the ignition. She looked at the neatly wrapped little package she had set down on the seat beside her. She must find a post office and mail it promptly.

All through the rest of that week and into the next Daphne stayed home, just as Julia had meticulously instructed, venturing out only for work and necessities. Most especially Daphne avoided going anyplace where she might encounter Georgie. Julia had been most adamant about that. For the best results she must wait a full week at the very least. With every day that passed, her anticipation grew and her expectations soared higher. She waited single-mindedly for the moment when she would see Georgie once again.

But when at last the week had passed, Daphne was filled with trepidation. What if it didn't work? She remembered the unconventional surroundings of Julia's shop and even Julia herself—so completely out of sync with everything she had imagined about hypnotists and how they would operate—and she couldn't help but wonder if she had gone mad, trusting a complete stranger and especially giving her so much money, money that Daphne had worked hard to earn. She had banked everything she had on a flight of fancy! But amid the doubt Daphne's hope still lingered, and it buoyed her spirits enough so that she was able to continue determinedly following Julia's instructions.

When she was satisfied that enough time had passed, Daphne began to prepare herself to see Georgie again, although according to Julia no such preparations would be necessary. She could show up in her shabbiest bathrobe for the same effect. Even so, Daphne primped and preened to her heart's delight, and when she was finished she was satisfied that Georgie would be impressed when he saw her. She strolled confidently into his favorite hunting ground.

Daphne's eyes scanned the crowded bar anxiously while trying to appear disinterested. Within seconds she spotted him. She moved purposefully in his direction, meandering in and around the throng of people. She had expected to feel nervous when this moment approached, but was pleasantly surprised to find that she was not.

Georgie was sitting at the bar, staring down at his drink in abject misery. Daphne drew out a cigarette and held it in midair seductively, saying, "Something the matter?"

Georgie's head came up and he looked at her in surprise. She put the cigarette to her lips expectantly and raised an eyebrow. He instinctively brought up a lighter and held it for her. She recognized the lighter instantly and smiled.

"I thought you were going to quit," he said.

"I'm surprised you remember that," she said with meaning. "I would have thought all those little details would be long forgotten once you finished with a woman."

Georgie just looked at her. He seemed momentarily distracted by her as his eyes scanned her face.

"I decided to deal with other matters first," she explained with a smile.

He couldn't take his eyes off her, and said, "You look beautiful tonight."

"Oh? I'm surprised you noticed."

Georgie shrugged his shoulders. "I guess I deserve that." He kept looking at her with a mixture of confusion and brooding contemplation. "Can I get you a drink?"

"Sure."

Not even a full hour later, the two stumbled through the front door of Georgie's apartment, struggling frantically to remove each other's clothes. Georgie kicked the door closed and enthusiastically thrust Daphne up against it. He was so beside himself in his desire for her that he behaved with an almost desperate urgency. Daphne's own passion raged out of control in response.

"I've got to see you," Georgie kept saying as he tore away her clothing. "I have to touch you!"

Daphne's body trembled for his touch. But when he finally had her fully unclothed, Georgie stood back, momentarily sidetracked by the sight of her. He let out a low whistle.

"I've never seen anything so beautiful," he murmured. Under any other circumstances Daphne would have balked at the words. But this time she pressed her arms against the door and pushed her body forward, toward Georgie, causing her breasts to jut outward. Georgie moaned at the sight of them, reaching forward and cupping one in each hand. As he caressed them his passion returned with renewed force, and he kissed her ravenously while he continued to squeeze and pinch the nipples. Daphne moaned loudly over the pleasurable discomfort he was giving her.

Georgie's kisses moved lower and he seared the tender flesh of her breasts with his breath as he licked and sucked each nipple in turn. While he consumed her with his mouth, his hands crept around her waist and moved purposefully up and down the length of her back, caressing and embracing her all in one stroke.

But soon his roving hands ventured farther down over her hips and greedily cupped her plump, round buttocks. He spread them apart and reached a curious finger in between the folds. While he was still holding her buttocks open with his strong hands, Georgie's finger adroitly located the folds of her labia and wiggled its way into the warm velvety passage within. When he felt Daphne's silky wetness he had another tremor of sorts, and in the next instant Daphne found herself on all fours, with Georgie still holding her buttocks spread wide apart in his hands as he leaned in from behind to replace the finger with his tongue.

"Ahhhh," Daphne moaned, shuddering as Georgie ravenously devoured her. His tongue meandered back and forth enthusiastically between her clitoris and soaking slit. It slithered and squirmed its way over her exposed flesh, expertly massaging her clitoris one moment and wriggling its way deep within her folds the next. Georgie worked on her tirelessly, forgetting, it seemed, his own needs entirely. Daphne did not worry over this as she normally would have done. She was suddenly convinced that whatever Julia had done had worked, and that Georgie would find more pleasure now in pleasing her. She threw her head back and languished in the wondrous feeling of Georgie's tongue as it worked tirelessly in and around her flesh, back and forth over and around her clitoris, bringing her closer to the edge with each new advance. Without even realizing she was doing it, Daphne began helping Georgie in his endeavor, feverishly thrashing her hips toward his face, grating her clitoris over his tongue and lips. Noting her increased passion, Georgie grasped her buttocks even more firmly in his hands and moved his tongue over her with even more steadfast determination. With all of her self-consciousness and anxiety so neatly put out of her way, Daphne was able to fully embrace the moment of her release. It spread its red-hot heat through her, beginning its tingling warmth in her quivering clitoris and radiating outward. She was too overcome to even cry out, and Georgie might not have even known what had happened had he not noticed the subtle and fleeting vibrations of her body, or the way her hips jerked away from him when his tongue tapped the now overly sensitive area.

Georgie released Daphne's hips and she fell onto the floor in a near swoon. He pulled himself up over her slowly, feeling half satisfied himself but not entirely. Daphne opened her arms and legs to him, all softness and yielding, as he drove himself into her. He was so hard she trembled from the invasion.

Daphne wrapped her arms and legs around Georgie, clasping him as close to her body as was possible. She pressed her body against him, luxuriating in the thrilling feel of having Georgie in her embrace. She felt a fierce possessiveness come over her. When Georgie exploded inside her she felt triumphant.

Georgie sighed contentedly as he rolled off of Daphne. "I thought I was going crazy," he murmured with a sigh of relief.

"Come again?" Daphne said.

He playfully turned her over and dropped a loud kiss on her bottom. "It's nothing," he said. "Just a rough week is all. But I'm back on track now."

"Sure." Daphne smiled in secret.

But Georgie was far from being tamed and it was another long, miserable week for Daphne before he finally called her again. She was resentful and angry, but relieved, too.

"Daphne."

"Georgie?" She tried to sound indifferent.

"How've you been?"

"What do you want?"

"Can I see you tonight?"

"I don't know, Georgie," but this was just for show; she knew she would see him.

"I really need to see you, Daphne," he said. The pleading note in his tone made it impossible for her to resist further.

"What time?"

But this time Daphne was hesitant to go to bed with him. She wanted to spend more time with him in a vertical position, and besides that, it was beginning to dawn on her that pleasing him sexually was actually working against her own wishes in the long run. "I don't think I should stay tonight," she said when they were standing outside his apartment door.

"Why?" he asked more tragically than he intended.

"Because if I do you'll turn cold again."

"What?"

"You're hot when you want me, but you turn cold after you have me."

Georgie thought about this. There was no denying it, so with a guilty grin he began to stroke her shoulder just the way she liked. "I've been a jerk to you, Daphne."

"Mmm..." She looked away indifferently.

He laughed. "God," he said in a strange new voice. "I guess I've been caught!" He said this as if it just occurred to him.

"What do you mean?" she asked. She wasn't sure if he was merely acknowledging her comment or if he was, as she suspected and hoped, admitting that she had captured his heart.

"It's you, Daphne," he said with cheery resignation. "You're the woman for me. I've been fighting it, but I can't deny it any longer." Daphne's heart leaped when she heard his words. She was speechless with astonishment and joy. Georgie took her face in his hands and tenderly kissed her. She melted in his arms.

They spent a delirious weekend in his apartment, much like a honeymoon, with Georgie never leaving Daphne's side. Georgie not only accepted what he believed to be his inevitable fate, convinced that he had simply fallen in love, but he actually reveled in it. He brought Daphne breakfast in bed on Monday morning, serenading her with corny love songs. Daphne laughed heartily, never having been so happy in her life. Had Georgie not been so delighted by what had happened, her part in it might have taken some of her pleasure away. But with both of them so content with the result, where was the harm?

Georgie and Daphne instantaneously became a couple. In Georgie's self-absorbed world, Daphne became like an extension of himself. Everything he had enjoyed in his former life alone he now wanted to share with Daphne. She accepted all of this euphorically, thriving under all the attention. She woke up in the morning and pinched herself, half thinking it must all be a dream.

Things continued to progress in this way, with Georgie doting over his beloved and her blossoming under his inexhaustible attentions, until one afternoon when Georgie accidentally stumbled upon Daphne's e-mail account while working on his home computer. Intrigued by something belonging exclusively to the one he adored, Georgie double clicked on the icon to open it. He wasn't surprised to encounter a request for a password; in fact, it seemed to present him with an interesting challenge. He was suddenly curious to see if he could guess Daphne's password. With a sly smile, he typed in the name of her first dog, remembering how affected she had become when she told him the story of how her beloved pet had been hit by a car. But it was not her password. Next, he typed in the name of the street where she grew up, congratulating himself on how well he listened to all the things she told him. But that was not her password either. He thought for a moment, certain that he ought to be able to guess the word she would choose. Then suddenly he beamed. He typed the word *Georgie,* and in the next instant he was in!

It was not his original intention to actually read any of Daphne's private e-mails but once Georgie was inside he was overcome with curiosity. He went into her in-box and slowly scanned the subjects, halfheartedly working his way down. All at once one of the headings caught his eye. It read, Re: Amazing results with Georgie. He did not hesitate a moment before opening the e-mail.

The e-mail began with a response to an e-mail Daphne had sent. Her respondent wrote, That's wonderful news Daphne…now what about the smoking?

Georgie scrolled down to the original e-mail that was sent from Daphne. Hardly able to believe what he was seeing, he read, Thank you so much for what you did to Georgie. It all worked out exactly as you predicted. I couldn't be happier. He actually still had the lighter with him the first night I saw him!!! He really believes that I am the only girl he can perform with because he's in love with me! Oh, thank you thank you thank you thank you….

Georgie could feel the blood draining from his face as the cold rage crept over him. The lighter! His eyes narrowed as he recalled the anonymous gift he had received in the mail. He had automatically assumed that the expensive cigarette lighter was an extravagant gift from a well-satiated lover. But thinking back now, he realized that it was immediately after receiving that lighter that he had all at once ceased being able to perform sexually. Daphne had gotten someone to put a hex on him!

Georgie rose up from his chair and began searching frantically through every drawer and shelf where the lighter might be. It had long since run out of lighter fluid and it could have been left in any number of places. He was still looking for it when Daphne came home.

She could see from his expression that something was terribly wrong.

"Where's the lighter?" Georgie thundered.

"Wh-what?" But she knew instantly what he was talking about. She wondered how he found out and how much he knew. "What lighter?"

"The lighter with the hex you put on me!" he yelled. He had forgotten every positive emotion they had shared in the interim between the time he had received the lighter and the moment he saw her e-mail.

Daphne took a step back. "I don't know, Georgie. What does it matter?"

"What does it matter? What does it matter?" Georgie was choking with indignation. "It matters because you're going to take off the hex."

"I can't."

Georgie stopped suddenly when she said this. He seemed to become calmer. He walked over to where Daphne stood and grasped her arms. Then he threw her up against the wall, hard.

"How do I get the hex off?" he asked her menacingly.

She remained silent.

"How do I get the hex off?" he asked her again, but she just stared at him. "Answer me!" he bellowed.

Daphne had started to cry. She was not upset by his anger. She was terrified of losing him. "You can't," she whispered.

"What?" he asked, whispering, too, all of a sudden.

"You can't get the hex off," she lied. "Ever."

"There must be a way," he said with desperation.

"There isn't."

Georgie stared at her for a very long time. He cursed himself inwardly because he could feel his body becoming aroused. It had been that way, he realized, ever since the day he got the lighter. He could not get hard without her, and he could not keep from getting hard whenever he was around her. Daphne could see it, too, and relief washed over her.

A menacing smile crept slowly over Georgie's beautiful features. He was beginning to shake with a mixture of anger and desire for her. He realized resentfully that there was nowhere else he could turn for relief.

Georgie reached for Daphne and his rage temporarily overpowered his desire. He grasped her head in his hands and plundered her lips with his mouth. She melted against him, relieved and reassured by his desire, but Georgie jerked away from her just as abruptly as he had taken hold of her.

"No!" he protested with a snarl. He took a fistful of her hair and dragged her down the hall to their bedroom. Once inside he released her, thrusting her from him so forcefully that she only just caught herself before falling. "Get your clothes off," he demanded.

Daphne was not pleased by the way in which this was happening, but it was, she forced herself to admit, better than she might have expected. She preferred the Georgie of yesterday but felt confident that he would come back around to that once he had gotten over the initial shock of what she had done to him. She undressed quickly, her body already tingling with anticipation. She was eager to help him get over his anger. She wanted him to accept the fact that he was hers now.

Georgie had stood by watching as Daphne undressed, and when she was finished he slowly removed his own clothing while she waited. He seemed reluctant, but appeared not to have the power to stop what was happening.

"Lie down," he said. "Facedown on the bed. I don't want to look at you." He was mildly surprised when she quietly complied.

In spite of his anger Georgie paused to run his hand along the length of Daphne's body, lingering on the curve of her back where it turned up toward her hips. Daphne held her breath. He moved his hand lower, working it over her buttocks and down in between her butt cheeks. She squirmed nervously as he moved his finger over her butt hole, circling it, round and round.

"Grab the headboard," she heard him say gruffly.

She moved up onto her knees in order to do as Georgie instructed. He continued to finger the outside of her anus menacingly. She waited breathlessly to see what he would do next. No man had ever touched her there before. She knew women accepted men there. She had even wondered about it, fleetingly, in her fantasies, but she had never actually meant to go through with it. Not until the very moment when Georgie pushed his finger inside her body. In that instant she knew she would let Georgie have her this way, but she was still afraid.

"Georgie," she moaned. He pulled out his finger. She heard him move to the bedside table and fish around in a drawer for something. She felt a tingle of arousal flit through her as she glanced over and saw him pull from the drawer a jar of lubricant. As angry as he was, she perceived that he did not wish to actually hurt her.

He began rubbing the lubricant into her anus.

"Georgie," she began, but the sound of her voice only made him rub the ointment in more vigorously. He was using two fingers now.

"Georgie!"

"Shut up," he said in a startlingly quiet voice. He continued in the same, maddeningly calm tone. "You want to possess me so badly, Daphne? You're going to get me then. All the way. For tonight, at least, it's not going to be about you. After what you did to me you don't deserve any consideration."

As he said this, Georgie began to gradually wedge his way into her body. Although his words were harsh, he entered her slowly and gently, careful not to hurt her.

"Georgie," she moaned. Sharp thrills of excitement pierced

through her in spite of the pressure as he penetrated her inch by painstaking inch. She arched her back slightly, pushing her hips outward in an effort to open herself more to him. This eased her discomfort considerably.

"That's it," he mocked her cruelly. "Push your hips out toward me. Show me how much you like it." He kept working his way into her little by little as he spoke, taking his time and clearly relishing every moment of it.

He grasped her hips more securely as he finally pushed himself into her body all the way to the hilt.

"Oh!" she cried. She was aroused, but the pressure temporarily surpassed her arousal, not extinguishing it but merely immobilizing it. She heard him laugh mockingly behind her and her former forbearance because of what she had done diminished considerably. With her arousal put aside for the moment, she felt somewhat violated. Suddenly, she was fully at odds with what was happening. "I hate you!" she blurted out impulsively.

Georgie had begun to painstakingly draw himself out of her now, leaving only the very tip of his raging hardness inside her. "So," he goaded her, holding himself back for the moment. "You hate me, eh? For mistreating you?"

"Yes." She braced herself to take him all the way again. Suddenly Daphne's arousal was returning with double strength. Even so, she continued in the same vein. "I hate you."

Georgie thrust himself all the way into her again. "Now you know how I feel."

Daphne moaned loudly, the pleasure increasing considerably with each new thrust.

"'Cause that's what you did to me," Georgie continued, pulling himself out again with agonizing deliberation only to thrust it all the way back in, again and again. "And like me you're just going to have to take it." And he just kept driving in and out of her, keeping a continuous, rhythmic pace that gradually increased in speed and intensity. "Can you take it as well as you can dish it out?" he mocked her.

"Yes!" she cried, suddenly fully aware of the exciting new pleasure into which Georgie was initiating her. There remained some discomfort and pressure, but this, too, given the circumstances, suited her tastes.

"That's right," he said. "You can and you will. Take it!" He began to drive in and out of her with the unrelenting intensity of a machine. She held herself steady and submissively accepted Georgie's thrusts. Eventually the discomfort was becoming manageable enough for her to focus on the pleasure. She slipped her hand down between her legs to further stimulate herself.

"Georgie!" she cried out, surprised that such an intrusive and demanding activity could bring such intense pleasure.

Georgie had warned Daphne that this was not for her, but he was nevertheless pleased by her response. And though his pleasure increased tenfold with the knowledge that she was enjoying what he was doing to her, his anger still burned steady beneath his overpowering desire.

Daphne, meanwhile, endured every bit of what Georgie dished out, even meeting some of his violent thrusts with wild little thrusts of her own. The grueling difficulty of it as he used her even more harshly gave her a delightfully perverse satisfaction. Perhaps she wanted to be punished for what she had done, and secretly hoped that her acquiescence to Georgie would make him truly forgive her.

The many emotions that Daphne had gone through that night, beginning with her terror at the thought of losing Georgie, ending with the couple's absolute and utter capitulation to each other, and encompassing all the incredible realities and sensations in between had their effect; Daphne's climax shook her to the roots of her existence. Afterward she could only cling to the headboard while Georgie continued to take pleasure from her, wondering over the tingling sensations that lingered for far longer than they ever had before. Georgie appeared to be shaken by the experience, too, until it was over.

Immediately afterward Georgie rolled over and drifted miserably off to sleep. But the next morning he was once again fully aroused by the sight of her. And so their relationship progressed, with Georgie going from hating Daphne, to yearning for her, to resenting her, and then back to hating her again. Sex, the chain by which she held Georgie to her, became for him an exercise in maliciousness, and he struggled to mortify and mistreat her in an effort to project his own powerlessness onto her.

Daphne made herself available to Georgie whenever he wanted her, but kept her distance when he did not, telling herself to give him time. She went along with his demands in the bedroom, finding that, once she got past the initial embarrassment, she actually enjoyed most of the things he did to her; but even the more harrowing things she also submitted to willingly. And once the worst was over she found that she was able to glean additional pleasure from the memories of those events after the fact. She walked around in a semiconstant state of arousal, even when Georgie wasn't around, thinking obsessively of the things he did to her and what else he might do. And in this way she became as trapped as Georgie was.

More than anything else, Daphne wanted to make the relationship between her and Georgie succeed. She was not content with things as they were. She yearned to once again see the love in Georgie's eyes that she had glimpsed there before he had discovered how she had trapped him. Another aspect of their former relationship that Daphne longed to get back was Georgie's willingness to spend time with her. Now, unless they were engaged sexually, Georgie wanted nothing to do with her. Georgie's resentment was still too acute to allow him to "give in" and share those other parts of his life with her. Whether or not he might have enjoyed her company wasn't a consideration for him. All that mattered was that he retain some small measure of control over his own life. He fought all sentiment he developed toward her. He reasoned that, although he had no choice but to be with Daphne, he didn't have to love her. He would give her his nights and his body, but he would not give her the affection she craved.

Daphne handled all this with amazing patience. At times she became angry, but she always forgave Georgie everything. She told herself that he would eventually come around. He would have to. He had no other choice.

Daphne's quiet reserve and unwavering perseverance frustrated Georgie even more.

In the meantime, Georgie tried everything he could think of to get rid of the hex, as he perceived it to be. Only a few days after finding the e-mail, it occurred to him that he could contact the woman that had helped Daphne and offer her more money to undo whatever it was she had done to him. But when he went online to find the e-mails and get the woman's e-mail address, they were gone. Daphne had deleted them and erased all the history. Undaunted, Georgie reasoned that another witch could counteract the hex as well as the first, but six "witches" later he had burned through frightening amounts of money with no results whatsoever. He even resorted to consulting several doctors, but they each recommended that he see a psychiatrist—who also refused to address the real issue, insisting instead that Georgie waste his time rehashing his childhood.

Eventually, Georgie was forced to accept the fact that Daphne was the woman he would be spending the rest of his life with. Very slowly but steadily, he shifted from genuine resentment to a pretense of resentment, put on more than anything else for his own pride's sake. He began spending time with Daphne more and more, but only when it seemed obligatory or unintentional, and doing so grudgingly, so as not to give rise to the suspicion that he wanted to. In the bedroom he became tender and loving, turning to the more decadent pleasures only when he knew it would please Daphne as much as him to do so.

This shift in Georgie was undetectable to Daphne, it being effected so slowly and deviously, and over such a long period of time. But just as she had originally hoped would happen, Georgie's anger and resentment had settled into necessity and acceptance, which had evolved into affection and then at long last, love.

One day this reality struck Georgie with stunning clarity. He suddenly realized that Daphne was good for him. She adored him. She had perceived something valuable in him and wanted it enough to fight for it. In the process, she had brought more pleasure into his life than anyone ever had before her, and all she had ever asked of him in return was for a little of his time. He had fought her every step of the way, and yet she had waited patiently for him to come around and accept all the goodness she had to offer. He knew that he had been cruel and hard to her from the start, even before the hex, when he had used her for the one-night stand. He marveled that she could have put up with so much negative behavior from him. He believed that she truly did love him.

For the first time in their relationship, Georgie devoted an entire day solely to Daphne. He began by going to the most exclusive jewelry store he could find and buying her an alarmingly dazzling ring. Next he proceeded to the grocery store, where he purchased the ingredients for her favorite dish, and then on to the liquor store and so on. With every stop that Georgie made he became more and more excited, rising up out of his self-centered existence and discovering the incredible joy of giving. His mind whirled with plans for the future as he rushed around making preparations for the night to come.

Daphne was fully disarmed by the spectacular scene set out before her when she arrived home that evening. It was so unexpected as to be incredible. There was candlelight and soft music. The rooms were immaculately prepared and delicious smells wafted out from the kitchen. Georgie greeted her warmly, looking vulnerable but exultant as he served her a drink. She was utterly taken aback and stood looking all around her, speechless. Something shifted imperceptibly within her.

She allowed Georgie to lead her into the dining room, following him dumbly. She was deeply moved, but it was bittersweet. How long had she waited for this? Perhaps if he had come to her like this a month ago, or even yesterday...but really, how patient was a person supposed to be?

Yet she realized that this wasn't the real issue, not really. The problem was within *her*. She couldn't help it. She didn't want him now. She hadn't wanted him for some time. And it suddenly occurred to her that she had noticed this change stealing over him for quite a while, and that was what had affected her. It had adversely affected her. Perhaps she was more like Georgie than she realized.

She was much more obsessed with the craving itself than the objects that she craved. It was just like with the cigarettes. Once she stopped obsessing over trying to quit and just accepted that she was a smoker, she no longer needed to have a cigarette in her hand every waking minute. In fact, she only periodically reached for them anymore. These thoughts flitted through her mind as she slowly sipped the drink that Georgie made for her.

If Georgie noticed her strange mood he did not remark on it. He remained cheerful as he served her dinner. Perhaps he was preoccupied. Upon examining him more closely Daphne saw that he was indeed preoccupied and quite nervous as well. She picked at the sumptuous dinner he'd prepared, aware that something unpleasant was about to happen but not really inclined to stop it. She waited attentively, watching the events as if they were happening to someone else.

She knew the moment had come when Georgie smiled at her.

"Words cannot begin to express what I feel," he told her, taking her hand in his. She remained silent, so he continued, "It might be easier just to show you." He set a small black ring box on the table in front of her. When Daphne still didn't move or speak he opened the box and revealed the glistening engagement ring to her.

Daphne felt as if she was watching a train wreck. With each moment that passed she was becoming increasingly uncomfortable. She looked at the ring he offered her dispassionately. She had dreamed of this moment so many times that there was no more magic to glean from it.

"I'm sorry, Georgie," she whispered. But she actually felt no remorse at all.

"What?" He was taken aback. It had not even occurred to him that she might reject him. "Daphne, I know I've been an ass since the first, but please——" He broke off in confusion.

There was a short silence.

"You can think about it," he told her hopefully.

She didn't respond to this.

"I can make you happy, Daphne," he said.

But the more anxious and desperate he became, the more far removed Daphne felt. She thought about that night when she went to his house to find him with another woman and shuddered with revulsion. It stung her pride even after all this time to recall how pathetic her behavior had been.

What a mess! How would she ever find happiness? At the moment all she knew was that she had to get away from Georgie. She snapped the ring box shut and got up from the table.

"Daphne," he said. "Let's talk about this."

"I'm sorry, Georgie," she said again. She picked up her purse and her phone and her keys.

"Where are you going?" he asked.

"I'm leaving you, Georgie." She was surprised by how good it felt to say the words.

"You can't just leave me like this!" Georgie was aghast.

But she was preparing to do just that.

"At least take the hex off me," he pleaded.

But Daphne found that, although she didn't want Georgie for herself anymore, she still wasn't ready to just hand him over to someone else. Besides, all of this was his own fault. It wouldn't have happened if he had just stayed the way he was.

"Daphne!" He grasped her arm and tried to pull her to him but she jerked him off her with a violence that surprised him.

"Please don't turn this into an ugly scene," she said, wondering if he would remember the words he had spoken to her on that night long ago.

He didn't.

"Daphne! Please don't go!"

She opened the apartment door and walked out.

"Come back!" he yelled after her.

Daphne walked out of the apartment building breathing a sigh of relief. She felt older but infinitely wiser. She reached in her purse and pulled out a cigarette, reminding herself absently that she ought to quit one of these days.

* * * * *

HOT CROSS BUNS

Hot cross buns!
Hot cross buns!
One wallop, two wallop,
hot cross buns!

Marcie slid into the passenger seat, shivering slightly with a mixture of cold, trepidation and euphoria. She jumped when Bill slammed the car door shut behind her, and then watched him anxiously as he walked around to the driver's side and got in. His lips were set in a firm line and a muscle in his jaw twitched furiously. Marcie knew that he was livid, and she also knew that it was her actions that had him fuming. A violent shudder shook her. Bill, with his inimitable attentiveness and remarkable ability to discern her frame of mind from even the least perceptible of her movements, noticed her shudder and turned to study her for a moment. His eyes searched hers. She felt the ever-present ache within her growing and spreading throughout her body, permeating every part of her all the way down to her fingers and toes.

Why had she done it? It gave her no pleasure or satisfaction to wound him. She loved him so much it hurt; yet she intentionally did these things in an effort to get this reaction from him. Was it because she knew that during these moments she was the sole object of all of his thoughts and feelings, and hoped that he would become as obsessed with her as she was with him? There was nothing in the world she craved so much as to have all his energies focused on her like this; no matter that she had hurt him to achieve it, or what the consequences might be for it later.

Marcie shifted in her seat in anticipation of the discomfort to come, aware that Bill noticed her movement and knew the reason for it. The drive home seemed interminably long. She found her thoughts drifting back to the very beginning of this extraordinary life they shared together.

She had fallen positively head over heels in love with Bill after only four months of knowing him. She could not resist the way he *cared* for her; always touching her, inquiring about her interests and feelings with genuine interest, and remembering her answers in minute detail, opening doors for her, and especially the way he looked at her. His attentive manner was like a soft caress to her harried mind, and she felt protected and soothed by his very presence.

In spite of all this, Marcie was, even back then, keenly aware of a subtle authority in Bill's bearing that all at once aroused and terrified her. Good things were not generally said about men who were controlling of women, and the very idea was appalling after women had struggled to come so far. Yet when the control was laced with genuine concern and such tender loving care…

Marcie was tremendously attracted to Bill's strong, take-charge manner from the start, but she began to wonder about his feelings for her when several months passed and he still hadn't tried to get her into bed. She began to think that perhaps his controlling nature was enacted to cover other deficiencies. Either that or he was truly in full command of his mind and body and was intentionally waiting until the right moment. Marcie's attraction for him continued to grow while she waited to find out which of these was the case.

The answer came one night Bill took Marcie to a very posh restaurant, where the waiters spoke in hushed tones and the guests followed suit. They were seated at a table in the center of the room, chosen by Bill, and surrounded on all sides by sophistication and elegance and quiet.

Up to that point, Bill had made no effort whatsoever to seduce Marcie. Now his eyes sparkled as he reached across the table to capture one of her hands in his. He caressed her skin sensually as they simply smiled at each other. She felt certain that this was the moment she was waiting for, but she remained outwardly composed, curious to see how Bill would carry it off. She knew him well enough by this time to realize that he would reveal his wishes when he was ready, and in his usual direct but considerate manner that was so appealing to her. She blushed with anticipation as she keenly awaited his speech.

"You've probably wondered why I haven't slept with you yet," he began. She remained silent, unsure how to respond, so he went on, watching her face carefully as he spoke. "It's not for lack of desire. I've wanted you since the first moment I saw you," he confessed, pleased by the deepening of her blush. "I've shown restraint because you may be reluctant to come to my bed once you hear what I have to say." He said this in an exceedingly gentle and quiet tone, but his words might have been shouted at her for the excessive effect they had on her. Nevertheless, she rushed to contradict him.

"I don't need—"

He cut her off before she could finish. "Don't be quick to commit yourself," he advised her. "You will want to know what you're agreeing to before you acquiesce." She gasped in surprise. He had caught her unawares, but even so, every word he uttered only seemed to make her ache for him all the more.

"I don't know what you mean," she admitted.

"Don't you?" he asked with a strange smile. "From what you've experienced with me so far, what do you imagine it would be like if you were to become intimate with me?"

She thought about this for a moment while he waited patiently for her to reply. He, too, had been anticipating this exchange, and he wanted to savor every word and gesture from this long-awaited night. Marcie, meanwhile, was suddenly becoming aware of the man sitting across from her. She felt she was just now realizing something she had known from the first. Bill saw her eyes widen suddenly, revealing her emerging awareness, and he waited for her to speak. But she was unable to articulate this new understanding or what it meant in physical terms. The dim lights of the restaurant seemed unnaturally bright to her suddenly. Their waiter came and went, but she had no idea why.

Perceiving her uncertainty, Bill at last intervened to draw her out, squeezing her hand gently as he spoke soothingly to her. His voice was especially gentle, melding with the hushed tones all around them. Marcie vaguely realized that he had requested the center table for a reason, but she still wasn't certain what that reason was. "This is not a test, Marcie," he told her. "Your answer cannot be right or wrong if it is what you feel. Have you realized yet that things would be...different, with me?"

"Yes," she whispered, knowing for a certainty that any intimacy she shared with Bill would indeed be quite different from any she had experienced before.

"How, Marcie?" Bill pressed her. "How will it be different with me?"

"We...I mean you..." The words were released in a stunted manner, but her embarrassment was slowly dissolving under his intense stare as she continued, "...will be...in...control."

The light in his eyes glowed with his pleasure. He had not been mistaken. She did realize what was in store for her, even if she was not yet aware of all that it entailed.

"It's more than control, Marcie," he told her. "You have to know that I would dominate you." She felt a stinging throb pierce the already soaking flesh between her legs when he said this. Heedless, he continued, "And I'm not just talking about in the bedroom. In all matters pertaining to our relationship I would make the decisions, though I would always take your wishes into consideration. And I would expect you to satisfy my wishes in return. And I would punish you when I felt it would benefit our relationship to do so."

Marcie was stunned speechless, so he continued, "I can promise you that everything you wish to do outside of our relationship would be encouraged and supported by me one hundred percent. I love that you are a strong, independent woman. It is only in matters relating directly to our relationship that I would dominate you."

There was silence. Marcie was still unable to find her voice. She stared at Bill while she struggled to identify the many emotions raging within her. It seemed she could feel her heart beating in every part of her body. Bill took a sip from his wineglass as he allowed her to digest all that he had said. Their meals were served but Marcie could not eat. She merely moved her fork over the food on her plate nervously. She knew that among the conflicting emotions within her there was arousal so potent it held her temporarily paralyzed. She struggled to gain control but failed.

Bill watched her, perceiving her struggle but not fully comprehending the reasons for it. "You haven't said a word. What are you thinking?"

"I hardly know what to think right now," she admitted. But she trembled and blushed and he attempted to read her body language.

He laughed lightly, saying, "Let me guess, my little speech turned you on but you're afraid of me now, too."

"Yes," she admitted, laughing with him.

"Look, it's nothing that out of the ordinary for a woman to fantasize about being dominated by a man during sex, but it's a whole different story when you're talking about this as a lifestyle. I want you to know what you're getting into right up front."

"I don't know if I'm the right girl for you. I'm not the submissive type."

"You're the right girl," he assured her confidently. His self-assured, masculine manner fanned the flames that were lapping at her insides. "The question is whether you're ready to admit that this is what you want."

"I'm not sure I understand what 'this' is."

He spoke to her kindly, with interminable patience. "I'm not looking for some mindless ninny to obey my every command. I want a strong, independent woman with a mind of her own. I will control our relationship, but not because I am better or smarter or any of that. I will control it because I am stronger. I am willing and able to take responsibility for your happiness and my own."

"But why couldn't we share that responsibility?"

"We can, but when there is a conflict of some kind, or a final decision to be made it will be me who makes it. I'm not saying you can't fight for your position...I hope you always do. I am merely warning you ahead of time that I will always win."

"So you're the sort of person who has to have his own way."

"It's not really about that, although that is true to a degree." He paused, thinking of how to explain his position. "I know that you're bright and I have a tremendous amount of respect for you. Believe it or not, I have already altered certain things in my life based on little things you have said. I can't imagine not taking your feelings into consideration."

She smiled when he said this. "Then where does the control come in?"

"You're not going to like this next part," he warned her. "But I have found women to be emotionally destructive to relationships when they are allowed to take the controls and dominate them. When the men in their lives are too weak to fight for what they know is right, the relationship is doomed. Next thing you know, these guys are cowering down and 'yes dearing' their women to death when the women aren't even making any sense." He put his hands up when he saw that she was going to object. "I don't care if it's politically incorrect or if I'm a jerk for saying it. This is what I believe. And although I would do anything for you if I thought it was in your best interest, I refuse to support destructive behavior. I particularly will not allow you to lure me into unnecessary conflict according to your moods."

"What makes you so certain I would even do that?" she asked, defensive.

"I'm just warning you of what would happen if you do."

"And that is?" she asked, raising an incredulous eyebrow.

"You would be punished." He said this with a small smile, but his words carried a ring of irrevocability that Marcie did not miss.

"Punished...how?" It was getting difficult to keep her voice down but she managed, aware that people were seated at tables all around them. Suddenly she realized why Bill had situated them there.

"However I deemed appropriate," he replied with an arrogant shrug.

Marcie couldn't suppress a laugh, even though she was assailed by conflicting emotions. Outrage was now mingling amongst the still-potent arousal and various other sensations.

"You're a wifebeater," she accused him quietly. The obligatory soft tones forced her to be more explicit than she might have otherwise been.

"First of all," he replied calmly, "I would never cause you physical harm or strike you in a way that could lead to physical harm. Second, I would never lay a hand on you unless you agreed ahead of time to accept the fact that I might do so. That is why I am having this conversation with you. Third, *you* would be the one who controlled whether or not you were punished, if you think about it. You would know ahead of time that if you acted destructively, I would punish you."

"…without causing me physical harm," she finished for him.

"Exactly." He smiled.

"Why?" she asked.

"Sometimes a person has to be willing to take control. And often taking control can get physical. If you want to be with me, Marcie, you are going to have to come to me in my home, and on my terms. You can stay forever if you want to, but for as long as you stay, you will always have to remember that I am the head of that household. I am the last word. I want you there, I will take very good care of you and I might even change a little for you, too, but if things get out of hand I will be the one to put them back on track."

Marcie stared at him, stunned. She felt a grudging respect for him even though she immensely disliked the things he was saying. Her desire, however, still reigned uppermost in her consciousness. She found herself wondering what being "punished" by him would be like.

"It's dishonesty that I am really trying to avoid here," Bill continued with her silence. "I will never betray you behind your back because I have allowed you to emasculate me to my face. If you agree to share your life with me, you will see that you will enjoy the simple truth I have presented to you here much more than you would have enjoyed the more traditional way people deal with each other."

Marcie was torn. She could definitely see that he made some very truthful and enticing points. The talk of punishment had shocked her but by no means turned her off. Bill seemed even more masculine and strong to her, in fact, and she felt an instinctual craving curling up from deep within her. On the other hand, it was all terribly frightening, too, if for no other reason than it was so unorthodox. She wished the throbbing desire between her legs would quiet down enough so that she could think more clearly.

"Perhaps I should give you more time to think about it," Bill suggested, perceiving her uncertainty. "It is extremely important that you realize what you will be getting into. You have to be in full agreement about this from the very beginning."

"Putting aside the punishment part of it—assuming I behave myself—" she blushed when she said this "—in other respects, when you say you will dominate me, what do you mean exactly?" she asked.

"My decisions in our relationship will be final. I will use force when necessary. That doesn't mean I expect you to simply 'obey' me without a fight. I expect you to fight. I would enjoy the fight in fact. But I will not patronize you. You will lose."

She felt a titillating thrill so powerful that she shuddered when she heard these words from him. She seemed to recall wishing once that she could find a man who wouldn't cower from the sight of an angry woman. Men had always found her intimidating. She wondered how Bill would handle her at her most extreme moments.

Bill paid the waiter with a self-assured ease that Marcie was all at once admiring and envious of. He was fully composed while she was aching with desire for him. In that instant she knew that she would be going home with him for that night at the very least, whatever the consequences.

"I don't need more time to think about it," she announced boldly.

Bill took her hand in his and led her out of the restaurant. They drove to his house in silence, a comfortable silence where both sat

thinking their own individual thoughts. Marcie trembled in anticipation of what was to come. She had never participated in any
sexual activities that deviated from the norm. She had never been
tied up, or spanked, for example, although she had read about such
things, and they always left her fascinated and aroused. Yet she
knew that she would never be the one to suggest them. Even to acquiesce had been terribly difficult and embarrassing. She stole a
glance at Bill and he smiled, reaching over to take her hand firmly
into his.

"Are you all right?" he asked her.

"Yes," she replied, looking away. He gently squeezed her hand.

"Good," he said. "Because we're here."

Bill's house was just as Marcie would have imagined it. Straight,
masculine lines formed rooms that were bathed in hushed brown
hues that clashed delightfully with the spatter of cold, steel-gray
accessories that were spread throughout. All was in perfect order
and exceedingly clean. The stark surroundings were made considerably more bearable by the disorderly encroachment of over-
growth that flowed out from the tropical plants that were placed
about everywhere.

"It needs a woman's touch," Bill admitted when she only stared
all around her in silence. She had been thinking how intimidatingly
perfect it already was.

"Would you like a tour?" he asked her.

Marcie followed Bill around his large house, noticing that he
saved the bedroom for last. She shuddered suddenly as she stepped

over the threshold into that room, thinking perhaps to find items of bondage within, and was even mildly disappointed to find nothing at all out of the ordinary in sight.

Bill approached her straightaway, taking her face in his hands and tipping her head back slightly for his impending kiss. His tongue penetrated her mouth with authority as his hands moved persuasively through her hair. Marcie had the comforting awareness that she was not expected to perform or impress or put forth any effort at all. Quite the contrary, she had only to allow Bill to take matters in hand and see to it that they both were fulfilled. She wasn't certain how she knew this, but that didn't matter. The feeling didn't appear to require substantiation in order to provide the incredible sense of bliss and well-being that came along with it. The feeling persisted and grew as Bill's caress meandered lower to glide along her shoulders and back, deftly finding the zipper to her dress and effortlessly easing it open. It was as if all the self-consciousness and pressure of the event were being stripped away from Marcie's body along with her clothing. All that remained was a feverish anticipation for what was to come and a genuine sense of freedom to experience it in absolute contentment.

When she was completely naked Bill lifted her into his arms and placed her onto the bed. He stood over her, drinking in the sight of her, while he removed his own clothing. She lay trembling before him, instinctively knowing not to cover any part of herself with her hands, or in any way try to hide herself from his gaze. He took his time undressing, and the possessive aspect with which he perused her naked body made her gasp. When he pulled off his pants she saw that he was fully aroused.

Bill joined Marcie on the bed, immediately capturing her lips in a passionate but exceedingly tender kiss. She was somewhat distracted and even mildly dismayed that there didn't appear to be any dominating or punishing forthcoming—for her curiosity had been peaked by his disclosure in the restaurant—but these thoughts were quickly being diminished by the overpoweringly gentle seduction of his kiss. She was once again enthralled by the self-assured yet considerate manner that originally captured her heart. Bill's confidence and strength seemed to become more pronounced with his mild handling of her. His earlier words were nearly forgotten but not entirely, for there were little reminders that thrilled her imagination and left her wondering. There was a conviction and determination in nearly everything he did, from the way he held her hands so carefully in his that she barely registered that she was actually being restrained in his iron grip, to the way his fingers gently titillated her tender labia while surreptitiously prying them apart. Slowly and methodically, his will became her own.

Marcie could do little more than cling to Bill as he skillfully and persuasively mastered her body. He took his time discovering all the little nuances of pleasuring her, gauging not only the places she liked best to be touched, but also the intensity and pressure that she preferred as well. Marcie lay back in a kind of delirious stupor, thoroughly captivated by Bill's seductive efforts on her behalf. He used his fingers, and then his lips and tongue, to lure her into a state of utter arousal. Once he had her fully impassioned, he let his tongue roam leisurely over her clitoris, again and again; pattering and prodding it until she felt the molten waves of exquisite pleasure roll over her. She cried out in stunned surprise.

Once this first passion had passed, Marcie lay dazed and pliant as Bill moved up over her and lovingly took her into his embrace. Forgotten for the moment were all thoughts of dominance as Marcie's body melted around him. He made love to her with such thoughtfulness and consideration that it was impossible to imagine him any other way. Marcie fell in love with him all over again.

And for the first few weeks of their being intimate together, Marcie could not imagine anything more wonderful than being with Bill. He was attentive, loving, kind and caring. He spared no expense to indulge her every whim. There were no disputes. How could there be when everything was exactly as she wished it? They talked for hours without end, and still he wanted to know more about her. He seemed to really understand her, continually amazing her with his insight. He cared for her better than she cared for herself. He accepted her. There was no part of her that he did not embrace.

One of the things that impressed Marcie most about Bill through this period of intense intimacy was that he always approached every matter that was set before him with integrity. He was a man who stood up for what he believed in. It was not just his integrity in and of itself but the way in which he fulfilled it.

He was thoughtful, firm and inexorable, acting with such strength and grace that it enchanted Marcie to observe him. Even more importantly it cemented her trust in him. He was not pushy or arrogant, but loving and kind. Had he been less loving, perhaps his gentle authority would have seemed more interfering and dominating. But if he in fact dominated her, she was not aware of it, except perhaps in the bedroom. He was becoming a more demanding lover, but she adored the attention, and so far it worked out in her favor, causing her to feel desired and needed, and making her ego soar.

But even as they grew closer, Marcie became increasingly overwhelmed by the sheer impressiveness of Bill, and over time a subtle voice began presenting doubts to her mind, intent on sabotage. Joined with this was a mild resentment of his unwavering self-assuredness throughout her own self-doubt and inner conflicts. She began seeking something that could transform her fears and insecurities from mere conjecture to reality.

One day, in this kind of a mood, Marcie wandered up into Bill's attic and began sifting through boxes, yielding at last to her accumulating suspicions and doubts. The more commonplace the items she found there, the more she felt—rather than relief—frustration. She scanned the items that marked Bill's former life contemptuously, certain that they must be concealing something she had a right to know about.

At last her eyes fell upon a clump of letters that were held together by an elastic band. She pulled one out and began to read it. After that another one followed, and then another. She was not surprised to find that they were love letters. They appeared to be remnants of a long-distance relationship from the past. They were all addressed to Bill and sent by the same woman. Marcie tried to glean what Bill's feelings had been for the woman by the inferences she made in her letters. She wondered why Bill kept the letters. Did this woman still mean something to him? More questions and doubts assailed her thoughts. She felt intense jealousy for the woman and fumed over the deductions she was making from what the woman had written.

By the time Bill returned home to her that night, Marcie was fuming with righteous indignation. All her insecurities and doubts had found an outlet through her anger. Even so, she knew she could hardly accuse him for something that had happened in the past—especially something she had no right to know about. This, too, irritated her; the fact that she must suffer with her new knowledge silently, knowing all the while that he was clinging to the memory of a woman from his past—this was one of the deductions she had made.

Bill noticed her mood instantly, although she was attempting to remain aloof. He pulled her into his arms and kissed her, ignoring her attempts to move away from him. "What's wrong?" he asked, holding her close and examining her face.

Bill's nearness was not conducive to Marcie's bad mood, but she couldn't extricate herself from his embrace without being openly hostile, so she turned her head casually and said the mysteriously magic word that had always worked wonders for her in the past. "Nothing."

But Bill refused to take the bait, holding her fast. "I asked you what was wrong and I would like an answer," he said matter-of-factly.

Marcie bristled. "And *I* said there was nothing wrong!"

"Okay, I'll take you at your word," he said good-naturedly. "So this is just a bad mood then?" He continued to hold her and meanwhile kept looking at her, searching her expression for the answer he sought.

"How dare you!" His reasonableness was antagonizing.

"I dare because you're clearly upset while insisting that there's nothing wrong. I can only assume from that behavior that you're in a bad mood. Is it or is it not the case?"

Marcie was becoming frustrated. This was not going the way she expected it to. She reminded herself that she was the one who was injured and tried to regain control of the situation.

"Am I a machine that has to smile all the time?"

"Not at all," he said. "If you're in a bad mood just say so. But I'm getting the distinct impression that you're upset about something. If you're upset, and especially if it's with me, that gets me involved and puts the ball in my court."

Marcie was becoming even more frustrated. She had never met the man who would not retreat guiltily in the face of an outraged woman, effectively surrendering under the confusion of it all and graciously granting her the advantage she sought. Her anger continued to escalate, even as her respect for him increased—or perhaps it was *because* her respect for him had increased. She once again felt the disturbing mixture of admiration and envy amongst the many other emotions.

"You're so full of yourself!" she erupted, raising her voice. "Everything has to be about you."

He laughed at that. "Last chance to tell me if there is something bothering you," he said, remaining fully self-composed and utterly unperturbed by her outburst.

"Go to hell."

In the next instant Bill picked her up and, before she was even aware of what was happening, he had slung her over his shoulder. Outraged, she kicked and screamed and jerked about wildly, trying desperately to get him to put her down. He laughed once again at her outburst, holding her tightly so that she could neither hurt him nor escape. He carried her into the bedroom and placed her carefully down on the bed. Then he got into the bed and climbed on top of her, gently restraining her. He was still amused by her struggles, chuckling softly as he easily subdued her. His indulgent reaction and patient resolve seemed to encourage her to fully let loose with all the pent-up aggression she didn't even know she possessed. She thrashed about vehemently, really trying to hurt him in her fury. But Bill controlled her effortlessly. Having captured her flailing arms, he held them firmly together, above her head, with one of his hands.

"It's okay, sweetheart," he said in a maddeningly calm voice. His unruffled composure, more than his words, inflamed her even more, and she thrashed about on the bed even more violently than before; but to no avail. Bill held her fast and there wasn't anything she could do about it. "Easy now," he said in a tone one might use with a wild animal. He waited until her energies were spent and her fighting stopped.

"Let go of me," she then demanded.

"Not yet," he said.

To Marcie's dismay she began to cry. "Please let go of me!"

"I haven't gotten you figured out yet," he said contemplatively. "I'm not sure what's going on, but I intend to get to the bottom of it." Marcie was alarmed by his words. Meanwhile her skirt had risen up during her struggles and Bill was slipping his free hand up her thigh. He wiggled a few fingers inside the leg band of her panties. "What's this?" he asked her, smiling, when he discovered that she was wet. Marcie was more surprised than he was by this discovery. Bill continued to stroke her for a moment but then, to her dismay, he took his hand away to quickly remove his tie. He then used the tie to secure her hands, which he had kept hold of the entire time with his other hand, to the bed.

Marcie searched her mind for the right words and realized suddenly that she had no idea what to think, let alone say. The truth was, she was genuinely conflicted about what was happening to her.

Bill, in the meantime, was sliding her panties down, handling her kicking legs with ease as he situated himself in between them.

He picked up her legs and spread them wide apart, holding them securely in midair with his strong hands. Once she was restrained in this manner, he leaned in between her trembling legs to kiss and lick her tenderly. He had learned many different ways to please her with his tongue, and he employed every single one of them now, painstakingly, and at an unhurried pace. Pretty soon Marcie was crying out with pleasure and gyrating her hips with the rhythmic motion of his tongue. He skillfully brought her to the very precipice of her climax, and then abruptly stopped before she was fully satisfied. Marcie watched him in stunned silence as he got up and began to undress. She noticed he was fully aroused and she began to ache with anticipation. She thought she ought to protest but most of her previous anger had completely abandoned her. He returned to the bed and once again moved between her legs.

"What are you going to do?" she asked stupidly.

"I'm trying to help you feel better. I don't know what set you off yet, but let's just get you feeling better first."

She was astounded. She had absolutely no idea what to think. His words rekindled her anger, even as they sent a fresh wave of desire coursing through her. She wanted him to make love to her, but she didn't want to yield to him. In her confusion she found herself halfheartedly resisting Bill as he approached her, making feeble attempts to kick him.

"Enough," he said firmly, but without anger. He rested himself between her legs without entering her, gently kissing her face and in between kisses searching her eyes. "What's going on with you, Marcie?"

Marcie couldn't begin to explain what was happening inside her, so she remained silent. More than anything at that moment, she wished Bill would simply make love to her, but she could hardly say so. When the silence became too much for her, she moved her hips against him enticingly.

"Say it," he told her.

"Say what?"

"Tell me that you want me to make love to you."

"I don't care what——"

He cut her off. "Look. I can see you're upset about something that you don't want to talk about. I can also see that you're very turned on and it is my opinion it would be good for us both to make love now. However, we haven't fully established the rules yet, and I want to make sure we understand each other. You don't feel like being agreeable or working things out. Okay. I'm more than willing to take charge of the situation, but you have to agree ahead of time to *let* me take charge and to trust me, *whatever* I decide to do."

Marcie stared at Bill in stunned silence.

With her silence Bill continued patiently, "We spoke of this already in the restaurant, so you must have known this moment would come. It's here, but I need your consent. You have to tell me that you trust me to take control of you—that you *want* me to take control of you."

She realized suddenly that she did want Bill to take control, but she still couldn't bring herself to say the words.

Bill sighed with her continued silence, but his tone remained calm and tender. "Either you agree to trust me, and give me free rein to do what I think is best for us, or I'll untie you now and you can get up, get dressed, leave here and never come back."

Marcie was both alarmed and hurt by his words. But she could not, in truth, say that she was entirely surprised. Bill had given her ample warning of his position, through not only words but actions. Throughout their time together, there was a clear leadership being established by him, and she had reveled in it. Until now.

Marcie was further confounded by Bill's proximity. Their bodies were pressed together, although he was careful not to lean his full weight on her. She marveled over how he always thought of even the smallest detail of her comfort and well-being. There was never a moment when her needs were not put as high in priority, or higher, than his own. Yet to give up control over her body and just hand it over to him carte blanche! But to get up and leave was too painful to consider.

Marcie did not like the position she was in one bit. Bill seemed to read her mind.

"I see that you don't like to compromise when you're upset." He still spoke to her calmly and with genuine kindness in his voice, although there was frustration there, too. "That is precisely why I want the authority to take control—so I can take over when you get like this. It will allow you to be as angry and unreasonable as you want, knowing I'll take care of us until you come around. I'm not going to allow you to dictate our relationship based on your moods. I thought I made this clear."

Marcie was once again torn between grudging respect, admiration and anger. Bill's words inflamed each of the emotions in question. She realized he was right about her unwillingness to compromise when she was feeling the way she did now. His mastery over his own emotions astounded her.

Taking her continued silence for refusal, he abruptly untied her. "Get dressed."

Had this been happening with any man other than Bill, Marcie would have got up and stormed out without a second thought, assured in the knowledge that he would come around eventually and that she would not only have kept her pride intact but also managed to make him suffer as much as she had. But she knew for a certainty that Bill would do no such thing, and she felt a sudden panic.

"No!" she cried vehemently.

He looked at her expectantly. She saw that he was losing patience with her. She was suddenly contrite, but terribly self-conscious and still hesitant.

"I do trust you," she admitted finally.

"And?"

She sighed in frustration. "What do you want from me?"

"I want your consent to take control of you when I think it is necessary. I want *full* control, over you and me."

"Okay." She realized faintly that she still wasn't one hundred percent clear about what she was consenting to. And yet she really did trust Bill. The uncertainty over what he would do to her once he took control didn't bring fear but anticipation.

"Okay what?"

"I give you my consent."

"Do I have your full consent to take absolute control of you and your body?"

Marcie nodded. New little pangs of sharp desire pierced the already engorged flesh between her legs.

"Say it."

"You have my full consent to take absolute control of me and...my body." She could hardly believe she had just spoken the words.

He smiled. "Thank you," he said. He took her face in his hands and waited for her eyes to meet his. She desperately wanted the discussion to be over and for him to resume the lovemaking, but he was not quite finished. "You've crossed a line with this agreement," he told her. "It has advanced our relationship to the next level. In the future you can be as unreasonable and out of control as you want and know that I'll protect us and our relationship. At any time if you want to take back your consent you may do so, but know that it will end our relationship."

"You obviously don't care about me at all if you can so easily threaten to end our relationship," she protested, suddenly bursting into tears.

He held her in his arms and patiently waited for her to stop crying. "I care a great deal for you," he said, embracing her more securely. "There are actually very few things you could do that would make me end this relationship," he told her. "You can do pretty much whatever you wish and express yourself in any way you like, but always know that I will do what has to be done to protect you, me and us."

Marcie had stopped crying so he gently laid her back down on the bed and, without further ado, began making love to her. He kissed away her tears as he took her tenderly into him. "Hush, now," he soothed, and she clung to him. She became more feverish in her lovemaking as a result of all the pent-up emotions that had been raging inside her. She found herself thrashing against him, even as she simultaneously clutched him to her. She became almost ferocious in her struggle to achieve the satisfaction she sought.

"That's it," Bill encouraged her. "Get it all out here and now." He spread kisses all along her lips and cheeks and neck as he lovingly consoled her. He easily controlled her unruly body as she fully succumbed to her passion, gently restraining her when she became too aggressive. All the while he moved in and out of her with long, even strokes, allowing her free rein to use his body as it pleased her best to do.

Marcie was feverish with thoughts of being dominated and all that that might entail, but thus far Bill had seen fit to be lenient, and frustration mingled and interacted with the other emotions that were scourging through her for an explosive effect. She imagined his strong hands, which up to this point had done little more than subdue her, actually turning against her to dominate and punish, and she screamed as her orgasm tore through her. Spurred on by her intense response, Bill climaxed right after her.

Afterward, Marcie felt as if she was immersed in a warm bath of tranquillity. She had never in her life felt so close to another person.

She thought about her earlier upset, and reflected that her anger was rather like a ravenous beast when it reared its ugly head. She had often allowed it to control her and those around her, never knowing how else to appease it. Certainly no man she had encountered before Bill had known how to manage it. For that matter, no man had ever even dared make the attempt. Bill had not only dared and succeeded, but he had actually *accepted* the beast within her. Still, Marcie was confused by her conflicting desires to both need and be self-sufficient.

But her thoughts were interrupted by Bill, who had not quite finished with the beast.

"Do you feel like talking about what upset you earlier?" he asked, still holding her tightly to him.

"Does it matter?" she asked.

"It matters to me if something is making you unhappy. If not, then, well, no, I suppose it doesn't matter at all."

Suddenly her earlier annoyance seemed ludicrous to her. Still under the spell of the intimacy they had just shared, she blurted out the cause of it.

When she finished, Bill leaned up over her so he could look down into her face. "You went through the boxes in my attic?" he asked in disbelief.

Her calm began giving way to dismay and she immediately regretted telling him. "Oh, God," she said.

"It's okay, Marcie," he reassured her. "But, why?"

"I don't know," she admitted. "I felt like I needed to."

"Were you already upset when you went up there?"

"Well…yes."

"So you were looking for something to fight about."

"I…oh, can we just forget about it?"

He laughed at her in spite of himself. "That's the kind of thing that would normally get you a good, hard spanking," he told her with good humor. "But I'm feeling rather indulgent tonight."

She balked at his words, but apprehension and new desire simmered beneath the hazy afterglow she was basking in.

After that night there was no denying that clear boundaries had been set, which Marcie loved and hated, both at the same time. She loved the sense of security she got from Bill's gentle care and attentiveness, and deeply admired his strength and confidence. She was strongly attracted to his positive energy; there was no job too tough for him to tackle, and no problem he wouldn't address head-on. She respected him immensely. She adored his power and melted in his tenderness. The only thorn in her side was the missing control that she had so readily handed over to him. Although it never really came up in the normal course of their lives she could not help thinking about it. There had not even been another incident where it had come into play since the night she relinquished it, but this did not stop her from thinking about the fact that it was no longer hers. There was something demeaning in it, as if she was not able to manage her own emotions and behavior.

In due time, for reasons she couldn't even fully explain, Marcie felt herself longing to challenge the subtle authority that Bill had developed over her. She felt strangely shackled by her contentment. Too, on the back burner, there simmered the tantalizing memory of how he had responded to her defiance on that previous occasion, actually seeming to taking pleasure in it and the battle that followed. She could not forget the exquisite struggle and all that came afterward, even including his gentle but firm mastery of her. Nor could she forget his offhand remark that her behavior might get her "a good, hard spanking." She wasn't entirely certain that he had been fully serious about this, but it continued to wear at her consciousness.

The moment of truth came one day when Marcie woke up feeling particularly out of sorts. In her present state of mind, the more challenging tasks of the day seemed overly disastrous to her. She had the sense that everything was working against her and she became more and more exasperated. The frustrations of her day crept under her skin and seeped into every part of her consciousness. They settled over her like thick thunderclouds, further darkening her outlook. An overall resentment arose and joined her malaise. Such was her disposition when she encountered Bill at the end of that day.

Bill sensed Marcie's mood immediately, and he became especially considerate. But she had passed the point where she could easily let go of the pain she was feeling. She was going to feel bad, and that was that. Furthermore, her mood had reached the stage where every action and occurrence could only further inflame her, especially Bill's inexhaustible composure.

"You don't have to treat me with kid gloves," she snapped at him, painfully aware of his efforts on her behalf. He merely raised an eyebrow at this. His lips twitched in an effort not to smile. This irritated her even more. Was there nothing that could rile him?

She began slamming things around the kitchen in preparation for dinner.

"Let's go out to eat," he suggested, not missing the point of the racket.

"I don't feel like going out," she replied shortly.

"Then I'll order in."

"I can manage," she insisted, but her tone was laced with martyrdom.

"That wasn't a suggestion. I *am* ordering in. Do you have any preferences?"

Marcie tightened her grip on the pan she was holding in her hand. Even though she was in no mood to cook and loved having food brought in, she was, for the moment, more preoccupied with an almost perverse desire to upset him. His control was making her feel entirely out of control. "Fine!" she snapped, lifting the pan off the burner and throwing it violently into the sink, causing a thunderous clash that startled even her.

"No preferences," he murmured, picking up the phone and calmly ordering dinner for them. "I don't want it right away," he added to the person on the other end. "Deliver it in a few hours, say, around seven-thirty."

Marcie felt a twinge of excitement when she heard him say this—in spite of her bad temper. Even so, when Bill hung up the phone and looked at her, she said testily, "I'm not in the mood, so you may as well have had it delivered right away."

He actually laughed at her. "If you think I delayed dinner to make love to you after what you just pulled you have another think coming," he said. "You're going to have to apologize to me first. Anyway, I have something else in mind."

Marcie's heart thudded violently as Bill approached her. "What's that supposed to mean?" she asked.

"Oh, I think you know," he said, abruptly picking her up and easily slinging her over his shoulder.

"Put me down!" she screamed. She kicked furiously with her feet and pummeled his back with her hands. He remained unperturbed, holding her firmly, and occasionally erupting into laughter over one of her efforts, causing her to struggle even harder. He held her legs securely with one hand while his other hand came up to caress the round fullness of her bottom. Then he raised that hand up and brought it back down, hard, on one plump buttock.

Marcie screeched, once again remembering his words from that earlier struggle, where he threatened a "good, hard spanking." She screamed again and beat on his back all the harder.

Bill, meanwhile, took her into their bedroom and dropped her onto the bed. She immediately flipped herself over—onto her back—and tried to get up, but he was too quick for her, grasping her arms and immediately turning her back onto her stomach the way he had originally set her there. Then he swiftly got onto the bed and straddled her, barricading her legs between his own. She was fully pinned beneath him.

Marcie continued to make a great effort to get away from him, in spite of the futility of it, wiggling and squirming and kicking and screaming. She was startlingly aware of his strength and energy as he held her. He secured both of her wrists with one strong hand and held them fast, even as he began lifting her skirt with his other hand. He did all this leisurely, playing with her, and actually enjoying her efforts to escape him. When her skirt was brought up around her waist, Marcie began her struggles anew, thrashing and bucking violently in an effort to throw Bill off of her. All the while she alternated between screaming and crying and flat out ordering him to stop. She held nothing back—something inside her knew she didn't have to—and Bill, very gradually, as it suited him to do so, subdued her.

When Bill had effectively restrained Marcie, having raised her skirt and lowered her panties, he began striking her buttocks with his bare, open hand, landing the blows hard with loud, resounding *thwacks*. Marcie screamed and fought like something out of the wild. Her whole body struggled in vain to escape his large, firm hands.

The spanking was not overly painful, but the blows were leveled with enough force to cause the flesh to sting and smart, leaving it sore and tender after the fact. The use of his bare hand instead of another object seemed exceedingly intimate somehow, and she was likewise jarred by the disparity of being struck by the hands that were usually so gentle and accommodating, and which normally brought her pleasure. She was aware, too, of the control Bill once again maintained, for she realized instinctively that his hand struck only hard enough to hurt her on the surface, rather than to actually injure her. That was the crux of the matter, really, that the worst part of it was the violation to her ego. Bill wasn't just punishing her; he was subduing her.

Marcie was panting from her exertions to fight Bill off, more winded than she had ever been. These exertions made her feel strangely alive, with every molecule pulsating vigorous energy. All her emotions of that day, the anger, fear, resentment and so forth, rushed together in a sudden spark that burned hot and then dissipated. And always lingering in the back corner of her mind was the awareness of Bill's ultimate strength and control, not just physically, but emotionally, too. Coming together with that awareness was the realization that she needed Bill to a degree that actually frightened her. At some point it occurred to her that her struggles, which she knew all along were in vain, were actually for her own benefit and indulgence. All the horrible sentiments that had been building up inside her throughout the day were disappearing; yet somehow she couldn't help feeling that she was losing a part of herself, too.

Marcie suddenly burst into tears, abandoning her struggles and weeping loudly in defeat. Bill stopped spanking her and took her in his arms. She clung to him with a raw need that left her feeling wide open and exposed. Her defenses had all been stripped away and she seemed incapable of getting them back. Her buttocks were sore and exceedingly warm. She wept cleansing tears, while Bill held her close, kissing her tears and tenderly hushing her cries.

Somehow, inexplicably, Marcie was no longer weeping tears of frustration but crying out with passion, suddenly kissing Bill hungrily while clinging to him in desperation. It was like a first, long-awaited kiss that took away her very breath. She gave herself to him completely, fully lost in her desire. It consumed her absolutely, and she could not have stopped herself from being swept up in the tide of it even if she had wanted to. But she had no thoughts of stopping. The spanking had broken down her emotional barriers, and it had shattered any remaining physical barriers as well. The sharp, stinging pain had awakened and warmed her flesh and the resulting heat had radiated into her womb, causing it to expand and contract and open to him. Her body was overwhelmed with moist warmth and yearning.

Bill took all of this in stride with his usual composure. He seemed to know that this would be the end result of what he had done, and he reveled in his utter victory over Marcie. He hadn't minded her angry words or her violent struggles. On the contrary, he was pleased; for without the struggle where was the victory? He felt his heart swell with love and desire for her. And he did not feel in the least remorseful over his treatment of her. Hadn't he given her fair warning that this was the way it would be between them? For him, this was much more than mere domination. It was his fundamental belief that it was a necessary part of their relationship to keep it fresh and new, for it cleansed away all the pent-up resentment and insecurity. For him, it was a lifestyle. He hoped that Marcie felt the same. She had responded the way he had hoped she would in all that had occurred between them so far, but he feared that she might feel differently afterward. This life was not for every woman, nor certainly for every man. But he had grown attached to Marcie, his thoughts were all of her now, and he wondered how he would bear it if she changed her mind and left him. As if the fear had been realized he suddenly clung to her more violently, causing her to cry out in surprise.

Their subsequent lovemaking was passionate and their movements in sync. Marcie was soft and yielding and he took her gently at first, but in the end succumbed to the delicious power of taking what he wanted from his victory, plundering all that she offered and more. His strength, which had stripped her down earlier, now filled her with everything that she needed. His unrestrained passion ricocheted off hers as they virtually consumed each other. Every limb seemed entwined within another; they were so closely joined that Marcie lost track of where she ended and Bill began. At one point, they rolled together across the bed so that she was on top. This was what she liked best, as it gave her the power to move over him in exactly the way that stimulated her the most. As she began working her hips against him she felt no sense of separateness in her activity. It seemed they worked together as one and that Bill derived as much pleasure from her movements as she did herself. There was no sense of urgency or of being hurried; she gyrated against him without a single self-conscious thought. Her intimacy with Bill was unlike anything she had experienced so far in her life. She was ever aware of his unconditional acceptance and love as she ground herself vigorously against him in search of satisfaction. Without warning, a thunderous upsurge of pleasure burst through her, startling her in its intensity. Her release triggered his, and he came together with her. She collapsed over him when it was over and he held her close. She listened attentively to the solid thudding of his heart.

But as wonderful as the moment had been, Marcie felt confused. How could she accept Bill's domination of her while she feared her loss of self?

"Tell me what you're feeling," he said, lightly drawing circles over her back with his fingertips.

"I'm afraid."

"What of?"

She wasn't sure, so she told him what she felt. "I feel like I'm losing myself."

"Why do you feel that?"

She hesitated, not withholding from him, but with uncertainty. She had never felt so free to express herself before and she believed she could tell him anything. Still… "I don't want to be tamed."

In one swift, gliding movement he rolled her onto her back and came up over her so that he could look fully into her face. "I don't want you tamed either."

"But…"

"When I took over tonight, I did it in order to bring us closer together, not to tame you."

"How can you say that?"

"Because it's the truth."

"But the spanking…" She was suddenly embarrassed. She couldn't believe it had happened. That spankings occurred in the world of sexual submission she was well aware, but this was more like discipline. She shuddered at the implications.

"That was the best way I could think of to subdue you."

"Right. That's what I mean."

"Okay, well, then we're talking about something else. I didn't spank you to change you, but to subdue you for that moment. I did it so my night would be more pleasant and because I believed yours would be, too. You were out of control. That doesn't mean I expect you to change the way you are. I dominated you this time, in this moment. Next time, I hope you will fight just as hard, even though I'll defeat you again." He smiled an evil smile when he said this. His smile annoyed her, but only mildly.

"I'm not sure I get it."

"Don't you?" he asked. "Let me ask you this then, did you enjoy the struggle?"

"Well…"

"I did, too," he said, knowing her answer already. "I loved it, in fact. It gave us both a chance to equalize things."

"But that's just it. I hate that you always get to win."

"Do you? Don't you *expect* me to win? I wonder if you would ever want me again if I lost even once." She wondered, too, astounded by his reasoning. It was true that his power and strength, so displayed, was an enormous part of what attracted her to him. She was momentarily too sidetracked by the happiness she felt to concentrate fully on all the other things she was feeling.

"I love this honesty," she admitted.

"Me, too. It's so much better this way. That's why I would never want to change you…or tame you, as you put it." His hand continued to move over her skin possessively as he spoke to her in his gentle voice. "It's kind of like a game, or a sport. If you were to let me win, where would the challenge be, or the fun? The struggle has to be real. For a man to truly dominate a woman he has to really be the stronger person, physically and emotionally. For a woman to submit to that man she has to genuinely feel that he has conquered her."

Marcie thought about this as she snuggled up close to Bill and drifted off to sleep.

* * *

In time, when the novelty of their extraordinary lifestyle wore off and Marcie became more comfortable with the unconventional peculiarity of it, she was able to more carefully examine it. She was then able to discern what it was that had initially attracted her to Bill, and how she really felt about his dominance over her. That it enhanced their sex life, drawing out and developing her innermost sensuality, she realized from the start. What she wanted to understand more fully was what this way of life would mean to her emotionally.

Each and every time Marcie submitted to Bill's dominance, one more barrier that she had built up over her lifetime came crashing down, and their intimacy grew. The things she believed in and wished for remained safe and intact, for she found that Bill did respect her, and he would even submit to her when it was in their best interest for him to do so. Marcie seemed to be growing stronger within herself with each capitulation in her relationship. As her trust in Bill continued to grow, she felt safer giving more of herself to him. The intimacy they shared inside the lifestyle was undeniably distinctive and outstanding.

Yet, even as their bond was strengthened, Marcie found that she would still become, at times, dissatisfied and unhappy. This was not exclusive to her relationship with Bill. It was simply the woman she was; hampered by the fears she had accumulated in her various experiences with men. In most of her past relationships, she would have acted on these feelings by simply pouting or blowing up, crying and ranting; using any recent occurrence that would serve as an excuse but really just needing to get her feelings out. But once the mood passed, she was left feeling empty and distant, with a wider expanse now to bridge in order to achieve intimacy. Her partners would often trudge back into her good graces miserably, never really understanding her or the reasons for their penitence, and the relationships would be marked for death. With Bill, she could rant, rave, cry or scream; knowing all the while that he would keep *them* safe, and even enjoy the challenge of it all while he did so. He had brought her to a place where she could express her feelings while all the while being accepted, loved, supported and protected. Even through the severest spankings, she knew that Bill was fully aware of her and her needs. He had been perfectly right when he told her that this kind of control had to be genuinely maintained. A man really did have to be exceptionally strong to pull it off. It was ludicrous to think that anyone could do it. If he had been a lesser man, she knew for a certainty the whole dominance thing would have bored her by now.

Instead, she was, overall, amazingly content and deeply involved. Bill was in nearly all her thoughts. And for days—and sometimes even weeks—after each submission, she walked around in a state of more or less constant arousal. Bill's presence was, for her, desire itself. She sometimes felt that she loved him too much, and desired him too much, too. She wanted him to an extent that frightened her. And when the fear became too much for her she compensated by finding ways to draw out his need to dominate her.

Marcie's thoughts came back to the present. After just over a year with Bill one would think she would have gotten past those fears. Bill had proved to her time and again that she was the priority in his life. He had made it more than clear that he would be there for her always. And she did not doubt it, not really. But the fear always returned, out of the blue, and often with such ferocity that it alarmed her. On this night she had merely glanced at him from across the crowded room and all at once it was there. His beauty and strength struck her like a terrible blow, and she felt horribly afraid. The other women at the party seemed so much more beautiful than her. She wondered if Bill noticed this, too, and she could imagine the soft, fluttering beauties yielding to his incredible determination and strength.

Marcie knew that she had gone too far this time, completely yielding to her insecurities and fears. She wondered if she had crossed one of the lines that Bill had warned her about that first night that he had dominated her. She kept asking herself why, cringing over the details of her behavior as the memories returned to harass her. She recalled her improprieties of that night in vivid detail. She had gone way beyond merely flirting with another man. She had thrown all concern for Bill's feelings aside in an effort to temporarily make herself feel more desirable. She had done everything she could think of to prove to herself that she was as attractive as the other women in the room, hardly caring if she hurt Bill in the process. She had publicly and brazenly taunted and humiliated him, leaving everyone who witnessed her performance with the impression that she would betray him. And what had he done to her? What had he done at all, besides simply being the devastatingly wonderful person that he was?

Marcie stole another glance in Bill's direction. His steadfast calm and inherent goodness shamed her. She didn't need him to tell her that she had crossed a line this time. She knew that she had. Had he treated her the way she'd treated him, even in retaliation after the fact, with one of the many beautiful women there, she could not have borne it. She would never have the strength to quietly endure such treatment from him.

She realized suddenly that it was Bill's strength that was most appealing. It drew her to him like a magnet. When something needed to be done, he did it. It didn't matter if it was unpleasant, difficult, painful or disturbing. He simply did it. He could always be relied upon. It was as if he was made of steel. His strength staggered her. And the tenderness that he was able to show for her, notwithstanding his overwhelming strength, made it all the more remarkable. With his strength he had managed to hold their relationship together without ever once allowing her to draw him into her own personal conflicts. He never lost track of his objective, always standing his ground and maintaining the control once he made the decision to take it.

But Marcie feared this time was different. She wondered how Bill would handle it. She felt that she ought to step up and admit that she was wrong without him having to point it out to her. But what if he rejected her anyway? It suddenly occurred to her that love wasn't about saving face.

"Bill," she began uncertainly, "I'm so sorry."

"I know," he said. He had calmed considerably since they had first gotten into the car. His anger was just about undetectable now. There wasn't a trace of malice in his voice, only understanding.

"You must be angry," she said.

"I am," he agreed. She once again marveled over his control.

Suddenly she was terrified of losing him. "I was jealous of you," she admitted. "Even if you never speak to me again, I want you to know that that other guy could have been a chair for all it mattered. I wanted to hurt you because I was jealous of you." There was never a man in her life, before Bill, that she could have admitted this to. She felt that she could tell him anything.

"I figured it was something like that." His voice was steady and thoughtful, but Marcie could not glean from it what he was feeling or how he felt about her now.

"I know I crossed a line tonight…" She could not go on. She waited for him.

"You certainly did, Marcie." He pulled the car into their driveway. She was frantic to know where she stood.

"Is it over?" she asked. Tears filled her eyes.

Bill looked at her then. He raised his hand to her face, capturing a tear as it slowly crept down her cheek. "No."

Marcie shut her eyes and breathed a sigh of relief, letting the tears spill freely down her face. She began to weep quietly, overwrought with emotion.

Bill leaned over the seat to comfort her, taking her face in his hands and kissing her tears away. "It's okay, Marcie," he reassured her.

"I didn't mean to," she wept.

"I know you didn't."

"I love you so much."

"I know you do." He smiled at her. "Come on," he said after giving her time to pull herself together. "Let's go in."

She couldn't wait to be alone with him in their bedroom. Once inside she waited for him on the bed with growing anticipation. When he joined her she melted in his arms. But he did no more than hold her close to him.

"Aren't you going to...punish me?" she wondered.

"Nope."

She squirmed against him, signaling to him that she wanted to make love.

"Stop that," he said, still keeping her close.

"You're still angry with me?"

"Yes. And disappointed, too. Now go to sleep."

"I can't sleep," she told him.

"Then you can read or watch TV and I'll sleep." He loosened his hold on her when he said this, but when she didn't move away he tightened it again.

She paused, frustrated and uncertain. "Bill."

"Mmm?" His voice reflected his steady temperament and soothed her soul.

"Aren't you going to do anything?"

He laughed, but immediately afterward turned serious. "Despite what you might think, Marcie, I'm only human. The truth is, I don't know what to do at the moment. One thing I know for sure that I'm *not* going to do is to punish you or make love to you, because I know you want me to do those things."

"That never stopped you before," she pointed out.

"True, but you never crossed this line before. Everything else I can accept from you, but this I can't. Maybe next time you think about pulling something like this you'll remember that it didn't get you what you wanted and it certainly didn't bring us closer together. I really hope you do remember it, because I don't see myself putting up with that again."

Marcie thought about what he said. "Well, maybe this time I should be the strong one. Maybe this time I should take care of you."

"You did already, in the car," he told her, tightening his hold on her.

And suddenly everything was exactly as it should be. For her, there was nothing else that existed outside of her life here with Bill. She could be herself here, and that gave her a tremendous sense of self-worth. All the second-guessing and worry, all the insecurities and fears, were a waste of time. This was her life to live as she wished. She had found a place for herself with Bill.

* * * * *

LITTLE MISS MUFFET

*Little Miss Muffet
sat on a tuffet,
eating her curds and whey.
Along came a spider
who sat down beside her,
and frightened Miss Muffet away.*

The world was surely a frightening place. Danger seemed to lie in wait for its victims, often where they least expected it. In the humdrum monotony of her life, Jessica pondered this as she read that day's news.

It had been a while since the last murder, but the papers still reminisced, counting the days and weeks and even months that passed like anniversaries. Six Months Since Last Victim Found in Park read the headline, and the caption below it asked, *Could the killer have found a new dumping ground?* Jessica shook her head, incredulous, and looked out her window toward the very same park mentioned in the newspaper. The reporters, much like the killer they spoke of, seemed impatient for their next victim.

The park was teaming with people on this warm and clear Saturday morning. It was difficult to imagine anything sinister happening there with the trees filtering warm, bright sunlight through their leafy limbs and people flooding the area with life. In fact, the murders themselves had taken place somewhere else; the park had simply been the victims' final destination. Why the bodies were brought here remained a mystery, along with the other troubling aspects of the murders, like why the victims were all women, and what, besides that and their deaths, they had shared in common. Most confounding of all were the markings left on the victims' bodies by the killer. They each bore the formidable image of a spider that had been crudely but carefully carved into their soft, delicate flesh just alongside the curve of their right shoulders.

Even though the murders had not actually taken place in the park, it alarmed Jessica to think that any aspect of the gruesome events had managed to drift so close to her home. It was frightening to think of such evil lurking right outside her door. What did the monster responsible for these horrors look like? How did such a person blend in with the rest of society?

Looking out over the park from her fourth-floor apartment at that moment it was hard to believe anything had happened at all. A shudder ran through her in spite of the cheery view. Suddenly, her own troubles seemed strangely insignificant. It occurred to her that this might be why people were still so interested in reading about the murders, even though there was nothing new to tell. One couldn't help feeling better about their own situation by comparison.

Jessica was disrupted from her thoughts by the shrill ringing of the telephone. She picked up the receiver, immediately recognizing the number on her caller ID as she answered.

"Your timing is impeccable," she said. She remained looking out over the park as she greeted her best friend, Linda.

"Is he gone then?" Linda inquired.

"Of course. He's probably on the third hole by now." Jessica allowed all her bitterness to come out through her tone of voice. It was a relief to be able to express it freely.

"So…?" her friend prompted.

"So…nothing," she replied with a tired sigh. "As usual, Steve managed to dodge the issue completely."

"I told you he would! Pushing him too hard is just going to push him away." Linda spoke with authority. "Men need to be handled with subtlety. You have to make him think the commitment is his idea." She was on her third marriage, so Jessica thought perhaps she knew what she was talking about.

"Call me crazy, but I would prefer to settle down with a man who actually *wants* to settle down with me," she said bitterly. This was a well-worn conversation spanning many relationships come and gone over years of friendship between the women.

"That's part of your problem," Linda told her. "A man never *wants* to settle down. A man has to be *made to think* he wants to settle down."

"I don't want to hear this."

"Well, I am really sorry about that, but it doesn't make it any less true. Your expectations are way too high. Men are little better than animals that need to be trained."

Jessica laughed in spite of her distaste for what she was hearing.

"I'm just not the sort of person to play the manipulative games required to train them," she said. But a sick feeling twisted in her gut. She couldn't deny that the women who did play games seemed to get everything they wanted.

"Don't think of it as games," said Linda, taking no offense whatsoever from the implication. "Think of it as coaching. We *encourage* them to want to do the right thing."

"Go team!" cried Jessica sarcastically.

"Exactly!" exclaimed Linda triumphantly, ignoring the sarcasm.

Jessica sighed. After years of dating in the same unsuccessful way, she doubted she had the stamina to change. She seemed to possess only enough willpower to complain about it. "I'm just so sick of trying," she whined.

"So *stop* trying! Back off and let Steve put forth a little effort."

"I'm not good at backing off," she admitted.

"It's not that hard. Just stop giving so much. You give way too much of yourself for a girl who's just dating. Then you get pissed when the relationship doesn't move forward. Think about it. You're actually taking away his incentive to move forward. Why should he? You're giving him everything you've got, right up front. He doesn't have to *do* anything at all."

"I know," Jessica conceded with another sigh. "I just don't know how to change things. It's always the same old story. I give and give while all this resentment builds up and then I explode, and then it's on to the next guy. I can already feel the anger building."

"So what did you say to him?"

"Nothing, really. We never got past 'I want to talk,' when all of a sudden we were arguing about why we can't ever talk. Last night his excuse was that he had to go to bed early so that he could get up for an early tee off—again. If he was half as committed to me as he is to avoiding these conversations—or to playing golf even— we would be married by now."

"You have to back off."

This frightened Jessica too much to think about. She hated to admit it but she needed someone to love. "I can't," she said. She wondered how other women did it.

"You have to. Otherwise it's going to end like all the other ones did."

"It's so hard!" But she was actually thinking about it this time.

"Find someone else to help you through the tough times."

Jessica blanched. "I could never...God, if he thought I had anything to do with another man he would never speak to me again."

"I don't see a ring on your finger. What do you really owe him?"

"Yes, but we agreed not to see other people."

"So, break it. It obviously doesn't mean anything. Your so-called agreement is simply you being loyal to him while he decides what he wants to do. You were stupid to make the agreement before he showed his intentions. Now you have no choice but to shake the sugar tree." Linda loved quoting euphemisms for prescribing behavior, her reasoning being that years of use and endurance had proved them to be tried and true. She had an endless supply of them at her disposal. This was the first time Jessica heard her use "shake the sugar tree," and she couldn't suppress a laugh.

"Did you actually *like* your husband before he married you?" Jessica asked her.

"Yes, as a matter of fact, I did," Linda said, nonplussed. "But I knew I wouldn't be able to tolerate just being his booty call. I knew if that happened I would become bitter and push him away in the end anyway, just like you're doing with Steve. You do have a say in what happens in your own life, you know. You don't have to give away your freedom to every man who happens to want to borrow it for a while."

"I just wish I knew what he was thinking. I feel like if he really loved me he would want to make it permanent. His reluctance to do that makes me think he is holding out for something better."

"You do realize that you go through this with every guy you date, don't you?"

"Yes."

"All right then. Just so long as you know what you're doing."

Later, while waiting for Steve to find time for her between golf, his friends and anything else he wished to do, Jessica found herself wandering the crowded park outside her apartment. She strolled among the throng of people, clinging stubbornly to a mood of resentment and self-pity. The warm sun and cheerful people actually enhanced her melancholy, giving it a bittersweet quality. She felt obscured from the crowd behind a pair of dark sunglasses. She sat on a park bench and was actually savoring her discontent when the man approached her.

He was older looking and disheveled, obviously unfortunate of circumstance, and her first thought was to wonder why he chose her for a point of contact. Perhaps it was simply her location on a bench that had another vacancy. At any rate, he sat down beside her.

"Lovely day," he said.

Ordinarily she would have ignored the man, especially given the circumstances of the park in months past, but her current frame of mind made her more receptive to wretchedness; the more wretched, in fact, the better.

"Yes, it is," she replied.

"You seem down in the dumps," he observed. She did not turn her head toward him, but cast her eyes in his direction from behind her dark glasses. He was not as old as she first imagined. He was more ragged than aged. She felt slightly irked by this, but more so by his comment. It was always, she thought, the most hopeless who wanted to offer encouragement to others.

"Just thinking," she said with a stiff, mind-your-own-business kind of smile. She was beginning to despise him already. She had hoped for lighthearted banter or perhaps could have even tolerated a harangue of complaints detailing the abundant problems the man quite obviously suffered with. But she could not abide strangers who became too intimate too quickly. Their lack of boundaries frightened her. She turned her face abruptly away from him.

"Having a bad day?" he asked. She silently fumed. She had been actually enjoying her misery until he came along.

"I *really* don't feel like talking about it," she said with emphasis.

"Ah, come on," he persisted. "It'll make you feel better to talk about it."

Why couldn't a man ever just give a woman what she asked for instead of everything but? That is what she was wondering, but she said, "I don't have anything to talk about with you."

The man laughed mockingly. She turned to watch him, focusing on his teeth, which were either rotted or missing. How ironic, she thought, unable to suppress a small smile in spite of her annoyance, that such a wreck of a man was actually mocking her. She couldn't help wondering how that was possible. She was beginning to think she might be cursed. *What the hell's so funny?* she wondered with a slight twist of her head.

"I'm sorry," the man said, turning serious. "I was only trying to be nice."

She stared at him, amazed. The fact that someone who hadn't bathed in a week or so had the ability to make her feel bad was disturbing. "Look," she explained slowly, her voice rising ever so slightly. "I just don't feel like telling my life story to a total stranger, okay?" And she wondered, *Why am I explaining myself to this loser?* And then she thought, *Why do I do any of the things that I do?*

"Well, if you don't want to talk, you don't want to talk," he replied, stating the obvious as if he were revealing a hidden truth.

"Excuse me," came a third voice from behind them. Both turned and Jessica saw that the voice came from an attractive-looking middle-aged man. She stared up at him. "I don't mean to inter-

rupt," he said with a slight grin. "I was just trying to remember...
aren't you...weren't you..." He turned his head sideways and
squinted his eyes as he acted out the part of the long-lost acquaintance to perfection.

Jessica stood up and struggled to bury her sudden mirth behind
her own imitation of trying to remember. "Yes," she agreed with
conviction. "It was...at the party...I remember...you were
with..." She had walked around the bench as she went through this
pretense and he kept it going by taking her hand in his for a firm
handshake while simultaneously leading her away.

"Nice to see you again," he said smoothly. His smile was perhaps
a little too perfect.

"Thanks," she said, laughing heartily now that they were out of
earshot of the scruffy man who had been sitting next to her. "So
stupid really...I couldn't seem to extricate myself from the conversation."

"That's because you're too nice," he said.

"Is that why you went to the trouble of pretending you recognized me, instead of just telling him to get lost?"

"That was part of it, sure," he said. "I figured it wouldn't impress
you to see another guy acting like a jerk."

"And the other part of it?" she asked him, curious. She had forgotten all about her earlier depression, along with her wish to be
alone.

"I wanted to see if you had a sense of humor," he admitted. "I
wasn't sure you would play along. And besides that, you had the

look of a woman who might really prefer to be left alone." He watched her face as he spoke to her, and she felt inordinately flattered. She was much more vulnerable to kindness when it was presented so eloquently and by someone with all of his teeth.

"That was my original plan," she confessed.

"Well, if you decide you would like to return to that plan, just say the word. I won't be offended. I come here to be alone a lot myself. Somehow, it feels more private when it's crowded like this." That was exactly how she felt about it, too. She admired his manner, at once so confident and correct. With impressive perception, he had picked up on her insinuation that she may have changed her mind about being alone, but he did it in such an unassuming way that she could not help but be impressed.

They had continued to walk throughout this exchange and ended up on a paved path that meandered all around the park for walkers and joggers.

"I'm Jessica," she said.

"I'm Derrick. It's nice to meet you."

They walked on in silence for a moment. Jessica breathed deeply as she took in the beautiful surroundings. A jogger came up behind them and Derrick moved closer to her so the jogger could pass by.

"Pardon me," he said as he brushed Jessica lightly. She liked him. When the jogger had passed, he asked, "Are you visiting the city or do you live here?" And all of a sudden they were talking. Jessica's mood had turned sociable and cheerful. Derrick was attentive and forthright, but he kept the topics light, never getting too serious or personal. Jessica found herself comparing him to Steve, who was often distant and introspective. Steve did not have the natural charisma that Derrick possessed. At first, Jessica had found Steve's reserved, detached manner intriguing, but lately it failed to charm. It was becoming apparent that what she had mistaken for depth was merely selfishness, and she felt cheated. She yearned for romantic overtures.

It had come to the point in their conversation where they would part ways, perhaps forever, or make plans to see each other again. Once again, Derrick managed the situation with expert aplomb.

"I would like to see you again," he told her honestly. The subject of Steve had never come up.

"I would like that, too," she said, blushing and slightly uncomfortable. Guilt twisted her insides, but she purposefully ignored it, remembering Linda's advice.

"Tomorrow night?" He was not one to waste any time, she noticed. A strange trepidation gripped her. She was not ready to set a definite time.

"I have plans..." she said hesitantly.

Derrick picked up on her hesitancy and once again exercised discretion.

"Why don't I give you my telephone number," he said kindly. "If you would like to get together, or talk even, give me a call." He pulled a card from his pocket and placed it in her hand.

Jessica left him feeling a disturbing mixture of giddy excitement and guilty anxiety. Instinctively, the conflict drew her to Linda.

"Okay," Linda began, trying to control her excitement as she settled them both on her couch with martinis in hand, never mind that it was still so early in the day. "Start at the beginning and don't leave out a single detail!" She stared wide-eyed at Jessica's face expectantly. Her enthusiasm was catching and the guilty feelings Jessica had been feeling subsided a bit in the exhilaration of something interesting to tell. She recounted all the minutest details of her morning in the park, leaving nothing out. Linda listened, enthralled.

"That is exactly the kind of guy you need," Linda announced when Jessica had finished.

"You don't even know him," laughed Jessica. "*I* don't even know him."

"Yes, but I know men," replied Linda with authority. She quickly began summing up the crucial details of Derrick's character, wrapping it all up with, "This Derrick sounds like he has the confidence to treat a woman right…unlike Steve." The mention of Steve brought back Jessica's anxiety.

"Yes…" She sighed unhappily and took another sip of her martini. "Steve."

"Forget Steve," Linda said with an annoyed little wave of her hand. "You have jumped through hoops trying to get a relationship out of him. He doesn't deserve you. You *have* to go out with Derrick."

"But...I'm not ready to lose Steve," Jessica said.

"Then don't tell him," Linda replied simply. "Personally, if it was me, I would rub his nose in it. But not telling him might be better. Wait until you're ready to dump him for good. Old Stevey boy won't know what hit him."

"I don't think I could do that to Steve." Jessica felt another pang of guilt.

"Why not?" Linda chewed thoughtfully on an olive as she prepared her next line of reasoning. "Don't you know that is exactly what he would do to you? Why do you think he can't commit long term? For God's sake, wake up! He's holding out for the bigger, better deal. He has the charm of a cockroach, which is probably why he hasn't found anyone else yet, but if and when he does, you'll be out like yesterday's trash."

These words had enough reality in them to stir the old anger and resentment that Jessica had been mulling over. "You're probably right," she conceded.

"Call Derrick!" Linda said, bouncing excitedly on the couch. "Call him right now and tell him you had a change of plans for tomorrow night." But Jessica was not ready to do that. She needed to think about it. What, really, was her obligation to Steve? It was true that they had made a mutual promise not to see anyone else, at Steve's request, but why not make a more permanent commitment then? What did their agreement really mean when one of the two kept it temporary? How could such an agreement be binding when they couldn't even discuss what it meant?

Later, when Jessica got home, Steve was waiting for her in an unusually gregarious mood. He greeted her with genuine affection for a change, holding her tightly in his arms for longer than was usual. Then he led her to the couch, positioning her on his lap and asked her about her day. Normally, this kind of attentiveness would have acted as a cathartic to Jessica's hungry soul. On this particular occasion, however, his romantic behavior had the opposite effect. She felt confounded by his sudden attentiveness, which reminded her of a bad hairstyle that suddenly looks fabulous on the day you go to the hairdresser's. Why couldn't he have made this effort the previous night, when she had wanted to talk? She wondered if he suspected something. But how could he? Even so, as the night wore on, Jessica became convinced that he must have sensed her inner detachment from him. Her friend's advice to "shake the sugar tree" came to mind. And once again the old resentment reared up inside her. His generous behavior seemed almost malicious to her when it was doled out for the purpose of controlling her.

Still, there was enough love remaining that she could feel herself melting somewhat, in spite of her misgivings. By dinnertime, Jessica was fully enthralled with Steve, and secretly sighed in relief that she had not stepped over the line by calling Derrick. And by the time they were ready to retire, she was filled with desire for him. At least there, between the sheets, Steve's quiet determination suited her to perfection.

Jessica pondered this in the shower, as she prepared for bed.

There really were so many things she loved about Steve. She shuddered as she thought about his hands, so lean and strong, embodying everything that she loved most about him. They were awe inspiring in their beauty and grace and precision. Like him, they were meticulous. In everyday life, it could be tiresome, his quiet insistence to have things so particularly his way; but at night it pleased her to have his sinewy and capable hands laboring over her body, effectively bringing it to life. They brought her pleasure and comfort and safety. She scolded herself for her earlier indiscretion. She had given the man from the park way too much credit. Anyone could be charming on a first encounter. What did she know about him, really? She felt embarrassed. This was always the way with her; she idolized the men she met too quickly, only to begin picking them apart once she had them in her life, searching for...searching for what? she wondered.

She told herself that she owed Steve the opportunity to prove himself as she crept into bed and his waiting arms. She snuggled close within his warmth. Very slowly and stealthily his hands began moving over her skin. They started at the small of her back and from there his fingers moved up along either side of her spine, not just moving, but meandering—almost crawling really—over and along her tingling flesh. He kissed her as his fingers made their way over her, and his kiss was hard and intense and warm, awkward by comparison to his expert touch, but pleasant for all that. There were no words exchanged between them, for Steve remained quiet in the bedroom, too, but when he touched her this way, it seemed to Jessica that his hands were saying what his lips could not.

She moaned and rolled onto her back as his hands worked their way round to her breasts. He was the first man who caressed her breasts without mangling them. He did not brutally crush them with his hands, disfiguring them, or pull at them greedily like a nursing child. With the same gentle expertise one would use to nimbly thread a needle, he tenuously approached her breasts with the tips of his fingers as receptive as antennas. They lightly grazed the tender undersides of the fleshy mounds, causing them to raise and tighten. Next, he flicked over the stiffening nipples and back again, only just teasing them to hardness at first, but then more methodically stroking and pinching them, applying just the right amount of pressure to coax and give pleasure. When he touched her like this she felt that he truly must care for her. She believed he was, at that moment, more aware of her needs than his own, to bring her pleasure with such painstaking precision.

But too soon his hands moved away and onward, stealing closer and closer to the object of his own need and desire. Like ten individual organisms acting of their own accord, his fingers crept systematically over her abdomen, inching over the entire span in their trail, leaving the flesh rigid with glorious bumps reaching out for more. By the time they tentatively probed between her legs she was shuddering with pleasure.

In spite of her ever-growing arousal, Jessica could not help feeling equal parts distress and pleasure with every advance of Steve's hands. Like the glass half-empty, she was aware of a loss whenever he abandoned one part of her for another. She was ever conscious of a poignant longing for something more. This longing was not for the climax that they both might shortly achieve, but rather, for a pinnacle never to be reached. It was a longing for the one thing that was always missing. Even now, while she reveled in his absolute attention and rigorous concentration as his fingers nimbly coaxed her clitoris to life, she sighed in mutual pleasure and discontent. Her pleasure was bittersweet; for she was always keenly aware that his efforts were bringing her closer to the end. It pained her that his flawless caresses seemed to be rushing her toward the end she was longing to delay. And she felt overall that for all his skillful lovemaking, he really cared little for her. This was the only time she received his full attention, and he spent it pining after the conclusion. It was not that he would find satisfaction before she did—he was far too cunning for that—but rather, that he needed nothing more from her once it was over. And she knew also that no matter how long it lasted, it would never be long enough for her. If only she could find a way to capture his attention so fully outside of their lovemaking she might not suffer so. And so, with the usual mixture of discontent and resentment dampening her desire, she opened her legs to his touch, and allowed her body to melt under his adept and perceptive caress.

As was the case with all of his caresses, upon reaching her most sensitive area, Steve did not disturb and annoy her with his fingers as other men were often known to do, but with that same meticulous precision of his, he carefully worked the length of one finger between the lips of her labia while expertly massaging her clitoris with another finger from that same hand. In this way he carefully gauged her responses to him, expertly tracking her progress by the swelling and wetness of her inner flesh. If his efforts were not achieving the desired effect, he would adjust his strokes over her clitoris accordingly, all the while keeping his finger securely inside her cunningly measuring her readiness for him. And even as she writhed in pleasure around the rigid finger that held her, Jessica had the sense that he was really only waiting, like a spider in a web, to open herself up enough for him to spring. He kissed her tenderly while his fingers kept coaxing her. By and by she succumbed, crying out and clawing at him feverishly as she climaxed.

Without a word Steve withdrew his finger and moved up and over her to straddle her chest, poising himself over her mouth. His breathing was ragged, but otherwise he made no sound. She opened her mouth and took all of his rigid fullness inside. Suddenly she was seized with a fervent desire to pull a reaction from him. If only she could incite the same passion in him that she was feeling. She began to suck on him more energetically than was usual. Still, he remained silent. She was becoming almost enraged by his lack of emotion, and was determined to draw him out there in her bedroom, even if she could not reach him in any other part of their life. She longed to have him feel what she felt, and was determined to make him feel it. She would have welcomed even anger from him if that was the only response she could muster and she began to nip at him, lightly at first, as she sucked on him even more vigorously. She felt him stiffen at the light nipping, and became more brazen with her teeth, careful not to actually injure him, but with the intent to give him discomfort. Steve pulled himself out of her mouth carefully, and moved wordlessly between her legs. With remarkable control and self-possession he mounted her.

Jessica wrapped her arms and legs around Steve violently as he entered her, still in a frenzy of passion, and she jerked his head down toward hers for a kiss. She sucked furiously on his tongue and bit his lip. Steve pulled his head away and looked down at her, slightly surprised. He was bewildered by the passion he found burning in her eyes. He became even more controlled and tender with her in response, slowly pulling himself out of her and then methodically pushing himself all the way back in. She struggled beneath him, moving her hips against his body in an effort to quicken his torturously slow pace and further titillate herself by stroking her clitoris aggressively against him. She yearned to make him lose control. It infuriated her to have him remain so composed while she burned so hot. Angrily she ran her nails down the length of his back, hard and with the intent to draw blood. Steve grasped her hands and held them securely at her sides. He continued his slow, easy strokes meanwhile as he continued to look down into her face. Jessica struggled to free her arms, grasping him more violently with her legs. Although she could not engage Steve in her rough play, his strength as he held her compounded her desire. But she was ever aware that she wanted more from him, and she felt herself wondering what Derrick, the man from the park, would have done in his place. Something in Derrick's manner caused her to think that he would have enjoyed the rough play and responded in kind. Somehow, in her overly aroused state, this thought took hold and she found herself imagining Derrick taking her aggressively while Steve looked on. These images were quickly escalating into a fantasy that Jessica fervently wished would come true. She clung to Steve as if he really were Derrick, and the look on Steve's face as he watched her with his expression of surprise enhanced the fantasy for her. She stared up into Steve's eyes as he watched her; he was always silently watching her. Suddenly she felt she was watching him watch her from across the room while Derrick made love to her. She screamed as she reached another orgasm.

Once the rush of pleasure passed, Jessica felt slightly disenchanted. Meanwhile, Steve, assured that she was at last appeased, threw himself into her. With one final thrust and a deep groan she felt him twitch and the warm wetness filled her.

Jessica clung to him in a sudden panic, but he was already moving away from her. He settled himself comfortably next to her in the bed, contemplating sleep. She stared at the ceiling, wide awake. She was never more aware of the increasing gap between her needs and what she was getting. She thought about Derrick again. Perhaps she should give him a chance. Difficulties immediately flooded her consciousness. She regretted giving Steve the key to her apartment. She reminded herself bitterly that he had not reciprocated by giving her the key to his.

"I have plans this evening," she blurted out the next morning, interrupting Steve in midsentence. He was running down the list of his activities for that day, as was his habit, to in due course let Jessica know when she could expect him that evening. What once felt like consideration for her now seemed like him taking her for granted. It was really more than she could endure silently on this occasion.

Steve stared at her in surprise. "Oh?" he inquired. "What are you doing?"

"I just have plans." She looked away from him.

He watched her in his quiet way for several minutes. She refused to meet his eyes. It was clear she was upset, but he couldn't even begin to guess why. "What's going on?" he asked her, and they both knew he wasn't talking about her plans for that night anymore. She was surprised to get this much out of him. She knew he abhorred confrontation.

"It's not like we're married or anything," she said defensively. "I don't have to answer to you." Her heart was pounding. She couldn't seem to remember any of the many things she wanted to say. She really wanted to fight, but knew he would never submit to one.

"Are you seeing someone else tonight?" he asked her, still in his calm manner but with genuine surprise. Regret over having said anything was already creeping over her. The truth was, she was not certain that she really wanted to see Derrick. She didn't even know if he was still available. She looked at Steve. Normally, his calm manner would have irked her, but now, at the prospect of losing him, it seemed terribly appealing. She absently wondered why she always had to be on the verge of losing something before she appreciated it. She was suddenly afraid and couldn't bring herself to answer his question, either to admit it or deny it.

Steve stood up. "I'll clear out then."

"Steve…" But he was already walking out of the room.

Now she felt panic. She didn't want him to go. She had only wanted to scare him into showing some emotion. But it was her who was scared. She stood in the kitchen, wondering what to do.

Steve came out in the next minute, carrying an overstuffed bag.

"Steve, can we talk about this?"

"I don't have time for your games," he said calmly.

"It's not games…it's…." But there was too much to explain and he was already reaching for the doorknob. Suddenly Jessica was angry. "I don't feel like we are going anywhere," she blurted out. "We never speak of the future at all, and yet, night after night, you're here, like we're married or something."

Steve turned to look at her. "If I don't come over one night you get upset," he reminded her.

"Yes, but…I don't know. It's just that it feels like our future is all up to you and nothing to do with me. I don't even know where I stand with you."

"You want to know where you stand with me?" he asked her calmly, looking directly into her eyes. His voice was soft and warm and calm, as always. "You were the woman that I wanted to spend the rest of my life with." He walked out the door.

For some reason this declaration did not have the effect she had imagined it would. In fact, it made her angrier. "So I was just supposed to wait patiently for you to tell me that?" she screamed at him as he calmly walked down the hallway.

But once Steve was gone the anger left her. She began to cry and simultaneously reached for the telephone.

"Well, well," Linda said with a self-satisfied little laugh. "A little push will work wonders."

"He said *wanted*. Past tense. And then he left me," Jessica pointed out.

"It doesn't matter. He's yours. *If* you want him, that is. We have to see what happens with Derrick." Linda was annoyingly cheerful, as if what Jessica had just told her was good news. The mention of Derrick made Jessica wince.

"Are you kidding?"

"Look, you already suffered the consequences for it. You might as well do it." Linda's matter-of-fact attitude made the idea seem more palatable.

"I don't even know if Derrick is still available."

"He is."

"He's probably forgotten about me by now."

"He hasn't."

And he hadn't. He was delighted to hear from her, in fact. "How are you?" he asked. He sounded as if he was smiling.

"As it turns out," Jessica said, gaining courage from his friendly tone, "I'm free tonight."

"That's great," he said, clearly pleased. Then, without a moment's hesitation he moved in to close the deal, "Is seven too late?"

"That's perfect," she agreed, hardly able to believe that she was doing it. And just in case Steve had a change of heart—he had not returned her key—she added, "Can I meet you out?"

Throughout the rest of the day, Jessica wavered between nervous excitement for the night to come and anxiety over whether or not Steve would call.

"Did he call?" Linda asked when they spoke later.

"No." Jessica was filled with remorse.

"Well, give him time," Linda said, unperturbed. "He will."

"I don't know."

"What are you going to wear tonight?" Linda asked, effectively changing the subject.

Jessica appeared at the designated meeting place—which was a posh restaurant she had often hinted to Steve about, but never managed to get him to take her to—wearing her clingiest little black dress and heels that she knew from experience she could stand in for no longer than fifteen minutes before collapsing in excruciating pain. But she felt terribly sexy and excited in spite of her lingering guilt about what happened with Steve. The fact that he had not called assuaged much of her guilt. Meanwhile, Derrick was waiting for her at the bar.

The date with Derrick should have delighted her; for the food and atmosphere were everything she had imagined and Derrick was a perfectly charming man who asked all the right questions. Even better, he listened to her answers with genuine interest. But Jessica discovered that she could not so easily enjoy another man's company while she was still so involved with Steve. Even so, she repeatedly found her attention being lured away from her concerns over her relationship with Steve and back to her charismatic date. He was almost too charismatic, she realized—and too attractive, too. She felt there was something contrived in his polite, funny, engaging dating technique. But she couldn't put her finger on it, and it didn't matter anyway because her thoughts kept returning to Steve.

Steve. At least with him she had something real. And now, more than ever, with the fear of having lost him, she found herself dwelling on only Steve's better qualities.

Somehow she managed to get through her dinner with Derrick without revealing her inner conflict. In fact, she could see that Derrick was completely enamored by her.

"It's still early," he said. "Why don't we go out dancing." Her mind immediately went to Steve, who hated to dance, and absolutely refused to go no matter how much she pleaded with him.

"I don't think so, Derrick," she said. Suddenly her mood was black and she was pining to see Steve.

Derrick paid the bill and walked with her through the parking lot toward her car.

"Are you sure you don't feel like dancing?" Derrick asked. "I know this great place that plays the best music."

"I'm not up for it tonight," she began, about to suggest that they do it another time, but instead she decided to come clean. "Actually, Derrick," she said, giving him an apologetic look, "I have a boyfriend." He stared at her, genuinely shocked, and she felt compelled to explain her behavior. "I was having some doubts about it, but…" Her voice trailed off.

Derrick had remained speechless throughout this garbled explanation, but all of a sudden he released a small derisive laugh. "So you went out with me…why?"

Jessica sighed. "Look, Derrick, I was confused when I called you. My boyfriend and I have been having some problems. But I want to try and work it out."

He laughed without humor. "That doesn't answer my question, does it?" Jessica could see that he was genuinely angry and she suddenly noticed that they were the only two people in the parking lot.

"I'm sorry," she said with as much calm as she could muster. They had stopped walking at some point, but she abruptly resumed walking to her car.

Derrick grabbed her arm, causing her heart to stop. "You women and your games," he said with disgust. The charming Derrick of a few moments ago was now an angry man. He spoke directly into her face, not talking to her but at her. Even so, he noticed the look of surprise in her expression, which made him even angrier. "How dare anyone question your behavior, right?" he said with another humorless laugh, shaking his head.

"Please, Derrick...I didn't mean—"

"Yes, you did," he interrupted her. She could smell the alcohol he'd consumed with dinner on his breath. "You knew exactly what you were doing. What was it? You wanted to piss your boyfriend off? So you used me."

"Let go of my arm!" She didn't like that he guessed so close to the truth.

"Next time you're complaining about what assholes us guys are," he said, "think about tonight." He released her arm then, actually thrusting it away from him vehemently. "Whatever you get, you've got it coming to you." His voice was filled with disgust.

Jessica rushed to her car, stopping so suddenly that she actually slammed into the side of it, and fumbled hastily for her keys. She looked over her shoulder as she pressed frantically on the unlock button on her key chain, but there was no sign of Derrick anywhere. He had disappeared. This frightened her even more, and she scrambled into her car and immediately locked the doors from the inside. Her heart pounded erratically as she turned the key in the ignition and quickly drove away. Looking in the rearview mirror, she saw that no one was behind her. She was trembling. Sometime during their exchange in the parking lot, she had become convinced that Derrick was a dangerous man. Now, her mind leaped to the killer from the park. Suddenly, it became apparent to her that the killer returned his victims there because it was the place where he had first met them. She had even come to the conclusion that Derrick was that killer.

She had been digging through her purse for her cell phone while she drew these conclusions. She had intended to call 911, but even though her eyes continued to scan the rearview and side mirrors to see if anyone was following her down the dark road, she was beginning to calm down. Once the initial terror subsided, she was confused. What did she really have to report to the police? She had gone on a date with a man who became angry when she told him she had a boyfriend after he had dropped a hundred and fifty dollars on dinner. The police would no doubt think she was crazy. The farther she drove away from the parking lot the crazier her fears seemed, even to her.

Besides, Derrick had not actually hurt her or threatened to hurt her, and there was no doubt that he could have done so if he had really wanted to.

Suddenly, Jessica was exhausted. She remembered why she hated dating so much. All those years of being single and going out with men, she had repeatedly vowed that if only she could find a good, decent, *normal* man, she would cherish him forever. And isn't that what she had found in Steve?

She remembered her sexual fantasy about Derrick while she was making love to Steve the night before, and she shuddered with horror. She simply had to speak to Steve. With impulsive finality she punched Steve's telephone number into her cell phone. "Come on," she whispered into the phone, but there was no answer.

Jessica cautiously made her way home. She was getting more and more anxious over Steve. Where was he? She dialed his number again. Once again he didn't answer. This time she let the call go to his machine. Tears came to her eyes, blurring her vision, as she listened to his voice on the answering machine; so calm and kind and simple. She wondered if he had gone out on a date, like her, and the thought brought with it a sudden surge of jealousy and uncertainty. She realized this must be what he felt like when he left her that morning. His recorded greeting had run its course and there was a long series of beeps.

"Steve...Steve...I love you!" She rushed headlong into her message without planning what she would say. The tears were running down her cheeks as she poured her heart out over his machine. "I was confused before because I was afraid. I didn't know what you felt and you weren't as communicative as I wanted you to be. But you are the man I want and only you. Please, forgive me...oh, Steve..." She began to sob, and finally hung up the phone.

At the other end of the telephone line Steve stood very still, staring at the answering machine while he listened silently to Jessica's voice. There was a slightly muddled expression on his face as he listened. He seemed worn out and uncertain.

An image of her came to his mind as he mentally said her name. *Jessica*. He was stupid to have trusted her. The rage rushed over him again. He had allowed himself to be made a fool of yet again.

Steve shook Jessica's image from his mind, pulling himself back to the present with a jolt. He reached over and pressed one sinewy finger firmly over the delete button, erasing the offending message. Then he turned back to the woman waiting beside him. He was not quite finished with her. She stared at the ceiling with an expression of euphoria. Carefully and meticulously he finished carving his mark into her cold, lifeless flesh.

* * * * *

PETER, PETER
PUMPKIN EATER

Peter, Peter, pumpkin eater,
had a wife and couldn't keep her.
He put her in a pumpkin shell,
and there he kept her very well.

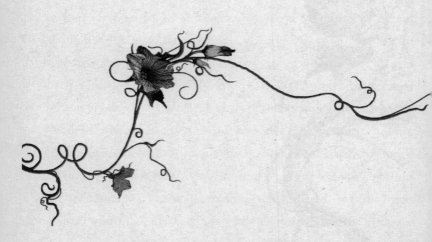

Joyce hurried through the house, anxiously putting things in order before Peter returned from work. Having just showered, she picked up her soiled clothes and stuffed them into the washing machine, setting the cycle to presoak. Next, she sat down in front of the computer and quickly and systematically deleted all the e-mails she had received or sent that day, and then, for good measure, she purged the computer's history file altogether. After that she made a quick detour to the kitchen, where she looked all around in the cabinet drawers for a packet of matches. Finding some at last, she took them upstairs into the master bathroom and, pulling from her pocket a collection of notes and letters, placed them along with a lit match in the small metal trash container that was kept there. She watched the paper burn thoughtfully. Had she forgotten anything?

When Peter arrived home a short time later there was nothing discernibly amiss and yet, no sooner had he stepped over the threshold than he was overcome with a sense of disorder. There was all around him the impression of unreality, and he faltered for a moment; puzzling, like a player over a game board. He dropped his keys and briefcase on a nearby table wondering where Joyce was, and in that instant she came into his view, greeting him with her usual Mona Lisa smile. Peter stared at her as she approached. Was there something different about her? Yes, as she crossed the room her eyes darted about the room, landing everywhere but directly on Peter, and he got the distinct impression that she did not want to meet his gaze. She seemed, to his heightened senses, affected.

"How was your day, darling?" she asked huskily, giving him a light peck on the cheek.

Peter didn't answer her. Instead, he grasped her wrist before she could flutter back away from him again, causing her to look up sharply and at last meet his eyes. He searched her face for a trace of duplicity, but she merely looked back at him with mild surprise. His eyes moved over her slowly and she saw something flicker in their depths when they settled on her hair. It was still wet, and hung in damp curls all around her shoulders. His brows furrowed together in thoughtful contemplation as he reached out to pick up one of the curls. He absently stroked the moist strands between his fingers.

"You showered earlier than usual this evening," he observed. This was not a thing of much significance but, even so, Peter felt his initial uneasiness unaccountably increasing, and a little knot of discomfort was beginning to form in his belly. He felt excessively suspicious all at once, without any clear, rational or explicable cause, except a nagging sense that everything was not exactly as it should be. Joyce did not comment on his observation, but her eyes once again shifted away from his. He knew it would be unreasonable to make an issue over the matter by questioning her further so he let it drop, albeit reluctantly, and pulled her into his arms. She was warm and soft and smelled good, but he could not get comfort from the embrace. He started up again, on a different tack.

"How was your day?" he asked in a casual tone, but there was an edge to his voice that he wasn't able to fully suppress. He continued to play with her damp hair, caressing it between his fingers as he spoke to her.

"The same as any other," she said, again with her strange little half smile.

"What did you do?" he persisted, trying to sound merely curious.

"Not a thing that would interest you, certainly," she replied shortly. He had dropped her hair so that his fingers could lightly trail along the curve of her neck. He touched her with excessive gentleness. She resisted the urge to pull away from him, remaining perfectly still. His feathery-light caresses along the sensitive skin of her neck affected her more than if he choked her. "I should check on dinner," she protested weakly, but Peter lingered another moment or two before at last releasing her from his delicate embrace, having scrutinized her face thoroughly as he held her until her cheeks turned a rosy pink. Once she was released, Joyce quickly escaped to the kitchen, trembling. A perverse thrill gripped her. She opened the oven and looked inside without thinking to notice the contents within.

Peter did not follow Joyce into the kitchen, so she supposed that he was making his way to the computer to check his e-mail, as was his habit after work. She closed the oven door and held her breath. Her heart galloped unsteadily. She busied herself with absently putting the final touches on their supper.

It wasn't until they met a short while later at the dinner table that Peter resumed his speculative manner with her. He was even more tense and pensive as he sat down opposite her. Joyce tried to appear nonchalant as she placed before him a hearty portion of his favorite dish.

"What's the occasion?" he asked, unable to keep the tone of interrogation from his voice. Everything suddenly seemed suspect to him.

"Do I need an occasion to cook for my husband?" she countered pleasantly, ignoring the implication in his tone. Peter could think of no reply. He took a mouthful of the savory food Joyce had so carefully prepared for him, but there was a bitter taste in his mouth that distorted the flavor.

"Was there a problem with the computer today?" he asked abruptly, effectively reopening the never-ending matter of contention between them. He approached it, as always, with equal parts dread and anticipation. Joyce tried to appear surprised by the question.

"No," she said, apparently considering the matter. "Why?"

"You deleted the computer's history," he explained. "I wondered why you did that."

"Oh, that," she said, appearing quite nonplussed. "I thought it might be better for the computer to clear away all that excess baggage. Less memory used...that kind of thing." She looked at him with wide eyes. "Should I not have done that?"

Peter examined her face and felt the innocent expression was contrived. The knot in his stomach was growing and it was with difficulty that he managed to swallow the food in his mouth. "But what made you think of it today?" he persisted.

"I happened to read online that it was a good thing to do from time to time," she replied, chewing thoughtfully on food that had long since dissolved in her mouth.

"Where did you read that?" he pressed on obstinately, becoming more determined with each evasive answer that she delivered. "What were you doing online that you happened to find that information?"

Joyce stared at him with an expression of restrained exasperation. "I can't remember," she said. "Does it matter?"

"Think about it," he said, ignoring her question. Her infuriating habit of answering his questions with one of her own acted like fuel on the fire that was burning up his insides. "What Web sites were you on today?"

"I don't recall," she insisted, still chewing and chewing.

"You must remember at least one of the Web sites you visited," he insisted. "What were you doing online to begin with?"

"This is ridiculous!" she erupted all of a sudden, tossing her napkin down violently and rising from the table. With amazing swiftness Peter was on his feet, and he grasped her wrist from across the table before she could get away.

"Sit down," he said in a quiet voice. His hold on her wrist was absolute without causing discomfort. He did not release her until she sat. They were both in a highly excited state. Neither made any further attempt to eat.

"What were you doing online?" Peter asked her again in a calm and determined voice that made it clear that there was no other way out of this but for Joyce to answer the question. Although he had released her wrist, his hand had remained on her arm, stroking it lightly with the tips of his fingers. His touch, at once so very gentle and utterly strong, was unsettling.

"I...don't remember," she insisted in a despairing tone. "I didn't realize I would be grilled about it later." She blinked and two small tears spilled down her cheeks as she told this lie.

"Take your time," he said kindly. "We have all night." He reached up to touch her cheek and captured one of the tears with his finger. Joyce's heart felt like it was in her throat; the furious pounding of it seemed to be making it expand. She wondered if it would explode. Surely there were too many powerful emotions flooding through her for her heart to endure it. The excitement was making her giddy. She was mostly anxious—unsure of what the consequences would be for what she had done, but as well she was impatient to see what those consequences might be. She was also surprisingly aroused, and terribly afraid. In spite of her attempt to appear cool and indifferent, she was painfully aware of Peter's every reaction and response. She watched him acutely, even when she appeared to be looking away.

The control Peter demonstrated with her throughout these proceedings enthralled her as much as it distressed her. She could see that he was frustrated and alarmed by her behavior, but he kept himself in check. She knew that he loved her and that he, too, was battling with emotions that raged within him. She could see the conflict in his eyes. His hand still lightly caressed her arm across the table, holding her there with a gentle influence that made the gooseflesh rise all up and down her arm. A painful yearning began curling its way through her entrails while her mind scrambled for logical answers.

She looked at her husband and sniffed. "I...there were some things that I was Googling," she began, quite obviously at a loss.

"What things?" Peter encouraged. She stared at him a moment and then licked her lips.

"Well...like...seeds," she said slowly.

"Seeds?" he echoed. In spite of the overall dread that enveloped him he could not restrain a small smile. Somehow, no matter how many little signs pointed toward something terrible, she could always lure him back to a sense of security with only the tiniest offering of herself. That she had, at some point, gone online—or intended to go online—in search of seeds he believed, though probably not today, but nevertheless it was a pleasing diversion for him to follow this thread for the time being, and see where it would lead. For even when he held her cornered like this, poised and ready to pounce, there always remained a strong bond between them that refuted even the most obvious signs of it being otherwise.

"Yes," she said more self-assuredly, gaining confidence from his change in demeanor. "I wanted to plant pumpkin seeds in our garden this year and so I went online to see what variety I should buy."

"And did you find the seeds you were looking for?" he prompted.

"Yes," she replied, but as usual, she did not elaborate about what they were. Everything must be drawn out forcibly.

"Well?" he prompted. "What kind of pumpkins will we be growing this year?"

"I forget the name of them at the moment," she said predictably, but added, "They are the ones that don't grow very large, but they're the best for making pumpkin pies." This sounded viable enough.

"Did you order the seeds?"

"No. I thought it would be quicker to get them from the nursery down the street."

"And yet you didn't bother to remember the name of them?"

he said, convinced that she was lying. Joyce didn't answer him, so
he continued on a different thread. "And is that where you found
the information about deleting the history from your computer?"

"Yes," she said.

"I bet if we went on the computer right now we could find the
name of those seeds and I could read about how deleting computer
history helps your hard drive." Peter waited patiently to see how
his wife would respond to this.

"I don't really remember which search thread I followed to get
there," she told him after another moment's thought. "I think it
was....it may have been four or five pages in."

Peter was now certain that she was lying. The anger that had
been temporarily assuaged during the pumpkin-seed diversion
returned, sending a red-hot heat through his bloodstream. He
grasped hold of her arm again and pulled her up in one swift
motion while he came around the table to meet her. Keeping hold
of her arm, he grasped her face by the chin with his other hand,
holding it firmly so that it remained very close to his and tipped
back so that she was obliged to look up at him. She could feel his
breath on her lips as he spoke to her, very slowly, and in a soft, low
tone of voice. "I think you're lying to me," he said.

Joyce didn't answer. Her hands had rested against Peter's chest
and she suddenly moved them up over his shoulders and around
his neck. She tried to move her lips closer to his for a kiss, but he
held her back. "I think you're lying to me," he said again, though
it was with less certainty this time.

Joyce didn't deny it. She whispered instead, "Let's go upstairs, Peter. It's late." He stared at her in abject frustration. Her words did not appease his fears, but they fed a need. He let her lead him up.

In their bedroom, Peter watched grimly as Joyce undressed. She took her time, getting much pleasure from the attention. She moved purposefully and gracefully, easing her clothing off and away from her body as lithely as a dancer while Peter simply gazed at her, mute with a harrowing mixture of frustration and desire. At length she wandered into the bathroom with him behind her, and she stood before the mirror in her sheerest nightgown and slowly brushed her hair. Peter stood at a nearby distance and watched, spellbound by the flawless rise and fall of her breasts beneath her gown with her movements of her arm as she brushed her hair. He was torn between desire and despair. Needing something to do, he removed the hairbrush from Joyce's hand and gently took up the brushing of her hair. His suspicions were slowly fizzling away under the heat of his desire for her. It was at all times this way, ever since the first time he set eyes on her, that his desire was ever present whenever he was anywhere near her. He knew that other men must feel the same.

Joyce closed her eyes and let her head fall back slightly. A low murmur of pleasure escaped her lips.

Suddenly Peter's eye was captured by the contents of the wastebasket. The dark ashes and charred bits of paper sounded a conspicuous alarm in the otherwise stark pastel coloring of the little bathroom container and everything surrounding it. His suspicions returned with renewed potency. As he stared bleakly into the wastebasket, an odd sense of déjà vu rushed over him, and he remembered distinctly telling her to burn his notes and letters, all those years ago. To see his own cunning at work against him caused him no small amount of grief, and he clenched his jaw firmly in an effort to keep his mounting rage at bay.

"What is that in the wastebasket?" he asked Joyce, keeping his voice remarkably calm, and even more curiously, continuing his slow, gentle brushing of her hair.

"Hmm?" she murmured, still under the glow of his attentions. But in the next instant she froze and her eyes flew open wide, automatically meeting her husband's in the mirror. "It's nothing, Peter," she said earnestly. "It's nothing."

"Why would you go to the trouble to actually burn something that is 'nothing,' Joyce?" The volume of his voice was menacingly low. "What were they?" he persisted.

"They...were...just some old notes I found," she said, adding as a second thought, "from Bob."

"Okay, letters from your ex-husband. Again, why not just throw them out? Why burn them?"

"I don't know," she lied.

"Why would anyone go to the trouble of burning notes unless they wanted to be absolutely certain that no one else would read them?"

"I don't know," she said again. Peter was outraged. "I don't know" seemed to be her ready answer for every question he put to her. He struggled for calm. Every sign seemed to point to what he dreaded most.

Peter had managed to contain his fears thus far, but he felt himself being seduced by the oddly alluring promise of something terrible to be discovered. In a dizzying rush of anticipation, he could even feel a simulated anguish for the injury to follow. Like a wounded animal he began to work over the injury, digging and picking relentlessly regardless of the pain—or perhaps it was to better get to the pain.

"What did you wear today?" he asked her, aware that he was about to cross a line but no longer caring.

"Peter."

"Before your *early* shower," he continued, heedless of her objection. "What were you wearing?" He had not stopped brushing her hair, but now the strokes of the brush, although still deceptively gentle, felt like sharp spikes driving into her scalp.

"What does that have to do with anything?" She watched him move the brush through her hair with fascination. Her heart had begun the erratic pounding again.

"Where are the clothes you wore today?" he demanded.

"They're in the washing machine," she said.

"In the washing machine? In the washing machine?" He stared at her, aghast. "With all the laundry you never have time to get to, *today's* clothes are already in the washing machine?" Voices from the past were now returning to his mind in a garbled rush, overlapping each other as his memory randomly replayed conversations gone by. He perceived foremost among them his own self-satisfied voice, advising Joyce to wash the evidence of him from her clothes and body the minute she got home so that Bob would not smell him on her. Icy panic swept over him at the thought of all evidence being gone. He was suddenly more afraid of never knowing than of finding out the worst. He was still outwardly in control when he set down the hairbrush and slipped his fingers through her hair, distracted for the moment by the thick masses and streaks of color as he absently massaged her scalp. With his enhanced awareness suddenly, he seemed to be seeing her hair for the first time, noticing every unique nuance of color as it picked up the light.

"Why did you feel the need to wash your clothes immediately after taking them off?" he persisted, still seemingly preoccupied with her hair. He was thinking about how Joyce was such a procrastinator about everything. He dragged his eyes away from her hair and met hers in the mirror as he waited for her answer.

"I don't know," she murmured futilely. She had no answers that would make any sense out of her behavior—at least not any that would appease him now.

"'I don't know,'" he repeated. "You must have been thinking something while you were burning notes and doing laundry and destroying computer history."

Joyce thought perhaps she had gone too far this time. It seemed that the tables had turned and she might lose him after all. But her clever mind, unfailing in its capacity to manipulate logic, seized upon a solution. She knew that, although Peter could not quite bring himself to admit it, he was thinking of each and every instruction he had given her in the process of seducing her away from her previous husband. This, she felt, could be used to her advantage.

Peter's fingers were still moving through her hair as he waited for her response, so she slowly reached up and began gently caressing his arms with her hands. Peter's eyes bored into hers in the mirror as he waited. Joyce knew that his desire for her was still strong; so much so that all she had to do was produce doubt, and he would grasp at it like a drowning man would grasp at a life preserver.

"Actually, Peter," she said, with more conviction now, "I started these little habits because of you." She let him think about that, and waited for him to draw her out as he chose. She did not want to say too much.

"What do you mean by 'these little habits'?"

"Well, if you'll recall, you were always telling me to burn everything, even if it wasn't important. I just got into the habit of it. And although I don't regularly get to all the clothes that are piling up in the hamper—it's true—I will often put that day's clothes in the washer immediately after taking them off just because I got in the habit of it before." She knew he could not for a certainty deny any of this, even if he still had doubts.

Peter was silent and thoughtful. Now that his anger had

emerged it wanted to take hold, but his desire had not quite been extinguished and his body was inclined to side with that latter emotion, giving it strength. Joyce continued to run her hands up along his arms as she watched him in the mirror. She allowed her body to fall back and lean against his. She moved her hips seductively up against him.

Peter struggled for a moment, uncertain. The pain, should he face it now, would be piercing and debilitating, while the pleasure, he knew, would be even more intense with the pain lingering so closely behind it. The pain could be pushed aside for a later time, if in fact it was merited at all. It was hard to believe the pain when her body seemed to tremble with desire for him, and her eyes burned with emotion that could not be pretended. He began to yearn for her.

Peter knew that he was losing control.

Aroused and angry and confused, he could no longer resist the hazy glow of desire in Joyce's eyes, or her parted and willing lips. He pushed the anger into a back corner of his mind where it mingled unhappily with his doubts. He succumbed to the only certainty he could extract from the ambiguous connection he shared with his wife; that her lips would soothe and her body temporarily alleviate the doubt and anger that regularly antagonized him. He gave himself over to his desire completely, and his simmering anger only increased the passion and intensity of his actions. Thinking only of tasting her lips, he pulled her to him, unaware that he had yanked her head around by the fistfuls of hair he still held in his hands. Joyce gasped as he ravaged her lips. He jerked her head back even farther to give himself better access to her lips and face and neck as he spread hot kisses all over her. Joyce delighted in his brusque handling of her, finding any discomfort brought on by his overzealous passion preferable to indifference. She did not think she could bear Peter's indifference. So she endured his violent attentions and actually enjoyed the discomfort they brought with them. His breath was hot and moist, and the sharp shadow of that day's whiskers grazed her skin as he moved his lips over her with both hands still buried deep within her scalp, holding her head firmly in place.

Joyce didn't struggle against Peter, or move at all in fact. She simply drank in his attentions as well as she was able, nearly drowning in the rush of sensations that were assaulting her as violently as he was doing. She shuddered helplessly as his strong hands finally released her hair and moved down along her jaw and lower, tentatively circling her neck. The sensation of his fingers curling around her neck left her feeling curiously safe and content. She arched her head back even farther and closed her eyes, giving herself over more fully to his caresses. Her mouth was open to his prying tongue, and the intense passion of the moment actually caused tears to flood her eyes. She waited eagerly for the pleasure to come. And all the while Peter could not help but wonder, *Was this how she responded with Bob when she returned home from an afternoon in my bed?*

This thought came to his mind just as his hands had moved

down toward the straps of Joyce's nightgown, and without really intending to, he tore the gown in his effort to remove it. But the sound of the tearing cloth only emboldened him, and he yanked it away from her body with renewed vigor, leaving it in shreds on the floor. Joyce shuddered again.

Peter immediately reached for her breasts, and he clutched one in each hand, tenderly cupping and fondling them, as if weighing them. His attentions caused them to tighten and swell, making them seem heavier and fuller. While he held them, he moved nearer and gazed at them attentively, almost as if he was examining them. She wondered. But in due course he turned his attention to her nipples, which jutted out to him teasingly, and he began to play with them, first pressing them firmly between his fingers and then sliding them lightly across the palm of his hand. Finally he bent his head and seized the tip of one breast carefully between his teeth, circling his tongue all around it and then drawing it into his mouth and sucking vigorously. The intense pulling of his jaws on her nipple caused a surge of tingling pleasure to ripple through her. She moaned with abandon, throwing her head back and leaning against the counter of the bathroom sink behind her. The strong flood of arousal left her feeling light-headed.

Peter continued to kiss and suck her breasts leisurely, each in its turn; with pleasure, yet not without also a sentiment of competitiveness to surpass in performance any other man who might have been there before him. While his lips and tongue were thus engaged, he let his hands roam over Joyce's stomach and hips, delighting in her soft roundness. She trembled with joy at his touch. How she loved it when his attentions stretched beyond his own needs, when he was striving after something other than mere sexual gratification. It was far more intimate and momentous for her when he touched her as he did now, with his hands gliding over her skin, down along the curve of her back and cupping her buttocks with reverence. She wished it would never end, but knew that it would, and far too soon to satisfy her ravenous soul. Already his fingers were running along the cleft in her bottom, dipping between her legs greedily, delving into her with a fierce determination. She moaned with pleasure over the contact, even as she lamented the loss of his earlier caresses.

Upon discovering her wetness as it poured over his fingers, Peter's attention was redirected. He gazed down at her in awe, fairly gawking. He picked her up suddenly and set her carefully on top of the bathroom counter, spreading her legs wide apart as he nestled himself in between them with his knees on the floor.

He took his time, examining her thoroughly, opening her labia wide and scrutinizing every inch of her. She had the sense that he was once again looking for evidence of another man. Nevertheless, his prying fingers and intense inspection was having a wonderful effect on her. She watched, rapt, as his eyes and hands thoroughly dissected her. Slowly his face inched closer, and his fingers opened her up even wider as he approached. He pressed his face right up into the cleft of her, inhaling deeply as he did so. She gasped. Peter turned his face ever so slowly to the right and then the left, unconsciously scraping her inner tissue with the day's growth on his cheeks. His prickly whiskers sent sharp stinging thrills of sensation rippling through her tender flesh. All the while, he continued to inhale her scent, burying his nose deep into her softness and breathing in long and hard as he held her squirming body firmly in his hands. She was certain now that he was looking for signs of another man but she no longer cared. The invasion into her secret self was far too exquisite to be insulting.

Seemingly satisfied with his findings, Peter began to dip his tongue into her, tentatively tasting her at first, but apparently finding it to his liking, he suddenly set out to devour her. He clung to Joyce's hips almost violently, with his powerful fingers pressed into her supple, white flesh so firmly that she could not move in any direction. She struggled against him all the same, moving reflexively in opposition to the force of his advances. Her struggles were barely noticed by him, but he did unconsciously slow his actions and become more deliberate, moving his tongue leisurely up along the center of her parted labia and at the top circling around to her clitoris and firmly pressing down over the peak of the little swollen flesh, making her jump. Then he descended back downward along her wet and gaping slit again until he reached her bottom. There he paused to tickle that nether opening with the tip of his tongue, causing her to jump yet again. Over and over again his tongue burrowed its way up and around and back again, lingering especially over the top of her clitoris to press and prod and provoke her with pleasure. He continued to work her over with his tongue in this way tirelessly, ever attentive to the pleasure she received and mindful not to allow her to climax. Joyce did not fret over this; on the contrary, she thrived on his careful attentions and simply allowed her pleasure to build. She clung to the sides of the counter with both hands and gave herself over to Peter's ministrations. All her concerns of the day were lost in the whirling sensations that came over her with the movement of Peter's tongue. She opened her legs wider for him and even raised her feet so they rested on his shoulders.

Eventually Peter's need, which was quickly becoming uncomfortable, overruled his wish to prolong Joyce's pleasure. He took one of her ankles in each of his hands and pulled her legs outward as he raised himself up in between. Then he rested her feet back on his shoulders, this time with him standing, as he worked quickly to remove his pants. He stared down at the spectacle of Joyce's body spread wide open to him and his eyes glazed over with desire. When his pants were removed he wiped his face with the back of one hand.

Peter approached her with relish, running his hands along the insides of her legs and then placing them beneath her lower thighs, just above her knees, to hold them steady. As he entered her, he bent her legs a little more and guided them down from his shoulders so they rested one in each hand. He spread them even wider apart as he pushed himself into her slick opening. Joyce cried out loudly as he moved slowly in and out of her. He held her legs in his hands, high up and apart as he kept slowly driving in and out of her. She wrapped her arms around his neck. She could still taste her body on his lips when he kissed her.

Peter increased the speed of his thrusts as his excitement increased, and he jutted his hips forward and up with each thrust, stabbing her savagely while forcing her legs up even higher with his hands. Joyce clung tightly to his neck, crying out with equal measures of pleasure and discomfort.

"God, you feel so good," Peter murmured. His anger was almost forgotten as he became more and more immersed in her softness. All he could believe for the moment was the pleasure she brought him. He was struggling to maintain control and forced himself to slow his pace to painstakingly protracted and unhurried strokes. She was clinging to him with her face buried in the warmth of his chest. Very carefully he let her legs fall, and she slipped them around his hips and locked her ankles together at the base of his back. He lifted her face tenderly in his hands and looked down into her eyes. He continued to slide his lower body into hers with long, even strides as they silently stared at each other. In the depths of his expression, lingering behind his desire, Joyce thought she glimpsed sorrow. Her heart stopped for an instant, and she was torn between her own fears and resentments and her love for Peter. How could she bear to hurt him?

But it was only fleeting, and in the next instant she even wondered if she had imagined it. Peter suddenly picked her up off the bathroom counter and, holding her with one hand on each buttock while her legs still clung to him, he carried her, still fully joined to him, into their bedroom. She wrapped herself around him like a vine and luxuriated in the way it felt to simply have him inside her. These short moments of shared intimacy in between the intense passion that brought them together were her favorite moments with Peter. It was what she lived for, from one sexual encounter to the next. If she had been a prostitute, this would have been the price she would have demanded for her body. But it was impossible to say what these moments were made up of or how they could be brought about. She only recognized them once they came to be, when the intensely soothing blanket of contentedness washed over her, leaving her feeling satiated and slightly stunned.

With the same measured carefulness that Peter employed to carry Joyce with him into the bedroom he brought them both, still joined together, onto the bed. Once settled there, he immediately resumed his long, easy strokes in and out of her. Joyce moved her hands over his shoulders and chest, admiring the feel and appearance of him. In the next instant a switch seemed to flip inside her and she felt an enormous upsurge of all encompassing passion rise up within her and rush toward her center with a warm flood of pleasure. She stared blankly up at Peter as it seemed to explode inside her, releasing the pressure in a balmy gush that dispersed into titillating little waves of contentment all throughout her. She lay motionless, trying to keep the feeling with her, but it was very quickly passing.

Yet, Peter was still inside her, strong and hard and hungry, and her climax seemed to ignite an explosive fire within him. Suddenly he gave himself over to all the yearning that had been building up throughout the night, along with everything else he had been feeling, including his frustration and fear. Joyce was soft and pliant beneath him, still wallowing in her earlier pleasure, and he plundered her softness with a passion-driven brutality. Joyce reveled in his loss of control, spurring him on even more with all the little touches and sounds she knew he liked best. She watched him, too, mesmerized by his strength and beauty as he struggled over her. She felt strangely detached now, making the rest of the act seem more intimate somehow, as if she was observing something very private that she had no right to see. Still, she couldn't take her eyes off of him, and so she gently clung and encouraged and stroked him to satisfaction while she trespassed into his most vulnerable moment in an effort to see inside. Peter stiffened all of a sudden and threw himself into her with a loud yell. Watching the intense pleasure cross over his features gave Joyce an overwhelming sense of power. She was delighted to have pleased him so. She realized he probably felt the same. This realization brought sadness with it.

Joyce rested sedately in Peter's arms. Normally he would be sleeping by now, but tonight she knew he was lying fully awake, wondering.

Her mind wandered back to the first time they were intimate together. She was still married to Bob, and he, too, had a wife at home. She had asked him afterward, perhaps unfairly, "Why are you doing this?"

"I don't know," he had replied. "I guess I'm not happy."

"You don't know if you're happy or not?"

"I don't think about it much," he admitted. "Maybe I'm just bored."

She had thought about his words many times since then. She could not accept the idea of such an incredible breach being made out of simple boredom. She herself had been excruciatingly unhappy in her marriage with Bob. Resentment and frustration had built up over the years to the point where she little cared anymore whether she hurt him or not. His lethargic attitude regarding her and their marriage had created an antipathy in her that grew and grew until it bordered on violence. She wanted to hurt him in fact. That was why she began the affair with Peter, really. And throughout their affair, Peter had admonished her to take more precautions so that Bob would not find out, but the truth was that she could not wait for Bob to find out. Her cautionary measures were all especially designed so that when Bob did finally find out, he would have many memories to recall with horror and dread, adding insult to injury once the cat was out of the proverbial bag.

Unlike the overwhelming majority of unfaithful husbands—for Joyce had researched the subject at length—Peter did leave his wife. Perhaps it was because Joyce was married, too, that it occurred to him to do so. Peter did not like having to share her with another man. It was decided that they had both made a terrible mistake with their first marriages, but that now that they'd found the "right" person for them, they could rectify the problem at once. And it was like a dream come true. Joyce had genuinely fallen in love with Peter, and she could not believe that something so wonderful could come out of her hatred for Bob.

But all too soon after she married Peter, it became apparent that he, too, could be terribly lethargic in matters of the relationship; and this is when Joyce began to call back to her mind his earlier statement that he was "bored." Only now *she* was the object of his apathy. She had fought the urge to give up and wallow in resentment, as she had with Bob. Yet in spite of her best intentions to make the best of it, she felt herself teetering back on the edge of hostility, and it simmered around and within her like a slow burn. It appeared to her that this was simply the way it was for men, that upon conquering an object of their desire, their interest in it would automatically be depleted.

Things progressed along these lines in the relationship between Peter and Joyce until one day Joyce happened upon, quite accidentally, a solution to the problem.

It came to her while they were out Christmas shopping together. Joyce was agitated and anxious, having won the war in getting Peter to go shopping with her, but having lost the battle—and all pleasure in being with him—for being obliged to fight for the opportunity. Just like the princess who was expected to spin gold from straw, Joyce floundered with the task of trying to make their outing cheerful and fun while being painfully aware that he had practically been forced to join her. She silently seethed at the injustice of it. She had focused all her attentions on Peter's gift-giving list, and now wondered how she could get him enthused about hers. He had thus far been sullen and distant. She was standing with him while he finished eating a fresh-baked pretzel at the food court contemplating this when a handsome, slightly younger man approached her.

"Hey…Joyce is it?" the man asked. She looked at him in surprise. She only vaguely remembered his face, but could not immediately recall where she knew him from. He laughed at her confusion. "It's Brian. I met you over at the perfume counter a few weeks ago. Remember?" He acknowledged Peter's presence while she was trying to remember the incident, explaining, "I think I frightened her a little. I was quite taken by her scent."

Joyce remembered the man when he said this. He had approached her slowly, grasping her arm suddenly and bringing it to his nose in a disconcertingly intimate gesture. She had been offended until he spoke to her, when she realized immediately from his explanation and his demeanor that he was quite harmlessly looking for a perfume for another woman. She had provided the necessary information and he had purchased the perfume and that had been the end of it. Until now.

"Oh, yes," she laughed now. "How did your friend like the perfume?"

"We'll find out Christmas morning," he said.

Peter moved closer to Joyce unexpectedly and grasped her hand firmly in his own. She stared down at his hand holding hers. Under the present circumstances it felt something like a foreign object clinging morbidly to her flesh.

"Well..." Brian faltered a little, becoming suddenly aware of the tension. "Merry Christmas, Joyce." She couldn't have said exactly why, but Joyce was suddenly so grateful to Brian that she could have kissed him.

"Merry Christmas to you, too, Brian," she said warmly, meaning it. He looked at her a moment before he walked away.

Peter and Joyce stood there a few moments longer before they resumed walking together, still hand in hand. Joyce was deep in thought. Peter mistook her thoughts and asked, "Who was that?"

Joyce looked up at him in surprise. "Why, he just explained our one and only encounter!" she said. She was still wondering over the sudden change in him. This was the most interest he had shown in her during their entire outing.

"He was clearly interested in something other than perfume," he said cynically. Joyce nearly laughed out loud, but something made her stop herself from doing so. She resisted the urge to immediately rush to the defensive and explain the situation more emphatically. It was slowly dawning on her that something of import had just happened, and she wanted to decipher what it was and, even more importantly, what it meant.

Peter, who had before the incident been like a sullen child forced on an unwanted excursion with his mother, was suddenly now the attentive and charming husband. It was Joyce who seemed to be only half present as she watched him with a detached inner eye. Here was the Peter she had originally fallen in love with. Here was the Peter she believed she was losing.

Yet he was back again, and all it had taken was a single word from another man! She marveled over how different Peter was from her. The same kind of encounter from another woman would have caused her to become distant and sullen. She suddenly realized that the constant reassurances she gave him were actually what *she* needed, not him. For her, those reassurances would have created trust and enhanced intimacy. But for Peter, they provided the cushion upon which he could rest his head in apathy.

All of this Joyce realized in a mere instant. But she watched Peter thoughtfully for days after the encounter, carefully gauging how long his interest remained piqued. It seemed that he needed a *reason* to be attentive, and for Peter, that reason was to keep what was his.

Joyce never uttered a single word about these realizations to Peter. It would do her no good to do so, and he would have adamantly denied them anyway. She merely adjusted her behavior so that it was not quite as straightforward as it had been before, adding a hint of mystery where before there had been none, and doing things that were improbable and inexplicable to keep Peter on his toes. She struck up conversations with strange men everywhere she went now, for those men became an excellent resource at the most unexpected moments. All of these little alterations in her lifestyle were relatively insignificant but had a powerful effect on the way Peter perceived her. She became, for him, a fascinating woman of mystery that both tortured and allured him. And when the effectiveness of any given behavior waned or failed, she would quickly find another. It seemed to her that the stakes were getting higher and higher in this game of theirs, but she could not stop. Even when it escalated to the point that she felt she had to resort to outright deception to get Peter's attention, well, so be it. She simply must continue to create the illusion that *she* was losing interest in *him.* And it was not, she reasoned, quite as much of an illusion as one might imagine. She had watched Bob lose interest in her for years, allowing herself to be treated as if she was no more important than an old piece of furniture. She knew she would never be able to just idly sit by and watch the same thing happen with Peter. Now that she knew firsthand how easily another man could be found, she could do it again if she had to. And, in fact, hadn't her outgoing behavior of late provided her ample opportunity to do just that? Her newfound appeal to the opposite sex not only piqued Peter's interest; it also caused her to realize how desirable and lovable she was.

As Joyce snuggled up to Peter, she secretly hoped she would never have to leave him. She loved him and being with him when he was attentive to her gave her everything she needed. A nursery rhyme from her childhood came to mind and a wicked little smile crept over her features as she mentally recited it, slightly altering the words as she went: *Peter, Peter, pumpkin eater, had a wife and couldn't keep her. He put her in a pumpkin shell, and there* she *kept* him *very well.*

* * * * *

HUMPTY DUMPTY

Humpty Dumpty sat on a wall.
Humpty Dumpty had a great fall.
All the king's horses and all the king's men,
couldn't put Humpty together again.

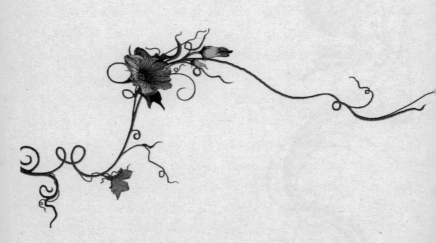

Sandra picked Joe up in a bar—that was the long and the short of it—although this simple truth bothered her. She didn't like the clichéd implications it brought upon her as a woman, or the idea of her and Joe beginning their life together on such a note. It bothered her so much, in fact, that she found herself modifying the event in the retelling of it, by changing a small detail here, or adding an extra feature there. These revisions seemed harmless enough; for what did it matter if people thought she met Joe in, say, a grocery store instead of a bar, or if it happened in the middle of the day instead of closing time in the middle of the night? It harmed no one, and made Sandra feel considerably better, to put aside the negative and focus on the positive, even if that positive did have to be manually incorporated into the event.

The end result of these machinations was charmingly romantic, with even Providence lending her a hand in the event, which had evolved into an in-depth encounter that began when Sandra's shopping cart collided with Joe's as they both came around the same blind corner in a crowded market, startling other shoppers and causing food to fly off a nearby shelf and roll onto the floor in all directions. Sandra's friends were as intrigued as the purported shoppers who lingered all around the incident to watch while she and Joe struggled to gather up the scattered items in the disoriented state that was brought on by the immediate attraction they felt for each other, and the palpable electric charge that sent sparks flying when their fingers touched as they both reached for the same can of peas, etc., etc. Throughout Sandra and Joe's relationship, this version of their meeting would only gain strength in the telling, in spite of the glaring reality that Joe almost never ventured into anything larger than a convenience store and that, even when he did, he never committed to the amount of items that would necessitate the use of a shopping cart. In fact, in all their time together the two would never be inside a grocery store at the same time.

Not only was it in a bar where Sandra first met Joe, but it was under circumstances where electrical charges and Providence were conspicuously absent. Joe was terribly drunk—so drunk that he had difficulty managing the most rudimentary of bodily functions, such as holding up his head without it wobbling disturbingly atop his neck, or keeping his comments along one single line of thought. He gazed at Sandra in confusion, slurring his words incoherently while babbling on about random topics. He was what her father would have called a "sloppy drunk" and had, at one point, even started to sob. Fortunately, this disturbing display of despair didn't last more than a second or two, and in almost the same breath he began laughing uncontrollably.

Sandra was captivated. Her sympathies were fully won over. To see such an attractive man—with seemingly so much to offer—brought to such a low filled her with compassion. She had been able to deduce in a matter of minutes that Joe was not only good looking and in excellent physical shape, but also gainfully employed. She had even caught the mention of a woman called Elaine, who she immediately presumed to be the cause of Joe's distress. The fact that such a man could be so affected by a woman told Sandra that sensitivity was yet another attribute she could attach to his character. All of this Sandra had concluded before she had time to finish her first White Russian.

Notwithstanding these qualities that Sandra was admiring in Joe, there was one thing in particular that captivated her heart. Joe, for all he appeared to have to offer a woman, was deeply wounded. Looking into his eyes, Sandra clearly identified a genuine pain and vulnerability. She immediately recognized a deep-rooted and urgent need in Joe, and her own need to be of use was alerted. She was certain she could help him. She already felt she understood him. He had obviously been hurt, most likely by this woman Elaine. No doubt he was afraid to get close to anyone else for fear of being hurt yet again. Sandra felt he must be terribly lonely. She knew that she could soothe the hurt and provide the loving care that would let Joe trust again. Her own past injuries had prepared her for this, giving her the ability to empathize. A strange sense of authority and control came over her at the thought of bringing all the wonderful things she had to offer to Joe. She knew she was capable of overwhelming him with her capacity to love. This was her forte. She was caring and considerate to a fault. What was more, she possessed a keen talent for doing things well above average when she put her mind to it. Where in other aspects of her life she could easily become bored and lose interest, in pleasing the right man she would be inexhaustible. And she knew every trick in the book for making a man happy—having read every issue of *Cosmo* since she was twelve—so she was more than up to the task of capturing this man's heart while expertly healing his wounds.

Sandra brought Joe home with her that very night. And really, what else could she have done? She could hardly have just stood aside and allowed a man of such potential drive home drunk. In the instant when she first decided this, she assured herself in all earnestness that she would not let herself be intimate with him. She would simply get him safely settled into the warm and cozy bed of her guest room. He would awaken the following morning alone but comfortable, nestled lavishly in the softness of her mildly scented blankets, lulled out of his sleep by the richer, more urgent smell of gourmet coffee brewing downstairs in the kitchen. There, he would be greeted with the cheerful sight of Sandra, perfectly groomed and wholesomely feminine, cooking him a hot breakfast and showing genuine concern for his welfare.

Upon arriving at her house several hours later, however, Joe seemed to sober considerably, and for the first time that night he was suddenly fully aware of Sandra. He reached for her eagerly—

almost desperately—and murmured earnest little observations about how beautiful she was. She was too flattered and delighted to rebuff him, and besides, having witnessed his pain in the bar over what she presumed was Elaine's rejection of him, she could not bring herself to further diminish his ego by turning him down now. But more than that, inside Sandra there was awakened the strong yearning to be wanted and needed and admired by a man like Joe. She rested limply against the wall and gave herself over to the wondrous feeling of him taking her face in his hands and breathing warm, ragged breaths over her skin as he spread passionate kisses everywhere. She moved her arms up around his neck and clung to him and his kisses became more demanding.

In spite of herself Sandra was aroused. Often, she would be so caught up in pleasing her partner—particularly on a first encounter—that she wouldn't have time to think about her own pleasure. But Joe surprised her with the intensity of his desire, and she found herself losing control under the influence of it. He was suddenly everywhere at once; with his one hand groping for a breast beneath her sweater while his other hand cupped one round buttock and squeezed it gently. All the while his lips burned a hypnotic trail along her jawline from one ear to the other. Once he had established her willingness to be more intimate with him, his passion quickly escalated. He seemed to be attempting to touch every part of her at once with his hands while his tongue devoured the inside of her mouth. Then quite unexpectedly, in a sudden impulsive burst of energetic decisiveness, Joe picked her up in his arms and held her cradled there, glancing all around them for the bedroom. Not seeing a clear path in that direction he looked questioningly into her face.

"It's upstairs, I'm afraid," she said with a nervous laugh. She bit her lip in expectation of the awkwardness when he put her back down—for she hardly expected him to attempt carrying her up the stairs in his condition—but Joe caught and held her eyes in that instant, really looking at her for the first time that night, and a slow smile crept over his features. It was a real smile, filled with genuine amusement that reached his eyes. She saw that he had nice teeth and noticed the dark shadow of thick stubble on his unshaven face. She was struck by the full force of his masculinity in that moment and it filled her with a kind of longing that went far deeper than her basic desires of the moment.

Without further hesitation Joe moved toward the stairs and effortlessly carried her up to the second floor. Sandra was impressed and delighted by his fortitude, and when he placed her gently on the bed she impulsively pulled him down on top of her. With this small gesture from her, the last of Joe's reserve melted away and he began eagerly pulling off her clothes, virtually tearing them from her body. His breathing was heavy and ragged but he was clearly determined. She let him undress her completely, and then lay sprawled out and shivering on the bed while he stopped unexpectedly to simply stare at her. His passion was suddenly subdued while he looked her over with extreme deliberation and keen fascination, drinking in the sight of her and then leisurely moving his hands over her flesh as if to confirm that what he was seeing was real.

"You're beautiful," he murmured. He seemed surprised by this.

She instinctively sucked in her waist a bit more, but aside from that, she really did believe, at that moment, that she was beautiful. She had no doubt that Joe found her to be so. There was no denying his desire. She wanted the moment to last forever. And it seemed as if it might as Joe merely continued to gaze at her body, moving his hand lightly down the length of it and then back up again as he stared, lingering over the sight of her nakedness much longer than any other man had ever done before him.

But in due time Joe's desire, which had been silently welling up inside him like the calm before a storm, became too urgent to delay. Without letting his gaze stray from where she lay, he quickly began removing his clothes. Sandra watched eagerly, noticing with delight how his hardness popped up conspicuously when he lowered his pants. Once his clothes were discarded Joe wasted no time in joining Sandra on the bed, immediately and possessively taking her into his strong arms, anxiously pressing his lips against hers, and forcing his tongue into her mouth. The sharp stubble on his face assaulted her skin, leaving it tender and vulnerable to even the feathery caresses of his breaths as they rushed out over her face in warm, irregular gusts. His excitement kindled Sandra's, filling her with intense eagerness as she clung to him, pressing her body vehemently against his. She tilted her head back, succumbing more fully to the never-ending flow of kisses he kept showering over her face and neck. She let her hands roam over his body, exploring his muscular back and shoulders with exquisite pleasure, delighting in the hard feel of him as much as he was relishing the delicate softness of her. She impetuously thrust her hips up to meet his hand as it meandered down the length of her stomach and ventured lower. She could not wait for his fingers to reach her; the entire area between her legs was alive with yearning, engorged and saturated and aching for his touch. When Joe felt her velvety wetness, he instantly stilled, pausing momentarily to look down and gaze contemplatively at the lustrous fluid that clung to his fingers. He seemed almost mystified by it. He gently spread her legs wider apart and once again worked his fingers in between the swollen folds, almost absorbing the silky moisture into his being as he probed and prodded her body with discomfiting persistence and deliberation. She waited, trembling, as he single-mindedly occupied himself in this way for what felt like an eternity.

But now again Joe's sense of urgency returned with renewed force, and without warning he flung Sandra's legs up high, pressing them as far as he could up over her shoulders, and plunged himself into her so vigorously that his testicles slapped against her buttocks in that first single thrust. She cried out in surprise just as his mouth came down over her parted lips to capture the cry in his kiss. She shuddered in response to being so utterly subdued by him.

Joe began vigorously moving in and out of Sandra's body with rhythmic force. He kept up a steady tempo of intense, arduous strides for several long minutes without hesitation. All the while, between gentle kisses, he commented with delightful insolence about how good her body felt, how soft her skin was, how large her breasts were, how wet she was and, most of all, how much he was enjoying what he was doing to her. Sandra received his inexorable thrusts and licentious remarks in a kind of stupor, shrouded behind a filmy haze of ecstasy that was tinged with a strange and painful yearning she knew would never quite be satisfied. She feasted on the pleasure she could easily grasp, constraining her limbs to become even more open and yielding to Joe, who seemed to be pummeling new bursts of sensation into her body with each and every thrust.

Eventually Joe stopped, once again curiously serene in the midst of his intense passion as he lingered, motionless but still joined with Sandra, for a long intermission where he simply held her, stirring almost imperceptibly every now and then to pull her closer to him, or to press his lips to hers. After a restful period of perhaps four of five minutes, during which he appeared to be gathering strength, Joe ravished Sandra all over again.

For more than an hour it continued in this way, with Joe, in turns, going from being violently passionate to tranquilly savoring the event, so that one minute Sandra found herself caught up in the heat of his passion and the next she was melting under his over-whelming tenderness. It was actually the effects of the alcohol that brought about the sudden bursts of energetic arousal in between slow, languorous periods of reverie, but for Sandra, it made for one of the most passionate and sensual evenings of her life. Joe's fiery outbursts made her feel desirable and enhanced her own excitement, while his contemplative tenderness in between caused her to feel, perhaps mistakenly, that he genuinely cared for her.

Eventually, in one of these bursts of feverish excitement, Joe climaxed violently and then collapsed almost immediately into sleep. Although she had not climaxed herself, Sandra felt triumphant. She knew she had given Joe incredible pleasure and was surprised that she had derived as much pleasure from the event as she had. For a first intimacy with a new partner it was more than she expected. Her self-consciousness and preoccupation would not allow for more. Throughout the encounter she had been secretly— almost unconsciously—evaluating Joe. The little things he did, the way in which he did them, the person he seemed to be; all of these appeared to be what she had been searching for her entire life. For the moment, it was crucial that she put her best foot forward to ensure that Joe realized how invaluable she could be to him.

Joe began to snore the loud, obnoxious breaths that alcohol induces, and Sandra listened to his snores with a strange mixture of anticipation and fear. She felt as though something significant was at stake. She tried to shake the anxiety that came over her by reviewing the details of their lovemaking. She trembled with pleasure when she recalled how Joe looked at her when her clothes had first come off.

But here now was another piece of her and Joe's history that would require some fine-tuning, although later, upon further reflection, Sandra realized it needed surprisingly little. The only thing she could find fault with, in fact, was that their first intimacy took place on their very first night together. This was easily modified to the more acceptable third date. As for the event itself, she realized with a thrill of satisfaction that she couldn't have come up with anything quite so exciting if she tried. In fact, some of it already seemed embellished just as it happened. It really was terribly exciting when she looked back over the details in her mind, which she found herself doing, again and again. Oftenest, she would call to mind the smile that came over Joe's beautiful features just before he carried her up the stairs. That was a moment so romantic that she would never have dared to make it up, fearing that no one would believe or even fully appreciate it.

The morning after their first night together Joe seemed somewhat flustered. He lingered over the gourmet coffee Sandra brewed in a sort of daze that bordered on incredulity. Sandra took this as a compliment, certain that he was undoubtedly taken back by her kindness and desirability. And as a matter of fact he was.

But after Joe left her she felt let down and empty. She wandered around numbly tidying the kitchen, but nearly all of her energy had been spent. She thought about Joe throughout the rest of that day, and wondered if he was thinking of her as well. That afternoon she tried to distract herself by flipping absently through the articles of her latest copy of *Cosmo,* but this just brought Joe closer to the forefront of her mind. She summarily scanned the key points from an article entitled "Sex Tips from Guys: Their All-Time Favorite Mattress Moves Revealed," but none of the tips offered any real hope for enlightenment. In fact, none of the men in the article had come up with anything she hadn't already tried—most of which had yielded little or no success at all. She couldn't help noticing, in fact, that the so-called tips hadn't been terribly successful for the women who had inspired them either, for although the sexual behavior had remained in the men's minds, the women had not. This was quite obvious from their comments as they enthusiastically described the sexual act itself, while offhandedly reducing the woman who provided the pleasure to "this chick," or "one ex I had." Sandra wondered that the editors didn't cut those parts out. It belied the idea that the sex tips held much value or promise.

And suddenly it seemed to Sandra that it was all a big lie anyway. All the articles in her favorite magazines seemed to constantly promise better results in life if only a woman tried harder to give men pleasure along with, of course, purchasing the products that would help her look better and younger and thinner. Sandra couldn't help but notice that the harder she tried the more elusive the love she sought became. Meanwhile, it truly appeared that the women who didn't try half as hard were just as able—or even more so perhaps—to capture and hold a man's attention. Sandra absently wondered if that was the case with Joe's ex-girlfriend, Elaine.

Sandra was momentarily distracted from this train of thought by a sentence that caught her eye in another article in the same issue of *Cosmo,* entitled, "Nine Erotic Tips to Rock Your World and His," which read, "As a rule, women take longer to get sexually aroused, so start by yourself before you get into bed. Spend thirty minutes taking a bath with candles and fondling yourself." For some reason this piece of advice angered Sandra so much that she hurled the magazine violently across the room, knocking over a lamp in the process. *Jesus,* she thought with indignation, *now we have to provide our own foreplay, too?* Ironically, this was already something that she often did with a partner beforehand—and sometimes even afterward, too, as a matter of fact—but it always seemed unfair that she had to do it, and seeing it served back to her in an advice column filled her with rage. Getting a man to love you seemed all at once as unachievable as winning the lottery. After all the years of searching, she was beginning to wonder if it was really worth it.

But then her mind drifted back to Joe and once again her heart was filled with that strange, powerful longing. Was she doing the right thing, repeatedly putting her best foot forward in each new relationship in the hopes that Mr. Right would recognize her value and appreciate her? Maybe this time she should try something different. Perhaps if she played "hard to get," Joe would find her more desirable. But that could also backfire, especially if he just came out of a relationship where the woman played games. It seemed to Sandra that she was always on tenterhooks with men, wondering which was the correct action to take, and suffering consequences for behaviors other women had exhibited before her. She shook her head, trying futilely to discard these thoughts from her mind even as she laughed at herself. She and Joe had shared one night together! She may never hear from him again. Yet something in the way Joe had carefully punched her phone number into his cell phone assured Sandra that he would call her.

But as several days passed without a single word from Joe, it was beginning to seem as if he might not call after all. By midafternoon of the third day Sandra was contemplating whether or not she should seek him out. She recalled an article in *Cosmo* advising women in her predicament that it was preferable to "run into" the man of her dreams rather than to call him outright. But the only place she knew Joe from was the bar where they met. She felt a sudden urgency to see him as soon as possible. She wondered what the chances were of him being in that same bar in the middle of the week. She didn't want to wait until the weekend to see him again, but on the other hand, if she went to the bar on a night he wasn't there she would be obliged to return again another night, and possibly even another. What if someone mentioned to him that she was in there every night?

As it turned out, planning an "accidental" meeting was not necessary. Joe finally called her that very afternoon. And even after three days to think about it, he still seemed nervous and uncertain.

"Would you like to get together tonight?" he asked after a few attempts at stilted conversation.

Sandra was so happy he called that she forgot to be upset over the short notice. She agreed to see him before she even knew what she was agreeing to. It wasn't until she hung up the phone that she realized she had no idea where they were going or if she was supposed to meet him somewhere or be picked up. She also knew from bitter experience that there was a chance that by "get together" Joe intended nothing more than a replay of their first night together. But for the moment, having gotten "the call" and knowing that she would soon be seeing Joe again was enough to make Sandra calm and self-possessed. She simply prepared herself for the evening to come, waiting for the next cue from Joe and, around six o'clock that evening, he knocked on her door.

Joe looked tired and a bit disheveled, but she caught the light of surprise in his eyes when he saw her. She could tell that her appearance pleased him and she was delighted. She would keep surprising and pleasing him and hope for the best.

To Sandra's surprise Joe actually took her on a "real" date, to an elegant and expensive restaurant. She wasn't sure what she had been expecting, but this threw her off kilter just a bit and she was momentarily uncertain. Joe seemed nervous as well, following the hostess several steps toward their table before catching himself and stopping abruptly to allow Sandra to walk in front of him. She moved by him awkwardly, feeling a sudden thrill when his hand lightly touched her back as she passed him. She glanced at his face and was delighted to find him watching her. She responded to each and every small overture from Joe with the same excessive appreciation and pleasure, again feeling the strange longing welling up within her. Her awkwardness was slowly leaving her and being replaced with a kind of euphoria.

At the table she sipped her water for something to do until the waitress arrived. She was feeling slightly giddy and found herself stealing glimpses of Joe as he examined his menu.

"Do you know what you're having?" he asked her, looking up from his menu to find her staring at him. She picked up her menu and scanned it briefly, hardly noticing the entrées.

"The veal looks good," she murmured absently for something to say.

"It is very good here," he told her confidently. "Their veal with linguine is the best around."

"Done!" she said agreeably, setting the menu back down on the table.

The waitress came over and Joe ordered the veal for Sandra and then ordered an entrée for himself. Sandra was inordinately flattered that he had ordered for her. In fact, that single gesture set the tone for the rest of the night, so that Joe could do no wrong. Everything he said had merit, and even his table manners appeared correct or, if not exactly correct, then at least terribly masculine. Even when Joe ordered his fourth martini Sandra found herself admiring how well he handled his liquor. He had pleased her early on, and that small pleasure would take her a long way. She could subsist on small pleasures, provided they came in a fairly steady flow that was at least regular enough to undermine any evidences of neglect, and prevent the bitterness of famine from setting in.

Sandra drove them both back to her house in his car. Upon arriving, she remained in the driver's seat, uncertain about how to proceed. He, too, seemed timid and unsure, so they sat side by side in silence for a few minutes. She interpreted his hesitancy as reverence for her, so she worked up her nerve to shyly lean over the seat in an attempt to make it easier for him to initiate a kiss. Only then did his passion from their previous night return, and Joe grasped her eagerly and kissed her. She immediately responded, filled now to overflowing with the strange longing for him. But as the kiss wound down Joe pulled away from her and hesitated yet again. He appeared to be struggling for control. Sandra was petrified that the date would end and so, even though she knew it was the wrong thing to do, she found herself impulsively asking him, "Would you like to come in?"

After that Sandra and Joe began seeing each other three or four times a week. Sometimes Sandra would cook dinner and sometimes they would go out to eat, but Joe always spent the night with Sandra afterward, and each and every time they made love. The sex was wonderful, although Sandra still was unable achieve an orgasm with Joe. Sometimes afterward, once he drifted off to sleep, she would masturbate right there in the bed beside him. It took strange fantasies for her to reach a climax, with bizarre encounters that often startled her, usually involving Joe in some way, but disturbing nevertheless, and always leaving her feeling empty and alone, and filled with an even stronger sense of longing than before.

Without their having discussed it, Sandra was fairly certain that she and Joe were exclusive, but even so it was difficult for her to achieve any real sense of security in their relationship. She wasn't fully certain that they were *in* a relationship. Aside from their habitual dinners followed by intimacy, there was little else. Both had their jobs and their lives, which she supposed was normal, but their time spent together never strayed from evenings into days, or from eating and sleeping together to venturing deeper into the other's existence. As time went by it was becoming more and more difficult for Sandra to imagine them ever doing so. She could not help but feel they were settling into a pattern that prevented a real relationship from forming.

After several months of this, Sandra suddenly came to the alarming realization that she had never even been to Joe's house. She asked him about this one day and was stunned to learn that Joe had no house. He had left his home when he left Elaine, taking up temporary residence in a local hotel. Sandra was more upset by the realization that she hadn't known Joe was virtually homeless than she was by the fact itself. It spoke volumes to her that she hadn't known; it seemed to her like a dreadfully obvious symptom pointing to a terminal disease. Yet she had known all along that Joe was not forthcoming with her. And each and every time she questioned him about his past, especially as it related to Elaine, he became even more withdrawn. It was the same when she tried to discuss her future with him. She could actually perceive him drawing away from her at those moments, cringing inwardly, without any discernible movement per se, but glaringly evident to her nevertheless. Seeing him retreat into himself in that way rattled her, but she knew if she pressed him too far he would become angry or, even worse, he was more likely to become antagonistic, expertly plucking at the strings that stirred up her own demons. The more attached she became to Joe, the more afraid she was to confront his past or their future.

Learning that Joe was living in a hotel, however, was so shocking to Sandra that she forgot to be cautious and diplomatic, and she let loose with all of the anger that had been secretly building within her in a sudden fury. Joe was taken aback by this side of Sandra, and for once he was the one to make the effort to appease her. She was almost immediately afterward contrite, afraid that she might have humiliated him.

"You should just stay here," she blurted out in the end. And suddenly she was calm and self-assured once again. "That's it!" she announced, genuinely pleased. "You'll move in here with me." She took his silence for embarrassment and rushed on in an effort to make him feel better. "It'll be fun," she assured him. "And it will only be until you settle things with Elaine and are ready to buy another house."

Later, she wished she hadn't added that last part. It made her offer sound more casual than she meant it. But overall she was happy Joe was moving in. And she was even more convinced that it was the right thing to do when he insisted on contributing to their new household by giving her money every week, further impressing her with the generosity and cheerfulness with which he gave. She could hardly believe the joy she felt to have Joe living in the same house with her, effectively wiping away the loneliness of her former existence and enhancing the quality of her life in one fell swoop. She found herself wanting to please Joe more than ever, and now, having the means to enhance her efforts, she lavished extravagant details at him from all directions, spending every extra cent that she gained from his moving in on making his stay more comfortable. She was certain that if she could make Joe see how wonderful life with her could be he would stay forever.

But here again was a part of Joe and Sandra's history that would need a bit of tweaking. So Sandra transformed Joe's need for a place to live into a need for Sandra herself, and she expanded upon his generosity so that it truly appeared that Joe was extravagant and indulgent with Sandra, rather than that he was merely paying his own way.

Sandra never thought to explain—or even mention—these little alterations she sometimes made to their history to Joe. There wasn't any reason to do so. There was little to no chance that either Joe or her friends would discover any of the discrepancies these alterations created, because there was little to no chance that the parties involved would have the opportunity to compare notes.

Sandra couldn't imagine Joe even meeting her friends, let alone his having a conversation about their life together with them. As their relationship progressed it became hard enough to squeeze out any significant amount of Joe's time for herself; Sandra never considered sharing any of that time with her friends. But even more to the point, Sandra recognized that Joe had no interest in spending time with her friends. It was one of the growing number of things that she instinctively knew not to ask for. And even if these circumstances changed—she supposed it was inevitable that Joe would eventually meet her friends if they were to stay together—it was so unlikely at the present time, and appeared to be so far off into the future, that there seemed ample time for her embellishments to have been softened significantly, or even perhaps, to have been forgotten altogether.

The new housing arrangement was working out splendidly. Many of the issues that bothered Sandra before she and Joe moved in together suddenly seemed to dissolve into nothingness. Their lack of time spent doing things together, for example, now seemed irrelevant because, after all, their living together brought about a dramatic increase in the amount of time they were actually together. Around the house, they ended up doing innumerable things together, if only to save time and make things easier. It now seemed logical to do outside activities apart, if only to have the opportunity to miss one another. Inevitably though, they began doing more and more things outside their home together, too, for it was often more convenient to do so. And Sandra loved every moment spent with Joe. She was convinced that she was slowly winning him over. Her own happiness gave her a sense of security and confidence that she could not fail. Besides, thanks to Elaine taking possession of the home he once lived in, Joe was now on Sandra's turf, and she felt she most certainly had the home-court advantage. In addition, she gained strength with each and every kindness she offered Joe, and it never failed to satisfy her to impress him with the depths of her devotion. Each little acknowledgment from Joe—whether it appeared as a mere light of surprise in his eyes or in one of his beautiful smiles of genuine delight—was for Sandra like a golden coin of affirmation that she could add to her store of self-worth, offering her the assurance that she was, in fact, in control, and that her efforts could earn her love and help her achieve a true sense of belonging.

With each little advance that she achieved in her relationship with Joe, Sandra always felt gratitude and joy, but these sentiments eventually faded into the same strange longing she felt on the first night she met him. It took several months after Joe moved in, but ultimately Sandra once again found herself wondering where she stood with Joe, why they never made plans for the future, and what exactly had happened with Elaine.

One night she cautiously broached the subject with him as they sat side by side, amicably watching television together on the couch. She took the practical approach.

"What is happening with your house?" she asked him casually.

Joe looked at her in surprise, but then gave her one of his playful smiles. "Are you tired of me already?" he teased.

"No!" She tried to match his teasing tone. "I was just wonder-

ing. Jeez! You'd think you were in the witness protection program
or something."

He laughed. "Come on now. It hasn't been as bad as that." She
realized suddenly that Joe had mellowed dramatically in the three
or four months that he had been living with her. He was considerably less defensive and much more cheerful.

"Hasn't it, Joe?" she continued, but still in the same teasing
tone. "Is *Joe* even your real name?" They were both laughing now.
But behind her humor she was determined. "Are you?" she asked
him, and to his questioning look she elaborated, "In the witness
protection program?"

"Come on, Sandra," he said, still amused but now withdrawing
from her a little.

"And yet," she continued, "for some reason you can't talk about
your past life."

"What do you want to know about it?" he asked. His tone was
agreeable, but he was still steadily withdrawing. Sandra knew that
it was only a matter of time before he closed up completely. It
caused her to become rash.

"Why is Elaine living in your house?" she asked him point-blank.

"Because it's her house, too," he replied. "We bought it together
and both our names are on the mortgage and the deed."

"Do you still make mortgage payments?" she wondered.

"Yep."

"Oh." This stumped her for a moment. "So how long were you
with her?"

"Six years."

"You never got married?"

"Nope."

"Why not?"

"She didn't want to."

Sandra could feel that she was running out of time and that at any moment Joe would tire of her questions, but ironically, now that he was submitting to her inquiries, she couldn't think of what it was she most wanted to ask.

"Why did you two break up?" she ventured.

But her time was up. Joe had remained sitting next to her on the couch throughout this brief discussion, and suddenly he got up. Sandra impulsively grabbed his arm. "Look, Sandra," he said. "That is all water under the bridge."

"Then what can it hurt to tell me about it?" she asked him.

"Why do you want to know about it?"

Sandra sighed. It was just like him to turn this around on her.

"Because I do."

"This is about you being insecure," he said.

"No," she disagreed. "This is about me wanting to know more about the man I'm living with."

"I don't ask you all kinds of questions about your past," he reminded her.

"Yeah, I noticed that, Joe," she said sarcastically, succumbing to another sore spot for her. "And why is that?"

"Because it has nothing to do with *us*," he told her.

"And what about our future, Joe?" she asked him. "Huh? That's another thing you can't talk about. Does that have nothing to do with us either?"

"Why can't we just take this one day at a time?" he wondered. "Why do I have to go through the third degree about things I don't even have any control over?" He looked at Sandra pleadingly. "I had very little say in what happened in my past as it turned out, and I have no idea what's going to happen in the future. I don't have a crystal ball."

"That's just an excuse!" she said, giving in to her anger. "Men *know* when they want to spend their life with a woman."

Joe was silent.

"If you can't bring yourself to talk about the future you could at least give me some idea of what happened in the past. Give me *something!*"

"It. Has. Nothing. To. Do. With. You!" he yelled, pausing significantly between each and every word for added emphasis. Then he turned and walked away from Sandra, retreating to the bedroom.

Against her better judgment Sandra followed him. She felt the urge to cry but the tears wouldn't come. She realized then that she was crying already, and she had been for a long time, on the inside. She wondered what she should say. How did a person get in? Why didn't *Cosmo* ever give advice for moments like these?

"If you cared about me at all you would communicate with me about yourself," she said. This sounded desperate, even to her ears, but she couldn't seem to stop herself now, and so she continued in the same vein. "I'm not asking you for a kidney here. I hardly ever ask you for anything, as a matter of fact."

"Let's not do this now," he said in a tired tone, continuing his retreat from her. He began to undress for bed.

"When then?" she asked in a shrill voice. "When would be a good time to bring this up, Joe, because I seem to be hitting all the bad times? Can I make an appointment for a better time so I'll know when that is?"

Joe moved around the room as he changed, still trying to get away from Sandra. His attempts to evade her enraged her even more, and before she knew it she had followed him into the bathroom. She stared at him, determined to force some kind of response out of him. He pretended not to see her. When he finished in the bathroom, he returned to the bedroom and pulled down the covers of the bed. But when he reached for the remote, Sandra, who had been trailing him and watching his every move, snatched it up before he could get his hands on it. Now Joe was forced to deal with her. She smiled in bitter satisfaction when he turned tiredly to face her. He seemed incapable of finding the right words and merely sighed as he looked at her.

"Are you still in love with her?" she asked him miserably. When he only just kept stubbornly staring at her she continued, with every word adding fuel to her anger and egging her on, so that she kept going on and on for much longer than she intended. "Is that it, Joe? Is that why you can't talk about her? Is it so painful that you can't even stand to hear the mention of her name? Because if you were really over her you would be able to talk about it. And what am I supposed to do in the meantime?" As she continued to talk, it began to seem as if she was really talking to herself, letting off steam and in the process drawing conclusions that were the culminations of all of her fears. "I suppose I'm expected to just sit here in limbo while you pine away after her. I'm probably just the rebound. I'm just supposed to fix all the problems, right? Even if you do get over Elaine it will be the next woman you meet who gets a shot at your heart." As she voiced these fears she waited for him to contradict her. She desperately wanted him to convince her that all her conclusions were wrong.

"You're pathetic," he murmured, turning his back on her. But she caught the hint of a self-satisfied smile curving his lips just as he was turning away from her and in the next instant she saw red. The sight of that smug little smirk on Joe's handsome features unleashed all the fury that had been building up in her throughout their relationship, a fury that came out of months of hard work performed on credit—credit extended on the flimsiest promises of payment, it's true—but even so it was extremely disappointing to discover that payment would not be forthcoming. And even worse was the realization that she had only herself to blame for granting the credit in the first place. Sandra was livid.

Joe slipped into bed as if nothing was amiss, just as Sandra suddenly flew at him, snatching the covers from his grasp and hurling them off the bed and onto the floor. Then, before Joe had time to register what was happening, she yanked the pillow from under his head and began to pummel him with it, not in the least seeing the absurdity of the situation as she did so, and only vaguely aware that if she had grabbed anything more solid than the pillow she might have actually bludgeoned him to death. Joe, on the other hand, was suddenly struck by the hilarity of the situation and he burst out in loud laughter, trying to dodge her blows during the first debilitating round of hilarity, but then grasping her arms with the pillow still in her hands and flipping her onto the bed on her back in one smooth maneuver. He quickly and easily positioned himself over her so that she was completely immobilized beneath him. She fought with all her might but her efforts brought almost no effect. His physical strength gradually subdued her. He was still laughing as he effortlessly plucked the pillow from her fingers like he was dealing with nothing more formidable than an amusing child.

Much of Sandra's steam had left her by this time, and the actual source of her anger—which was her fear and pain—now surfaced. Large tears formed in her eyes as she stared up at Joe in stunned surprise. When Joe saw the tears his smile faded.

"Hey there," he said softly, dropping the pillow and taking her face in his hands. "What's this?"

To her horror she started to cry in earnest. Her sobs sounded contrived to her ears and she hated herself even as she reveled in the comfort Joe was offering. He kissed her lips and cheeks and eyelids as he gently shushed her. As always, she acquiesced, pushing her hurt aside and recklessly grasping the gratification of the moment instead of following through with what she had started. She suddenly felt too tired to care where their relationship was heading. It suddenly seemed inopportune to worry about tomorrow when today held such pleasure. Without even realizing it, she was earnestly kissing Joe back. And why not? she asked herself. Why not just focus on how much she loved him?

And then it was like their first time together all over again, with

Joe tearing at Sandra's clothing in a sudden frenzy to have her. Both gave in completely to the heady feeling of succumbing to an exquisite pleasure in spite of the pitfalls surrounding it. The pleasure was made all the more intense by the pitfalls in fact. Neither thought about, or even fully realized this. Sandra didn't consider that she was simply relieved to have been temporarily distracted from the terrible pain and worry that Joe didn't love her, any more than Joe was aware that much of his pleasure was derived from the simple fact that he had subdued her for the moment.

What Joe couldn't seem to say in words he had no difficulty expressing through his lovemaking. He went far beyond his ordinary efforts to give Sandra pleasure in every way that he could think of. He knew that she loved to be touched and so he put his warm hands all over her, taking his time and, for the moment, getting more satisfaction from the pleasure he was giving her than what he was feeling himself.

Sandra let herself believe that Joe's attentions during their lovemaking proved that he valued her, and she would not allow her mind to wander into the more pragmatic passages that questioned the validity of any real value to be gleaned from this kind of intimacy with a man. For now, she decided to steer clear of all forms of reasoning that required more evidence than her feelings in that moment, which in and of themselves created a very compelling argument indeed.

To her astonishment Joe suddenly confirmed those feelings, whispering dreamily as he gazed down at her, "I love you."

Sandra's heart overflowed when she heard Joe's words, and the benevolence she felt for him in that instant surpassed everything else, even her previous anger. She couldn't even respond, she was so utterly overwhelmed.

Joe became even more affectionate with Sandra after his declaration, as if to give it emphasis. He slipped his arms all the way around her, spreading his hands over her skin and holding her very close to him in the most intimate manner while he gradually and leisurely worked his way into her body. She was soft and pliant beneath him, almost melding into him as she accepted him into her. His arms tightened around her even more when he felt her liquid softness as he penetrated her, lifting her up off the bed in an embrace so encompassing that virtually every part of her flesh was touching his. He continued to hold her in this way as he slowly moved himself in and out of her, cradling her in his arms while lightly rocking her with the gentle force of his thrusts. She turned her face toward his and he dipped his tongue in between her lips, devouring her mouth hungrily. She clung to him feverishly as he gently ravished her, trembling and murmuring incoherently that she loved him, too. Joe shushed her gently, whispering tenderly and repeatedly, "I know, sweetheart...I know." His words, combined with the heartfelt kindness with which they were spoken, seemed to pick Sandra up and transport her into a tempestuous sea that thrashed her about amid violent waves of euphoria, contentment and disbelief; all washing over her and threatening to pull her down into the dark, murky depths. But Joe kept bringing her back up to the surface, cradling her in a warm, comforting shield of well-being.

Joe's movements as he made love to Sandra became so restrained as to be nearly imperceptible. He drew himself out of her slowly—so slowly and stealthily that it was almost as if he wasn't moving at all—and then in the same unhurried manner he gradually inched his way back into her again. He, too, was genuinely affected by the unexpected intimacy of the moment. His senses were heightened by his awareness of it, and his deliberate movements were designed to enchance and extend it. Neither wanted the moment to end.

With this in mind, Joe continued to stretch out every single stroke and caress to almost maddening lengths. It was as if he were experiencing a part of lovemaking that he had never experienced before. He noticed things he had not noticed before, from the arch of her back to the feel of her legs as they clung to his body. Everything seemed different and new. He observed nuances in every aspect of her being. He almost believed he could feel the very pores on her smooth skin as it brushed up against him. His heightened awareness had sharpened his senses to the point that it seemed as if he were absorbing her very essence while making love to her body.

Sandra felt it, too, and she clung to Joe helplessly, unable to do more than simply bask in the warmth of the surreal moment that enveloped them both. Somewhere in her conciousness there lingered visions of home, and comfort and children—her and Joe's children—and happiness without limitations.

All of this was contained in that one single moment, like a dream that exists for mere seconds but seems to encompass unlimited spaces of time. Like a dream, the moment was almost over before it had fully been achieved.

Yet it was the tenderest lovemaking they had shared. The

goodwill between them was palpable, and the bad feelings they had both pushed aside seemed to make it even stronger. Sandra felt so blissful that she forgot all about appearance, or performance, or even to respond. She just held on to Joe as she slowly let down her guard, allowing herself to trust him completely. And although she vaguely realized that she would not climax—she was far too preoccupied to even try—she was as content as if she had. But even so, when Joe's thrusts came harder and thicker, indicating his own impending release, Sandra heard a distant cry within her, calling out from the depths of her very soul it seemed, and she thrilled to it even as she pushed it aside. *Next time,* she assured herself.

It was as if a part of her was being severed when Joe ultimately disengaged himself from Sandra and rolled away from her. She remained still and quiet, except for a slight trembling that continued to rock her. She struggled to console herself from the disproportionate amount of loss she felt. She waited for the soothing sound of his snores and was surprised when he spoke.

"I'm not in love with Elaine," he said slowly. "I can't say for certain that I ever was."

Sandra was too surprised to speak. She held her breath and waited.

Joe rolled onto his side and leaned up on one elbow, looking down at her. This new intimacy overwhelmed her, and she had to bite her lip to keep the tears at bay. His voice was almost a whisper, husky and low. They gazed into each other's eyes as he spoke and she listened.

"I was involved with her. That's the best way I know to describe it. Then one day I came home to find police officers with restraining orders telling me I couldn't come back. So I left, and shortly after that another guy moved in."

There were numerous questions running through Sandra's mind, but she couldn't seem to find her voice, so the two just looked at each other in silence for a few minutes.

"And in case you're wondering, I never laid a hand on her," he said as an afterthought.

She had been wondering about that but replied automatically, "I knew that." And in that instant she realized that she had. Still, she found herself torn between the desires to both condemn the other woman and defend her. "But if you didn't really love her— I mean, that still doesn't justify what she did—but….didn't you realize that it might end somehow?"

"At the time I couldn't have been more surprised," he told her, but after a moment he conceded, "I suppose now, looking back, I can see that we did have problems."

"What were they?" she dared to venture.

"I was happy so I assumed she must be, too…" He seemed to be considering it as he spoke. He continued slowly, measuring his words as he went on. "Maybe 'happy' is too positive a word," he said upon reconsideration. "It's really more that I was content. I thought I was doing everything that needed to be done. I figured if I fucked up too badly she'd definitely let me know, because she didn't seem to have any trouble telling me about it when things bothered her. I sure didn't know she was so unhappy, or that she was out looking for my replacement."

"She should have been honest with you," Sandra said, even as she silently wondered, was she, herself, being honest with Joe? There were always so many little acquired injuries to her heart that she nursed in private. With Joe——or was it the same with all her lovers?—— she felt the need to tread lightly, carefully picking her battles, for fear of losing him altogether. But where did that leave them?

"Yeah, well," he said softly, and Sandra knew that he had shared as much as he was able to. She put her arms up around his neck and pulled him toward her. She felt all at once safe and secure in the warmth of his embrace and she sighed happily. She felt more certain than ever that she was the right woman for Joe.

Joe's breakthrough, as Sandra came to think of it, marked another change in their relationship. Joe became noticeably happier, laughing more and drinking less. This, in turn, made Sandra more secure within their relationship, giving her the confidence to pour even more of herself into it. These positive aftereffects lasted several months, during which Joe appeared to get stronger even as Sandra seemed to get softer.

But after those months had passed, it once again appeared to Sandra that she and Joe were settling into a pattern of being together that, although comfortable and pleasant, offered no real commitment or permanence. He still refused to discuss their future together. He seemed to think that saying "I love you" was the end-all to relationships. Sandra yet again found herself feeling dissatisfied with her relationship. As was also a pattern for them, Sandra allowed these feelings to build up until she could hold them in no longer.

"Why do we never make plans for the future?" she asked him one day.

Joe looked at her. Did she imagine it, or did he actually cower away from her? On his face was a look of genuine frustration. His body language seemed to be saying, "God, not this again." At least that's the way Sandra perceived it, and she suddenly felt the buildup of resentment within her begin to bubble.

"It's a pretty simple question, Joe," she said, her tone full of condescension. The constant struggle to achieve even the tiniest advance in their relationship left her feeling utterly disillusioned and cynical. But these feelings actually seemed to empower her now, and she was struck with a strange sense of irony as she moved right up under Joe's nose and stood her ground with her back held rigidly straight and an expression of utter disgust on her face. When she spoke, her voice was dripping with sarcasm. "I mean, it's not like I just asked you to come up with a brand-new theory for solving integral equations, is it, Joe? No, no, I'm not forcing you define the elements of an isosceles triangle either, am I?" Sandra was practically out of breath when she completed this tirade, but somehow it had made her feel better. She realized vaguely that she had no idea what she had been talking about, especially in regards to the isosceles triangle, although, in the back of her mind it dimly occurred to her that an isosceles triangle had only one element she herself could identify, and that was that it possessed two sides of precisely the same length. What struck her most was that she had thought of the isosceles triangle at all, let alone the way it had smoothly glided off her lips as if she spoke of it every single day. What was she—in fifth grade—when she last thought about an isosceles triangle?

All this was a tiny and fleeting undercurrent of thought scurrying along the edges of Sandra's mind, but at the forefront there remained the source of her anger, and she would let nothing distract her from it.

Joe, meanwhile, looked bewildered. Perhaps he, too, was momentarily stumbled by the unexpected reappearance of the isosceles triangle.

"All I asked for," Sandra went on, "was a little information— no—a little *hint* about where I stand." Her sarcasm quickly metamorphosed into sarcastic martyrdom. "Not that I have the right to know anything about my own future, I guess," she said in a long-suffering tone of voice. "Why should I? How *dare* I ask the all-wonderful, all-desirable Joe to explain his intentions? No, I guess I'm just supposed to keep sucking his cock until something pops off in his big head instead of in his little head."

In spite of himself Joe laughed. He knew when her sarcasm became funny she was close to the end of her outburst and then he would be able to reason with her.

"Yeah, it's funny, isn't it?" she said. "A big joke." Her outburst was winding down as Joe predicted it would, but something was different about this time. She looked at him with tired eyes. "Why don't you want to be with me in the future?" she asked him.

"I never said that I didn't," he told her.

"Yeah, but you never say you do, either. And we never make any plans. Your refusal to talk about it is clear evidence that you don't want it."

"You don't know that," he said.

"Then tell me now. Do you or do you not want to be with me in the future and…like…someday…marry me?"

"I can't answer that."

"So the answer is *no!*"

"I didn't say that."

"You don't say shit. What is the answer now, at this moment? If you had to make the decision today, would you marry me?"

"No," he said. She looked at him, shocked, and he felt compelled to continue, to explain. "At this moment, I would not. But if things were to change…"

"Change!" she suddenly screamed. "Change? Is that what you've been waiting for? Change? *You* are waiting for things to *change?*" She laughed hysterically at this. She continued to laugh even after the tears came. "I bet you are waiting for change," she ground out between her teeth. "Why the hell not, when I'm the one doing all the work? I guess I'll have to try harder, right? Yeah, that's it. I'll try harder and you can continue to evaluate how well I'm doing." She had moved away from him while saying all this, wandering around the room, picking up random items and throwing them in the middle of the floor.

"What are you doing?" he asked her, noticing that all the items on the floor were his.

"Things aren't going to get better, Joe. Sorry to have to be the one to tell you that." She continued to rummage around and collect more of his belongings to add to the growing pile on the floor.

"Look, Sandra, there's no need to…"

Sandra stopped in front of him and flipped open her cell phone. "Don't make me call 911, Joe."

"What? Sandra, come on!"

"Get your shit and get out, Joe, now, this minute, before I dial the numbers." She held one finger poised over the number nine on the dial pad.

"What just happened?" he asked.

"I just figured out that the payoff is never going to come, Joe," Sandra said with a smile. "Would you believe it took me this long— what's it been? Eight or nine months? To figure it out."

"What are you talking about?"

"I'm talking about the things that *I* want out of life. To be with a man who is certain that he wants to be with me. To be married. To have security. You keep dangling these things over my head like a carrot, but come to think of it now, why would you ever give me these things? You are getting all the things you care about right now. Yeah. You want a girl who won't cheat…you got that. You want good sex…you got that. And you want someone you can talk to who cares about you…you got that." She laughed again. "Waiting for things to change, *my ass.* The only one who wants change around here is me."

Joe seemed genuinely stumped and it suddenly occurred to her that he might not have led her on. It probably never even occurred to him that she was expecting a payoff for all her hard work, or that the desired payoff was a loving relationship that developed into a trusted partnership. He seemed to really be thinking they were simply having a good time.

Joe bagged up his possessions in silence. He seemed genuinely surprised by Sandra's attitude and behavior. He didn't feel that he had misled her. What made her think he would be staying forever anyway? It was her who said he would only be staying until he settled things with his other house.

Later that night, after Joe had dumped all of his belongings in the same hotel he had taken up residence in after his split up with Elaine—in the same room, too, as it turned out—he found himself back on the same bar stool he had occupied the night Elaine dumped him, too. He ordered the usual round of drinks, back to back, for the first hour or so until the pain was numbed enough so that he was able to ignore it. Only then did he bother to lift his head to glance around the room and take in his surroundings. There was a woman at the end of the bar who was watching him with interest. He tried to smile at her but his neck failed him in that instant by suddenly giving out, causing his head to flop idiotically onto his chest. He felt dizzy, but after much struggling he managed to haul his head back up straight and hold it steady so that he could look at the woman in the corner again. This time his head remained upright as he flashed her his most attractive smile. But he needn't have exerted himself quite so much, for she was already on her way over.

* * * * *

ABOUT THE AUTHOR

Currently living and working in Newburyport, Massachusetts, Nancy Madore achieved enormous critical acclaim with her debut, *Enchanted: Erotic Bedtime Stories for Women*, which hit several best-seller lists and has quickly become a fan favourite. A feature writer for local newspapers, Nancy is also in business with her son and is working on her next collection for MIRA® Spice.

EROTIC BEDTIME STORIES FOR WOMEN

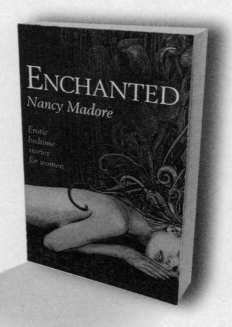

Allow yourself to be drawn into a fantasy world like no other, where a beautiful princess is seduced into a love triangle with a handsome prince and her winsome maid…where a mysterious gentleman's young bride is deliciously disciplined for her unchecked curiosity…where a naïve daughter is married off to a beast of a man whose carnal appetites awaken her budding desire…

www.mirabooks.co.uk